Love is the Magic Elixial.
Never let a Day go By
without To lling that
special someone that
yn love them !

Bradley J.

I Apologize

To all the women I've loved, and, through no fault of their own, I've lost—

I Apologize

A novel by
Bradley Booth

AFFLUENT
PUBLISHING

Published by:
Affluent Publishing Corporation
1040 Avenue of the Americas, 24th FL
New York, NY 10018
http://www.Affluent-Publishing.com

Library of Congress Control Number: 2008910706
ISBN: 978-0-9822111-9-9
Printed in the United States.

Chapter 1

I LOVE THE SPRING NOW, BUT IT WASN'T ALWAYS THAT WAY. I can recall being so busy that I would go to the park with a cellular phone, laptop, and unfinished paperwork. There I would sit with all my twentieth-century electronic gadgetry, not realizing that I was strangling life. I thought then that climbing the so-called ladder of success was the most important thing in life. But fortunately, sometimes when you're headed in the wrong direction, as I was, people come into your life as a sort of warning, and may God have pity on your soul if you don't heed them. I can remember my warning now, since hindsight is the best of all visions. "Be not deceived; I will not be mocked: whatsoever a man soweth, so shall he reap."

Let me take you back to the beginning. I was a loner, not by choice, but by circumstances difficult to explain. Perhaps later I will be able to fully explain it, but for now I ask you to allow me to tell this story in my own way and at my own pace.

Since the day tragedy struck, I buried myself in work for solace and I decided that for my life to take shape. To keep from brooding over a past that I could not change, I would immerse myself in cultural activities with visits to art galleries, museums, and

Broadway plays, and also develop my interest in jazz and classical music. But plans are sometimes a double-edged sword. At least they were for me.

I decided to spend an evening being entertained by the compositions of Beethoven, Haydn, Mozart, and Schubert at Avery Fisher Hall. Listening to the radio as I drove home from the office, I could never have guessed that I would set in motion events that would change my life. But I had better not get ahead of myself.

On that particular night, I dressed rather casually, given the occasion, in a bluish-black checkered sports coat, a maroon merino-wool sweater, brown slacks, and my new tan alligator shoes. To round out my attire, I decided to wear my Omega Deville instead of the sportier Yacht-Master. In a good mood, I got in my car and headed to Manhattan to enjoy a night on the town, purposely arriving early enough to have sufficient time to eat.

There is an eating establishment in the hall; however, I believe everyone had the same idea to dine there before the concert, which left me to find another restaurant nearby so I could make it back in time.

The restaurant's décor was designed to depict Italy with all its old world charm; the staff was decked out in attire reminiscent of that of a gondolier, and the tables were covered with red and white checkered table cloths. Although that bistro would never be mistaken as being pretentious, the smell of marinara sauce had my mouth watering.

The maître d' ushered me to a table for two at the rear. From this vantage point, depending on the seat you sat in, you could either see the kitchen doors or the big column that blocked the view of the other patrons' tables. Ah, I felt so at peace in that setting. I was exuberant with where I was seated: close to the kitchen to get the aromatic scent that drifted by when the doors swung open and sequestered off to the side so as not to be disturbed.

I ordered a virgin piña colada from an attractive young lady with long black hair tied into a side pony-tail, the sort of waitress who adds charm to any restaurant. I exchanged a few pleasantries and couldn't help noticing her lovely, petite shape when she went to get my drink. I make it a business of mine to study people—an exchange of only a few words can yield so much information about the true contents of their character. But, of course, sometimes I reach the wrong conclusion.

The maître d', who had been so self-composed, returned soon after I had been served my drink, rubbing his hands together nervously.

"I hate to intrude, sir," he announced, "but we are in a little bit of a jam. One of our regular patrons who usually lets us know ahead of time when a table is needed has arrived without a reservation. Would it be too much of an imposition if I were to seat her at your table?"

What to do? I thought. I could tell him that it would indeed be an imposition and refuse his request, or I could be gracious and comply. I decided on the latter.

"Sir," he sighed, "please accept our apologies, and, for this intrusion, your meal will be on the house."

Well, something good has come from following the Golden Rule, I told myself. But that was not the end of my reward. The valued customer who was promptly seated across from me turned out to be a very alluring woman.

She couldn't have been more than twenty-two. Her most appealing feature was her bewitching green eyes, which seemed to look right through me. Her lips were sensuous and inviting, highlighted by an enchanting smile. She thanked me and ordered a bottle of Evian water with a slice of lemon. We introduced ourselves, and I barely caught her first name through the din of noise from the kitchen. I extended my hand and told her my name was Tony. She smiled and repeated her name, Christina. It occurred to me that this dubious "imposition" might turn out to be a very pleasant interlude.

"Are you going to see any particular show tonight, or are you just dining in the restaurant?" she asked.

There was nothing coy or flirtatious about the way she approached the conversation, so I relaxed. It seemed that if we had to dine together, she intended to make the best of it. But before I could answer, she asked another question—this one more direct and personal.

"I hope you are not going to take offense to this," she said, "but why is a handsome man like you dining alone?"

Bursting into laughter, I began to look at this young woman in quite a different light. She was, apparently, unusually outspoken; perhaps I had been wrong in my assessment that she wasn't being coquettish. I decided to respond in kind.

"I could say the same of you," I countered. "Why is such a beautiful young woman sitting in a restaurant with a total stranger?"

I detected a look of sadness in her eyes when I

said that, but the waitress came with our food and the expression faded. I decided not to pursue the matter, although, I must confess, it made me curious.

"Actually," I said, sensing that I needed to uplift her spirits, "I'm going to the concert at Avery Fisher Hall."

She smiled. "I heard that it is sold out. I believe they're presenting the works of Schubert, Beethoven, Haydn, and Mozart."

"Are you interested in classical music?"

"I dabble in it from time to time," she told me.

Then, suddenly, our conversation took a more intimate path. Christina confided in me that she had lived a very sheltered life with parents who had forced her to devote most of her time to her studies.

"My father is really the stricter of the two," she told me. "I wasn't allowed to have many friends. They required my total dedication to my schoolwork. The friends I did make found me strange, I think. They teased me about being a wet blanket, since I did not share their love for mischief . . . "

Never before had a stranger provided me with such insight about her life in so short a time. And it was not just because she was passionate; certainly she was that, but every word she spoke struck a chord in me, perhaps since I also knew what it felt like to be hopelessly unhappy.

The hint of sadness resurfaced as she spoke, and I sensed a longing in her to be understood, even if only by a stranger whom she would never see again. I kept quiet and let her continue.

When dinner was over, I insisted on paying her check. It was then, when we both rose to leave, that she began to act strangely, as if she wanted to say something more or reach out to me. Her face was flushed, and she turned away dispirited, perhaps sensing the intensity of the conversation she had just had with a stranger.

I tried to brush it off, believing that having confided in me must have embarrassed her. But why feel embarrassed? After all, we would never see each other again. But strangely enough, when she left, I felt as though she was taking a part of me with her. Dismissing it as total nonsense, I watched her round the corner.

Checking my watch and noting that I only had ten minutes before the ringing of the bells, I thanked the maître d' for his auspicious intrusion and bolted out the door.

Avery Fisher Hall is a prestigious place. Here you find the movers and shakers of the world, as well as the pretenders. And then there are people like myself who just want to enjoy the music. I arrived just as the bells began to peal and made my way to the prime orchestra seats.

The maestro tapped on his stand and the orchestra came to attention. All eyes focused on the conductor. He lifted his wand and then lowered it; the orchestra began to play Schubert's *Overture Italian Style in D*, a piece that, according to the program, he had written to show up the composer Rossini.

It is said that music has the power to sooth the savage breast, and that night I understood this as never before. I was so engrossed in the beauty of the sound that it came as a sudden shock when I realized that the first violinist looked familiar. Could it be? Certainly, it looked like Christina. According to my program, she was Christina Jaloqua, a world-renowned violinist, once a child prodigy and now considered one of the world's masters.

Mixed emotions rose within me. Joy at the way this young woman could play, and astonishment that earlier I had shared a table with someone of such prominence. At that moment, I realized she was looking directly at me. Our eyes met for only a split second and my body shivered, but anger was the cause of it, I'm sure; she had said that she "dabbled" in music from time to time. Dabbled!

Why had this lovely lady been sitting in a restaurant talking to me, a total stranger—and why had she not felt the need to tell me who she was?

Lost in these musings, I didn't realize that the piece had ended until I heard the audience clapping. The maestro took a bow and pointed his wand at Christina, whereupon the audience applauded louder. He left for a few minutes while the stagehands pushed a grand piano in front of the orchestra. When he returned, he extended his hand toward Christina. This time she rose to even more boisterous applause, and I could see her more clearly. Dressed in an elegant black gown, she was even more radiant than she had been in the restaurant.

The applause subsided, the maestro again tapped on his stand, and the orchestra came to attention. The second selection was about to start: Beethoven's Piano *Concerto No. 4 in G.* As the pianist began, I imagined a child lost in the wilderness, calling out for someone to respond, which the rest of the troupe did eloquently. Again the pianist played and waited for the troupe to answer. This exchange mesmerized the audience and me. I smiled; the evening was more than living up to my expectations.

The pianist, another internationally known figure, received a standing ovation when he had finished. The stagehands started removing the piano as the bell sounded for intermission.

This time I had an opportunity to look around the lobby. There was a concession stand in the middle where concertgoers could buy books about famous classical artists. Next to the booth where I had purchased my ticket were programs for upcoming events; I stopped there for a few minutes to peruse the schedule for the rest of the year before going to the bar where they were serving wine, champagne, and soft drinks. The crush of people reminded me of feeding time at the zoo. Not able to get closer, I had just decided to venture back upstairs when my pager went off. I reached in my pocket and realized that in my haste I had left my phone in the car.

The usher pointed out the phones and I dialed the strange number, only to discover it was an old friend, Jackie, calling to say hello. I hadn't heard from her in quite some time and wondered if she realized why I had distanced myself from her. I was trying to think of a way to rush her off the phone when someone tapped me on the shoulder.

It was the same usher who had led me to the phones. He looked around curiously then handed me an envelope. I hesitated before taking it as Jackie screamed out my name. I told her to hold on and turned to ask the usher what this was all about, but he was gone. I didn't know which disgusted me more: the fact that I couldn't find him or that I would have to call Jackie back.

I decided to open the envelope, although I was convinced that it must have been meant for someone else. On top of this distraction, which had me anxious and nervous, the bells indicating that the concert was about to resume began to peal. I ripped open the envelope and quickly read the note, only to be pleasantly surprised by its contents.

> *Tony,*
>   *Please do not be angry with me for not telling you who I was. You treated me like a normal person, and I cannot begin to tell you what your little act of kindness meant. I would like the opportunity to talk with you again. I am enclosing my number. I would be very happy if I could see you again.*
>
>   *Christina*

Receiving a letter like that made me very happy indeed, but it also filled me with trepidation. After all, her world was different from the quietness and anonymity of mine. Tabloid and fan magazines chronicled her every movement, which meant that anyone entering her life would be put under the media's scrutiny. It occurred to me that, since we had dined together, it might already have begun. I began thinking of all the worst scenarios for tomorrow's headlines: "Mysterious Stranger Dines with Christina Jaloqua . . . The Marriage of Figaro?"

Coming to the conclusion that my problem was no real problem at all, since I simply need not call her, I headed back upstairs to enjoy the concert, pleased with myself for coming up with a quick solution.

Taking my seat, I started reading the program. This time it stated that a famous cellist, Boris something-or-other, would be making his orchestral debut. A tall man in his mid-thirties, with long, curly black hair and a well-groomed moustache, took his seat directly in front of the violin players with the other cellist, ready to begin Haydn's *Cello Concerto in C.* Taking his cue from the maestro, he started playing, and a melodic sound permeated the hall.

It was turning out to be a wonderful evening. While waiting for the last piece to be played, I pondered my decision not to call Christina. After all, there might be a way to make her acquaintance and still maintain my love for privacy. Finally, deciding that my original decision was the best course of action, I prepared to listen to the last selection, Mozart's *Symphony No. 38 in D.*

As the violinists began to play, I focused most of my attention on Christina. Watching that delicate flower rest her face gently on the violin, I started imagining how wonderful it would be to one day sit at her feet, marveling at the way she played.

When the last selection came to an end, everyone rose to his or her feet and gave the orchestra another boisterous ovation, which lasted several minutes. When the maestro came back the final time, he handed a bouquet of roses to Christina, whose smile ignited the audience again. This time the applause reached a crescendo that was ear shattering.

People lingered when it was over, as though they could not bear for the evening to come to an end. I did likewise, recalling with pleasure all the events of the past few hours.

Christina's note still bothered me. It was an odd thing for her to do. No, I thought to myself, no response would be the most prudent course of action. I simply couldn't let another woman be of any importance in my life again.

Chapter 2

I WAS A MARKETING CONSULTANT LIVING A VERY ORDINARY life at that time. I had become a creature of habit, and prided myself on my emotional stability. I got to my office by eight every morning. I arrived before my secretary so that I could have an hour to unwind by playing works of the great composers, such as Vivaldi, Bach, Strauss, or Mendelssohn, music that I have always found uplifting. My secretary, on the other hand, preferred listening to golden oldies. We had a longstanding agreement not to try to convert the other to our particular taste, although, if the truth were known, I sometimes found myself listening to her favorite radio station.

Mrs. Bickerstaff had been in my employment for about five years. I had placed an ad in the *Times* and a slew of women showed up, most of them sadly lacking in qualifications. I was wearily concluding an interview with yet another applicant who clearly would not do, and I found that everyone except the lady I came to know as Maggie had left the outer office. It transpired that she had taken the vacant secretary's desk and told the remaining applicants that the position had been filled. Handing me her résumé, she went about straightening up my waiting room, while I, dumbfounded by her audacity, went into my office and pored over her résumé in an attempt to find some reason not to hire her. I am, after all, a man who has his own ways, and I had no intention of being manipulated. This was, I fear, how I saw it at the time. However, no matter how hard I searched, there was no doubt that she was ideally suited for the job.

"That was a bold move on your part," I said, calling her into my office. "Suppose I would have taken offense?"

"It would have been a great loss," she said, simply enough.

And of course she was right. It would have been foolish of me to lose her, this I knew. Fortunately for me, so did she.

An intimidating figure, although only five feet tall, Mrs. Bickerstaff had short, reddish-brown hair with a smidgen of silver protruding at the front, and wore old-fashioned glasses that, most of the time, dangled from her neck on a gold chain. A former executive assistant for a Wall Street broker, she had left her job to care for an ailing husband. Now widowed, she was adamant that she would never return to that stressful environment. Her professional demeanor and perfect diction gave my office a large degree of respectability.

Maggie has been my confidant and my best friend for five years now. She is still full of fire and brimstone but possesses a most loving touch. She has gone head-to-head with me on numerous occasions, one of which immediately comes to mind.

"You simply cannot keep up this pace," she told me the day after the concert when she discovered that I intended to stay in the office until midnight, if necessary, in order to make up for the work time lost during that evening of pleasure. "You know what you need?"

"No, but I am sure you will tell me."

"You need to find someone to settle down with, someone who will help you take a much needed rest from work."

"They stopped making your model a long time ago, Maggie," I told her. "Besides, who could put up with a workaholic like me? How many times must we go through this?"

"Why push yourself so hard?" she demanded.

"Because I have nothing else in life," I told her, "but my work. I didn't plan on anything else."

"One does not plan love," she admonished me. "It has a way of coming at the most inopportune time."

Self-assured, I told her not to worry. I was, after all, far too busy to fall in love.

If only I had taken her warning more seriously.

The week was going well. I was trying to close a big deal with a well-known company. Several larger and more prestigious advertising firms were bidding against me, but what gave me the edge was our personal service. Maggie and I have an eye for details, and we constantly double-check each other to ensure that, when I make my presentation, everything is accurate. More important, she concentrates on their personal lives: their likes and dislikes and the clubs that they frequent most. Armed with this information, we go to work to ensure that I am able to meet these clients on their home turf. Pooling resources with other executive assistants, she knows where their bosses will be, giving me the opportunity to be there as well. I have closed more deals on golf courses, at tennis matches, or over lunch at some exclusive club, than I care to remember.

Let me give you an example of her Machiavellian manner. Last month she discovered that a particular client always plays a round of golf on Wednesdays. John, a rugged man with features more resembling those of a lumberjack than a suave businessman, was very competitive. I had purposely fallen behind on the front nine while he teased me about my game.

Although we talked about a wide variety of subjects, I was determined not to bring up business unless he did. When he asked, I explained that even though mine was a small and growing company, we have found our niche by offering personalized service. We decided to take a break and finish our discussion over lunch. He then felt compelled to give me some pointers on how I could improve my game.

After lunch, the game turned decisively in my favor. It is amazing how a man's disposition can change when his shots are not falling. I began to reveal the full compliment of my game and stood in awe of the debacle that unraveled before my eyes. John's ire grew with each missed shot and he began to mumble profanities.

John snatched his clubs and threw them into the lake when I birdied the final hole. I quietly withdrew as he stood frozen, staring into the lake. Part of me admired how he played with zeal, while part of me wondered if I could ever get that passionate about anything again.

I filled Maggie in on what transpired on the golf course and told her that she couldn't have picked a better site for me to see John. I was so sure that we wouldn't be venturing into business together when she told me he was on the other line.

"I can't remember when I've been outfoxed and outclassed like that," he told me. "You put one over on me, coasting the way you did. And after you hooked me, reeling me in—you showed your real game on the back nine. I felt like a fool going into the lake to retrieve my clubs."

I maintained my innocence and told John that it's that obsession for winning that has guided his company to the success it now enjoys. He started laughing and told me that he would not underestimate me again.

We cemented the deal on Friday, at which time he lavishly praised Maggie. Jokingly, he told her if she ever became tired of working for me, he would be glad to have her on his team. Whereupon, being the consummate professional, she assured him that she was quite happy where she was.

The only problem working with someone with Maggie's perspicaciousness is that she misses nothing, absolutely nothing, and I had made the mistake of telling her about Christina.

"You don't have any excuse not to call that young lady from the concert," she reminded me a week later. "She must be wondering why you haven't called. Don't tell me you haven't been thinking about it. I've noticed that you have been doodling her name all over your notepads."

Before I could open my mouth to utter a word in my defense, she continued. "It is no good trying to deny it," she said. "You can bluff others with your straight face, but I have worked with you for over five years now and I know you better than you know yourself."

There is an eerie silence that pervades a building when all of its occupants have gone home. One could usually find me at my desk on Friday nights, recapping the week that had just passed and planning the next week's objectives. I opened my planner and there was a note in which Maggie congratulated me on the closing of another deal, along with these words of wisdom:

> *We do not always look for love,*
> *Yet love finds us.*
> *We believe it is our right to choose,*
> *Never realizing we were chosen.*

She was right, of course. Love had found me. I had carried that envelope with Christina's note for over a week, taking it out whenever I had a quiet moment. Reading it one more time, I decided I would make that call.

Nervously, I began dialing . . . only to stop halfway through and put the phone down. It was difficult to believe that a man who had outmaneuvered a CEO to land a big contract for his company would be here with butterflies knotting up his stomach, trying to make a simple call. Disgusted with myself, I tried to make the call several more times, always with the same result.

I was glad that Maggie was not there to see me, because then she would know that I cared more than I was letting on. Determined not to be deterred, I picked up the phone and dialed the entire number.

Christina was direct, as usual. "I am glad that you called tonight," she told me. "We're having a few close friends over. I would be happy if you came."

"I was really looking forward to going home and unwinding," I told her. "It's been a very hectic week."

She persisted with a tenaciousness that would

have made Maggie proud. I offered an array of excuses, from having to fight traffic to get a change of clothing, to feeling out of place. Her pertinacity was unbelievable and before I knew it, I had consented to join in the festivities.

What is this strange power she has over me? I asked myself as I turned off the lights, at the same time becoming aware of my renewed enthusiasm and vigor.

It is usually a forty-five minute drive from my Madison Avenue office to my home in Lynbrook. Unlike my other associates, who had chosen to live in Manhattan, I had opted to leave the bustle of city life for a town with shopping centers and a nearby park with a clean pond. At night the park is illuminated, and one can sit there and think, undisturbed.

Most of them had queried if I was getting old and had wondered how I could leave the nightlife behind. Ironically, five years later, all of them have followed suit, though they may have done it for different reasons, since all are either married with children or engaged.

I had chosen a simple, single-family home made of brick and vinyl siding, with an attached garage. Arriving home, I opened the garage from the car and drove inside, wanting nothing more than to flop down on the couch and go to sleep but knowing that I had better not, since I had given Christina my word.

I turned on the stereo and was about to go upstairs, when my Abyssinian cat nudged my leg. As I poured milk into her bowl, I couldn't help but recall how she came into my world. Shortly after moving and getting everything squared away, I had been alone one night listening to music as I reviewed some reports on my computer. A habit of mine back then was to have the television running while I worked in my den. As I worked through the night, a commercial ran several times about cats that were being offered in Port Washington, Long Island.

I decided that was what my home needed: someone quiet to share my world. Two weeks later I found myself in a dreary brick building crammed with people obviously there for the same reason. That day everyone seemed intent on getting a Persian or Siamese cat.

"Those cats are the favorite pets of prominent figures and nobility," the attendant, a young woman in a white smock, explained. "I will be glad to put you on the list for either."

Demurring, I began peering into every cage until I was irresistibly drawn to a pair of almond-shaped green eyes—and thus I met Lady, who was to become an important part of what could otherwise have been a lonely life.

Chapter 3

Leaving Lady to enjoy the milk, I headed upstairs to shower and shave. Wrapping a towel around my waist, I went back to the bedroom to dry myself, taking a few minutes to admire my washboard stomach. Reaching the conclusion that my medium build would prevent me from ever resembling Arnold Schwarzenegger, I had long since decided to work on a perfect midsection.

I was undecided on what to wear to Christina's informal gathering but settled on a charcoal-gray sports coat with a silk handkerchief, a white merino-wool sweater, blue trousers, and tan Italian loafers. The only thing left to do was to spray on some Fahrenheit and see, as Steve Cole's song suggests, "Where the Night Begins."

Arriving at the Waldorf, I elected to go through the Astoria entrance. Nothing could have prepared me for the lovely setting which the lobby presented with its glittering chandeliers, Rockwood stone columns, and the most magnificent bronze and mahogany clock I had ever seen. Definitely impressed, I went to the front desk and gave my name. As the clerk looked down the list, I saw that what was supposed to be a small party had apparently ballooned to over one hundred people.

Great! I'd been hoodwinked again, and I had no intention of going up there and feeling out of place. I would have made it out the door and gotten clean away if it hadn't been for Helen Fosdrick, a social wannabe who seemed to be at every event in Manhattan. She was a middle-aged blond with a raspy voice who tried to hide her considerable weight with loose-fitting gowns.

How her husband Harry—a likeable chap with grayish-black hair, cold, piercing eyes, and a jaw of granite—had managed to stay married to her for so long was still a mystery to me.

I saw Helen first and tried to duck behind one of those Rockwood columns, but it was no good—she had seen me already.

"Yoo-hoo, Tony," she called. "Yoo-hoo!"

"Hi, Helen," I said, not wanting her to think I was avoiding her. "Is Harry with you?"

"He is outside talking with the valet," she said cheerfully. "You know how he is about that car of his."

Harry's pride and joy was his blue and gray Bentley, which, as I often tease him, he treats better than he does Helen.

When Harry appeared, he enveloped me in a bear hug. One thing I have always admired about him is the fact that he is so down-to-earth.

"Son," he had told me one day when we had been out sailing, "You can always spot a poor man, because he is trying to impress you with what he doesn't have. His house is mortgaged to the hilt, and his credit cards are all maxed out from trying to keep up with the Joneses who aren't even aware of his existence."

"Son, what are you doing here?" he asked as he released me. "I've never known you to be out on a

Friday night. You're usually in the dang office playing with that computer."

"Harry," I said in a low voice, while Helen tried to comfort the wife of a drunk who had sought refuge in an elevator, "help me to get out of here."

"What's your rush?"

Before I could finish, Harry cut me off.

"So you were invited by the young gal that plays the fiddle," he said, slapping me on the back. "Good. You can keep me company since . . . Helen, will you leave that poor woman alone? How many times must I tell you to stop meddling in other people's affairs?" Harry demanded, as we made our way to the Palm Room.

Christina stood by the entrance, greeting her guests and wearing a clinging black evening dress with a split that revealed her lower thigh.

It wasn't long before we were face-to-face, staring at each other. Her eyelashes stood up as if at attention. Above her eyelids, I could see traces of a soft reddish color that complimented the rouge on her face, and below her eyebrows was a faint green, matching the color of her eyes. Her lips were sensuous, more inviting . . . the color of a delicate rose. Those sultry and bewitching eyes were drawing me in again. Her face glowed. Her very presence radiated throughout the . . . Stunned by her beauty, I found that I could not speak. I could have stood there gazing upon her forever.

"Darling," Christina cried, taking my arm and pressing herself close to me, "I am so glad you could make it."

I was a bit bewildered, particularly since Harry was looking at me with raised eyebrows; but then again, this woman was part of the show business world in a way, and everyone knew how effusive they were, even with relative strangers.

What to answer? I thought to myself, as the cameras flashed in my face. Why had I accepted her invitation? My worst fears were suddenly upon me. Harry and Helen on my heels, I reluctantly took Christina's arm as we entered the Palm Room.

A tremendous round of applause greeted us when we entered the lavishly embellished room. Everyone who greeted us, oddly enough, expressed how happy they were for her and congratulated me.

I thought, perhaps vainly, they had mistaken me for a celebrity. Christina held on tighter to my arm as she waved to the crowd. Before I could ask her why they were applauding, she had led me to the dance floor.

It had been so long since I was locked in a woman's embrace. Was it her perfume or how tightly she held me? My palms started sweating and a tingling sensation traveled through me.

"You are not leaving now, are you?" she demanded when I tried to step aside at the conclusion of the song.

"No," I said, thinking quickly. "The room has become warm all of a sudden, and I think we both could use a drink."

"Congratulations, son," Harry said, slapping me on the back at the bar. "Why didn't you tell your old friend that you were dating Christina? You had us all fooled. You made it sound like work was the only thing you had time for. Helen really thought . . . "

"What the—what are you talking about?" I exclaimed. "Whose coming-out party is this?"

"The fiddle is not the only thing that the young

lady can play, son. While you danced with her, Christina's agent told us this would be a joyous occasion and that shortly she would be showing off her beau. Imagine my surprise when I saw the way she clung to you on the dance floor."

"What in God's name are you talking about, Harry?" I demanded.

"Son," he told me, "I hate to say it, but it looks like you were set up from the word go."

"What possible reason could she have for doing this? I hardly know the woman. We briefly shared a meal at a restaurant, and when I called her earlier today she extended me an invitation to this small, informal gathering."

My mind was having a hard time grasping those seemingly unrelated events. I needed to escape, get to my car and sort this out. I kept looking at Harry for answers.

"Don't you think you're asking the wrong person?" Harry asked me. "I agree with you, it doesn't make sense, but you can call this party anything except small."

"I have had enough of this!" I exploded. "Why is she using me? I am getting out of here now! Let her clean up the mess she created. This is what I get for almost falling for a pretty face."

I was about to turn and leave when Helen appeared, her face flush with excitement.

"Tony! Tony!" she cried, edging in between us. "Why didn't you tell me? Imagine—your and Christina's coming-out party. You could have at least told me. How long has this been going on?"

"Helen—Helen."

"You sure are a cool one. But you're getting a

wonderful girl. She is so incredibly talented. Everyone knows that Christina . . . "

"Helen, leave him alone," Harry interrupted. "Tony has to tend to some unfinished business."

Turning from them, I headed toward Christina, intent on setting the record straight. I was halfway there when Harry yelled, " . . . hard a starboard, son—hard!"

I ducked just in time. Returning the blow, I connected with the chin of the drunk we had seen in the elevator earlier. The room erupted in bedlam.

"Now this shindig is getting exciting!" I heard Harry shout.

Suddenly, three men were attacking him from the right, while I was occupied with two on my left, and then Helen was in the middle of things, hitting Harry's attacker with the heel of her shoe.

Total chaos ensued on the floor of the Palm Room and someone shouted, "Call the police!"

I saw a clear path to the elevator and yelled out to Harry and Helen to follow me. Helen quickly asked for Harry's phone and let out an earsplitting scream. She told someone at the front desk that Harry had been attacked by a drunk and demanded that my car be brought to the front of the hotel immediately. Harry wondered about his car, but she told him not to worry, since the most important thing just then was to get me out of there.

At their Park Avenue apartment, Harry got the fire started while Helen fixed us something to eat. I couldn't believe what had just happened. If it wasn't for Helen's quick thinking, what a mess I would have been in. I could imagine tomorrow's headline: "Businessman Brawls over Debutante."

"Harry, I always wondered why you stayed married to Helen. I guess that tonight I got my answer. You should be commended on your choice of wife. I hope that one day I am so fortunate."

He smiled and pointed toward the kitchen. "Then you better go and thank her, for she chose me. I'd be lost without her, even though I kid her a lot. She means the world to me."

"Helen, I want to thank you for your quick thinking tonight," I told her. "I confess that I had you all wrong. I only hope that someday I am as fortunate as Harry."

"Go on, Tony," she said, flicking a dishcloth at me. "You don't know what you have gotten yourself into. But let me finish in here. I will be out shortly."

I went back into the living room where Harry was pushing the poker into the fire. I wondered what Helen was talking about. I didn't do anything. Why was Christina acting so strangely? Why give the impression that we were more than strangers? I hoped it would all blow over and that no damage had been done.

"Son, are you sure . . . ?"

"Excuse me?"

"You didn't do anything else with that young gal, did you?"

"I am absolutely . . . "

"Tony, don't think you're innocent in all of this!" Helen interrupted, as she passed me a plate.

"But what did I do?" I said, curious about Helen's remark. "We briefly shared a table before her concert."

"Sometimes that's all a woman needs to fall in love," she told me. "Don't underestimate the power of your charm, young man. A woman doesn't need a man just to jump on her pelvic bone from time to time."

"She doesn't? Now that's news to me."

"Tony! Will you be serious!"

Harry and I began laughing.

"So you find it funny, too." She threw a napkin at him. "Never mind. I am not saying another word."

"I'm sorry, dear. But this is a serious matter for Tony. All of this is apt to be plastered all over the tabloids tomorrow."

"I'm serious," Helen assured him. "A woman wants a man to listen to her, to console her, to let her know that her needs are above everything in this world, to shower her with words of affection, adoration, and endearment, and back that up with loving deeds. But when you do that, you'd better make sure you care about her, because you'll not only have unlocked the key to her heart, but to her body as well."

"Son," Harry said, "even though I've been laughing with you, an old phrase comes to mind. If you're going to play with fire, expect to get burned. You have lit that young woman's pilot light, so what are you going to do now?"

"Nothing! Are you two forgetting what happened tonight?"

Before going to bed, Helen told me that when she first met Harry, he had been engaged to another woman, a woman whom his family thought would be fitting for the business empire he would eventually inherit. She smiled as she related seeing him for the first time. It had been his first day out of college, and he had been walking through his father's plant. She had felt uneasy whenever he had been around and hadn't taken notice of the fact that he would always stop and say hi before going to his father's office until one of the girls had pointed it out.

Helen said she had become the butt of everyone's

jokes for sitting in the park opposite the building. She had been known as a wallflower who lost track of time by reading romance novels on her lunch hour. One day Harry had snuck up behind her. He had covered her eyes and told her to "Guess who." She had known it was him, she sighed, by the scent of his cologne. They had started talking and naturally she lost track of time. When she realized it, she had jumped up and ran inside, unaware that Harry had been behind her.

Helen's supervisor yelled out her name and Helen had closed her eyes for a severe tongue-lashing, but it had never come. She had opened her eyes to find the supervisor's mouth wide open and Harry standing behind her, smiling.

"Harry didn't know what he started that day, but he released passions in me," Helen concluded. "My days were consumed by thoughts of him, and even though I knew he was to marry another, it made no difference."

Helen went on to point out that a woman could be just as conniving, resourceful, and cunning as me on one of my business deals when going after what she wanted.

"I vowed to be his wife," she said emphatically, "and nothing he or anyone else did was going to prevent me from living out my dream."

"But, Helen," I protested, "that was you and Harry. Christina couldn't possibly feel that way about me."

"Then you have a lot to learn," she said, kissing me gently on the cheek. "I hope you are prepared to handle the fire you have lit."

I wanted to go home, but how could anyone refuse Helen's hospitality? Besides, there was another reason. Looking back on it now, I realize how silly I was. I couldn't shake the feeling that tabloid photographers lurked around every corner and that, somehow, I would be safer and better off staying with Harry and Helen. Even though Helen had prepared the guest room, I fell asleep in front of the television waiting for news of the night's fight. Harry woke me up early the next morning and invited me to jog with him through Central Park.

"Tony, this is far more serious than you think. A determined woman will do everything in her power to have what she wants."

"Harry," I said, "you and Helen are making a big deal over nothing."

"Then why didn't you go home?" Harry asked as he trotted over to a bench. "I know Helen's persistence and I know your determination."

I didn't know how to answer him. What could I say to make him believe otherwise? I was confused about last night and wished more than ever that the two of them would just drop the subject.

"I can't begin to tell you all the things Helen did to win me over," Harry told me in earnest. "All I know is that every time I turned around, she was there. I wonder if you've really given any thought to the gravity of the situation you now find yourself in."

What was he trying to tell me? Could a simple dinner conversation have led to all this? I decided to defer to his experience and felt it best to remain quiet and listen.

"You're a proud and obstinate man who loves the challenge of competition," he continued. "I must warn you, though, that if you try to be as cunning as a woman at her game of love, you most certainly will lose."

I became intrigued by Harry's theory. He may have lost with Helen, I thought, but I'm never going to see Christina again.

"Shucks, son, they don't play fair, and given their emotional temperament, they think of things that the logical minds of men cannot. Greater men, with far superior minds than ours, have attempted to understand them and failed. That is one of the great mysteries of the world that God probably never will allow man to solve."

I listened to him as a child would to his father. When he finished speaking, I had only one question: "Harry, what if I choose to ignore everything that has happened?"

"Son," he simply answered, "I am afraid that you are in for a rude awakening."

We were on our way back to the apartment when we saw Helen waving frantically from the balcony.

"It seems that all hell broke loose after we left!" she said, as we came through the door. "The police detained a lot of prominent citizens, since the Waldorf's security was unable to stop the fracas. No one was arrested, though. And no one knew who started the fight. The media has gotten wind of the story, and now the faces of some of New York's outstanding citizens are gracing the front and back pages of every tabloid in town. So, my dear, we got out in the nick of time, with no bad publicity to look forward to."

"The drunk may have started the fight," I said, "but all the blame lies with me. I made two idiotic mistakes."

"What are you talking about?" Harry demanded.

"Didn't you hear what Helen just said? Her quick thinking saved us from all that bad press."

"Don't the two of you see? I should have never agreed to let her dine with me, and worst of all, I should have never accepted her invitation. Our reputations could easily have been dragged through the mud. I'm truly sorry for the trouble I've caused. Thanks for your hospitality. I must be going home!"

The open road has always been a sort of refuge for me. I opened all the windows and stepped on the accelerator. My life was complete, albeit bereft of passion. I couldn't afford to be entangled again. I had suppressed my emotions all those years. I would never let another woman drive me down that road again.

Chapter 4

Aʜ, Mᴏɴᴅᴀʏ ᴍᴏʀɴɪɴɢ, ᴛʜᴇ ʙᴇɢɪɴɴɪɴɢ ᴏғ ᴀ ɴᴇᴡ ᴡᴇᴇᴋ. Maggie called before I had had my morning cup of tea. "Have you seen the morning papers?" she said. "That commotion at the Waldorf is all over the news. Every television and radio station claims to have the exclusive on what happened and who caused it. What on earth happened?"

How could I tell her that a pacifist like me had gotten himself into a fight with a drunk? And, worst of all, that I was unnerved by the prospect of seeing Christina again? I told Maggie everything about the night before, except for the private talks I had had with Harry and his wife, not wanting to taint her judgment on what would be my best course of action. When I had finished, she, quite uncharacteristically, said nothing. Curious, I pressed for an explanation. "Maggie," I said. "Are you all right?"

"I'm perfectly fine," she told me. "I was just reflecting on the miracle this young lady has managed to perform. She's come into your life and actually added some excitement to it. I hope you really did sweep her off her feet, you know."

I was surprised and disappointed by her reaction, having thought she would be helpful in getting me out of this predicament.

"It seems, Mr. Richardson," she added, "that you have finally met your match. For five years I've warned you—to no avail, I might add—that one day a woman was going to take your charming nature too seriously. I hope this one does pursue you. I might finally get to see a crack in that unemotional façade you hide behind."

I had not expected an attack, and my first reaction was to be angry.

"Listen here, Mrs. Bickerstaff!" I said. "If you're not going to be any more helpful than that, we have business to attend to."

It was true that we had a very busy week ahead of us, and I was determined not to let anything impede its progress. Opening my planner, I prepared to return to my peaceful existence.

Around noon, Maggie interrupted me. "Mr. Richardson, you have an important call on line one."

Deep in thought about a slogan for John's company, I grabbed the phone without noticing that she hadn't let me know who was calling.

"Tony," a woman sobbed, "I—I'm so sorry."

It was Christina. My first impulse was to protest. Why did she feel that she had a right to intrude into my life, particularly after what had happened on Friday?

"Why are you calling me?" I demanded. "How did you get this number? Why won't you leave me alone? What did I ever do to you? Please, don't call here again."

"You should have told me who was calling," I told Maggie as I held on tightly to the receiver. "Don't you ever do that again! For if you do, so help me God—and I am not being belligerent, ma'am—I will have you replaced. How is that for speaking the King's English?"

She opened her mouth as if to say something then turned and walked out of the office.

Wow, I thought. My blood must be curdling. Never could I recall being this angry. Clearly, I could do no more work today. These same walls that had harbored me for so long were stifling me. Hurrying outside, I jumped in my car and headed for the highway, en route to some quiet haven where I could have some peace . . . although it was beginning to dawn on me that wherever I went, Christina's spirit would seek me out.

The radio station's announcers kept repeating the "Waldorf exclusive" as one of their top stories every ten minutes. Disgusted by the whole thing, I turned it off, impatient to get to the marina where I could sit on the dock and watch the boats sail by. But first I knew that I had better make amends with Maggie, and so I called to apologize.

"Richardson's and Associates," she answered, ever the professional.

"Maggie, I am so sorry." I felt like the drunk in the hotel who repeatedly told his wife he would never touch another drink. "I had no right to take my frustrations out on you. I haven't lost my temper that way in a long time. Please forgive me."

"I'm happy that it happened, Tony," she told me. "I'm not exactly thrilled about what you said, of course, but it's nice to see that you're human after all. I am glad you called for another reason. You're not going to believe this. Christina is here and she is not leaving until she speaks with you."

"She—she is *where*? This can't be!" Why wouldn't this woman leave me alone? Would I never be rid of her? "Maggie, tell—say—make up something."

"I'll do no such thing, Mr. Richardson!" she told me firmly. "You pay me to manage your financial affairs, not to get involved in your love interests."

"Love interests! Love interests?"

"I have a hunch she'll be waiting no matter how long it takes," Maggie assured me. "Shall I tell her that you're on your way, sir?"

"What a brazen young woman!" Irritated that I had to abdicate my excursion to the marina, I sped to the next exit, not knowing what to expect to find waiting for me.

"No such luck, sir. I put her in your office," Maggie said, noting my expression of relief at not seeing Christina in the foyer. "I knew you wouldn't want her attracting attention out here."

I have always admired Maggie for her quick thinking and sense of professionalism. I would have told her so, but all I could think of were some choice words with which to lace Christina.

I opened the door to find Christina gazing out my window. Upon my entering, she turned, and once again we stared at each other. Today she had on a simple, cotton, fitted tee with an expanding V-neck, dark-blue denims, and short, black boots. Even simply dressed, she was a breathtaking sight.

Trying to get the upper hand on the situation, I spoke first. "Mrs. Bickerstaff informs me that there is a matter of great urgency that you wish to discuss." I motioned her to a seat while I took my rightful place behind the desk and assumed a businesslike expression.

"I don't blame you for never wanting to see me again," she said.

You don't know the half of it, I thought.

"I never meant to cause all this trouble for you."

I wondered what she could have done if she had really tried. Still, I forced myself to listen as she continued. No matter what story she told, I was going to make sure that we never saw each other again.

"Remember that I told you my father was stricter than my mother?"

I nodded, not wanting to say anything that would prolong this interview any further than was necessary.

"Well, at the age of five, my mother and father discovered I had a talent for music. According to mother, my father used to bring home all sorts of odd things he bartered for in order to sell. His greatest triumph, she said, was when he brought home an old violin. He dreamed of selling it for a great deal of money. But he decided to make money from me when I grew attached to the instrument."

She continued by telling me about the torturous hours of practice, how her father forced her to play all over town, how he dreamed of getting rich and so brought the family to America, how everyone except she had slaved in sweatshops and restaurants, working two or three jobs in order to educate her.

Sitting on the edge of my seat, I listened more intently.

"When I began touring around the world," she continued, "I longed for a different way of life. When you're on stage listening to the audience applaud, it feels so good . . . but no matter how loud they clap, it can't take away the loneliness of an empty hotel room."

A lonely hotel room, I thought to myself, can feel just as lonely as an empty house.

"I confronted my father," she said. "He told my

mother that I was ashamed of them, that I no longer respected their wishes or the old world values they were accustomed to."

I wanted to reach out to her, but how could I? I had retreated to the business world to forget the tragedy of my own past.

"But what hurt most," she said, fighting back tears, "was when he closed the door in my face as he told my mother that they only had one daughter left— my sister."

She was, I saw then, as lonely as I, but I knew she would have to seek comfort from someone else.

"Christina, your story is very touching," I said. "But what does it have to do with me?"

"I usually eat alone in my room before a concert. But on that particular Saturday, I decided to go for a walk to clear my head and wandered into my favorite restaurant. Georgio told me, if only I had called . . ."

"Georgio?"

"The maître d'. He said he would have saved my favorite table for me, but he'd just given it away no more than five minutes ago. 'Funny,' he said. 'Must be a night for people to dine alone.'

"I saw that he was swamped with guests, but I had to know what he meant. I wondered who you were and decided to see for myself. I stopped before you could see me. I felt warm all of a sudden and was surprised to find Georgio beside me."

Christina's eyes glistened when she told me how Georgio had returned with a devilish grin and stated that I had consented to have her join me.

"I will never forget his words," she said, "as he pushed me forward. 'Opportunity knocked, and faith answered.'"

Opportunity for what? I wondered. Surely, Georgio couldn't have thought he had been entrusted with Cupid's arrow? I struggled with whether or not to ask her, but curiosity got the better of me.

"One thing I don't know," I said, "is what happened while we were sitting there. What did I do or say that made you take an interest in me?"

"There was something about the way you listened to me, Tony. I know that I never should have bared my soul to you. But I sensed something—sympathy, an understanding—as if you knew exactly how I felt. You seem so controlled, and yet there is a dark side to you, a side you never allow others to see. I'm sure of it."

"You could tell all that from a forty-minute conversation?"

"A woman can tell that and more," she said. "Especially when a man pretends to be preoccupied when all the while he is sneaking a peek at you."

I should have focused more on the paper.

"But the best way a woman knows," she said, leaning closer to my desk, "is when a man tries to avoid her."

How could she know that I never wanted to see her again? I wondered. How long was she here before Maggie called me? Did they have a chance to talk, to scheme together? But what was I thinking? Surely Maggie wouldn't . . .

"Mr. Richardson," she said, "It must be very easy sweeping a woman off her feet with your charm and grace. Excite her about the possibility of sharing her heart and body with you. Then, stopping short, leaving a void where hope once lingered. You may have done that in the past and gotten away with it, but make no mistake about this: now that I have found you, I have no intention of ever letting you go."

She picked up her jacket and left me. I was bewildered that she had actually come into my office, *my* place of authority, and tried to gain the upper hand in what was apparently a struggle of wills between us. Harry had warned me about playing games where love was concerned and that if I did, I would surely lose. However, I felt the slap from the challenge issued, and there was no way I could refuse.

Five years ago when I was struggling to get my business started and still shackled to working for someone, I hired a young woman to assist me. My concern over her traveling home alone late at night found me on more than one occasion giving her a ride. To my surprise, her husband showed up at the office one day to pick her up himself, and we became friends. His wife, a woman of strong character, kept such a tight rein on him that I would constantly tease her about holding on so tight.

"He will never leave me," she would say complacently. "Never!"

Attitudes such as this always troubled me and were part of the reason that, ever since my loss, I had stayed clear of emotional entanglements.

"He was a wild man once," she told me. "But as you can see, he's become as docile as a lamb."

I could remember assuring her that that would never happen to me.

"I can't wait till you find a real woman," she told me. "When you fall truly in love you'll become like the rest of the men. She'll have you wrapped around her little finger."

Strange how that thought so often came to mind,

so often, in fact, that I actually worried about the possibility that someday I might lose my freedom. Finally, I decided to go on the offensive to preserve the sanctity of being single and made a five-year plan to gain financial success and to acquire more money than I would ever need. Nothing was going to impede my progress toward my future goal, least of all a woman.

And suddenly this virtual stranger was trying to enter my world and disturb my carefully laid plans, which simply would not do. I had worked too hard and fought too many battles to give up. Besides, I was too set in my ways. Even if my life was bereft of passion, it was a safe haven for me, free from either euphoria or depression. I had only known Christina for two weeks, and already I had been involved in a brawl, had crossed swords with Maggie, and to top it all off: I had had an emotional outburst.

Immediately after Christina's departure, I started formulating a plan to extricate myself from this predicament. So naïve was I back then about affairs of the heart that I actually tried to solve the problem logically. Forgetting Harry's claim that men with far more intelligence than I had fought and lost this battle, I was determined to emerge victorious.

Maggie entered my office with a big smile on her face. "I see that the lion has been bearded in his own domain," she said.

"Very funny," I replied. "We have work to do. You know the goals that I have set for the company. Nowhere in my five-year plan did I factor in the intangible of choosing a wife. In fact, I have deliberately abstained from becoming romantically involved so that my full attention could be given to my business."

"You're considering getting married?" Maggie asked me, raising her eyebrows.

"What the—what are you talking about? Who mentioned anything about getting married?"

"Tony," she said, leaning across my desk in a confidential manner, "I have never heard the word 'wife' come out of your mouth before."

As quickly as I reassured her that I had no intention of getting married, she collapsed into a chair.

"Maggie," I said, "is something wrong?"

"No, Mr. Richardson, what could possibly be wrong? You were saying that you have no intention of getting married."

"No intention, of course. Christina told me a very interesting story which explains some of what she has been going through, and she dropped a bombshell of a statement before leaving. She's not letting me go. In fact, she suggested that I'd better get used to having her around. And that, my dear Maggie, is my ace in the hole."

"I'm not following you," she said, frowning.

She was usually so perceptive that it exasperated me that she could not see what I meant at once. I am afraid that I was becoming rather quick-tempered with anything that concerned Christina.

"Get me a copy of the performance schedule for Lincoln Center," I told her. "Talk with your contacts and pool resources to let me know where Christina is scheduled to appear when she is not playing there."

"I see," Maggie observed. "By knowing where she is, you hope to avoid her completely?"

"Not only that," I replied, "I want to see if she can make good on her claim. Get me the schedule so I can call her bluff."

Feeling that I had prepared for every contingency, I plunged back into my work, unaware that I was to learn why the use of logic serves no purpose in affairs of the heart.

On the way home that night I decided to go to the marina after all. I love going there for two reasons: first, to gaze at the boats and dream of being able to sail into the sunset, and second, to gather my thoughts when I am confronted by a taxing situation with no easy solution in sight.

Walking toward the dock, I could see the rising moon silhouetted against the backdrop of a purple-blue sky. I enjoyed the gentle breeze across my face. I watched the tide as it slowly came in. It was so serene there, listening to the faint roar of the ocean, that I wondered if I could forget the tragedy of my past and let anyone into my world again.

Looking at it from every angle, I decided it could never work between Christina and I. Beautiful and talented as she was, her world was far different from mine. Then those two voices decided to join in again. One reiterated how lovely Christina was and how even when simply dressed, she still managed to take my breath away. The other countered that with the difference in our ages, she deserved to be with a younger man.

Yet I continued to struggle, weighing each opinion: that the beautiful and vivacious young woman would add some zest to my life, and that, being malcontented, because I did not achieve all my goals. And what of the promise I had made to another?

And through it all, no solace from the past could I find, even from the ever present and resounding Biblical saying: "Whatsoever thou hand findeth to do; do it with all thy might."

Jarred by those musings and feeling utterly helpless that the tragedy would again befall me, I headed home, more determined than ever to put Christina out of my mind.

Breaking from my customary routine, I didn't put on the television, opting instead for the calming effect of soft music. Lady was nowhere in sight, but I refilled her bowl. I was in a melancholy mood and playing Peter White's "My Prayer" didn't do much to help.

Suddenly, Lady jumped into my lap. I massaged the top of her head, and, for the first time in quite awhile, I felt like crying. But being taught as a boy that men do not cry, I lay on the couch hugging Lady as the music filled the room.

On the way to work the next morning, I decided to start the day on an upbeat note with Grover Washington Jr.'s "Take Five (Take Another Five)" since its rhythmic bass had a way of revving me up to start the day.

Figuring to make up for the lost time of the previous day, I was surprised when the phone rang. "Maggie," I said, "what are you doing there so early?"

There was a long pause. "I wanted to have those schedules you asked for on your desk," she finally replied.

"Are you okay?" I asked her.

"Yes." Her voice became, if possible, even more businesslike than usual. "Why do you ask?"

"Can't really put my finger on it, but you sound a bit odd."

"I stayed up late last night," she told me, "and then I rushed out early this morning. As a result, I'm famished, not to mention a little irritable, because I haven't had my morning cup of tea yet."

"I'll tell you what," I told her. "I'm thirty minutes away, but for you, lady, I don't mind being sidetracked. I'll call ahead to that little place on the Lower East Side and tell them to have our order ready: two Earl Greys and a half a dozen bagels with butter and orange marmalade."

"How well you know me," she said, and I thought she sounded more cheerful already. If there was anything that I didn't need that day, it was an irritable woman on my hands.

Going to the Lower East Side is always difficult in the morning, given the amount of traffic coming into the city. One could spend a half hour in one spot and not even move an inch. Parking conditions down there are ridiculous, particularly since you have to watch out for the beat cops who love to give the owners of luxury cars tickets. When I got there, the delivery boy was in front of the restaurant. After taking the bag and tipping him, I started toward the office, already a half hour late.

As soon as I opened the office door, Maggie motioned me into the conference room.

"We'll eat in here," she said. "It's more comfortable."

Perhaps being famished accounted for Maggie's earlier mood, but she still seemed uneasy. After we finished our bagels and tea, I wanted to remain in the conference room reading the financial pages, but she insisted we get to work. Something has her irascible this morning, I thought to myself, and not wanting to add to it, I followed her to the foyer. Immediately, I detected a strange but sweet, odiferous scent coming from my office.

"Maggie, what is that scent?"

"Am I to account for every strange smell around here?" she asked, while moving toward her desk.

Opening my office door, I was astonished to see the room inundated with flowers. Everywhere I turned there was a beautiful floral arrangement. On the desk on top of what I assumed to be Maggie's report was a pink envelope that contained a card showing a couple standing by a lake holding hands, with a figure of cupid silhouetted against the moonlight.

Underneath was a poem entitled "Straight to the Heart."

Straight to the heart, Cupid's arrow flew,
Bringing the hearts of two who never knew,
Who were headed to the brink of despair,
Both searching for love and never knowing where.

Was it around the next corner, or staring us right in the face?
Both hoping it would be wonderful, all the lonely feelings erased,
Straight to our hearts, Cupid's arrow flew with care,
Turning what was one into a lovely pair.

At the bottom of the card she had written, "Dearest, I can't stop thinking of you. Love, Christina."

What a way to be thought of—*Dearest!* "Maggie," I said sternly, "she had to have help to pull this off."

"I'm sorry, Tony, but I didn't have the heart to refuse her when she told me what she intended."

"When did you know?"

"Yesterday. How was I to know her 'little gift' was going to be a van full of flowers?"

"Don't worry about it," I said, amused at the

situation in spite of myself. "I can't blame you for this." It occurred to me that it might be better to change my strategy and give in, since the more I resisted, the more determined she became. I wonder if I should?

"Maggie," I said, "please get her on the phone."

I had, you see, decided to lull her into a false sense of security. That should, I thought, reduce her tenacity and allow me to get back to work. Vowing to keep my emotions under complete control and armed with Maggie's list of concert dates, I was going to beat her at her own game.

Maggie's voice on the intercom interrupted my train of thought. "Mr. Richardson," she said, "Miss Jaloqua is on line one."

"Hi, princess," I said, mustering as much enthusiasm as I could. "That was definitely a nice gesture on your part."

"Then you're not angry?"

"No, on the contrary, I'm speechless," I told her, about to put step one of my plan into action. "I know that you have a concert tonight, but if you're not busy on Thursday night, maybe we can get together."

She was free. How could it have been otherwise, given the circumstances? The relief in her voice actually made me feel a little guilty.

My plan was very simple; I would spend time with her, show her that my world was as busy as hers. As we were pulled in different directions due to our schedules, surely she would see that we weren't compatible. I needed to focus on my business; she, enlightening the world with her music.

But if all else failed, I also had her father on my side, spouting off about family honor. Confronted with all these obstacles, she was certain to see that the odds were insurmountable. Then again, she might *think* she was in love. Since she was an artist, that was understandable, but in the end I was certain that practicality would rule the day.

Relieved that I had found the solution to this, I called Maggie into my office to get some work done and started working on the campaign for John's company. I was in a lighter mood for the rest of the day, although maybe working in what had become literally a garden had something to do with it. Whatever the reason, I didn't realize it was five until Maggie came to bid me good night.

She gazed at the flowers. "Tony, what do you want me to do with them?"

"Put them in the spare office, but leave a few in here."

"You don't mind if I have one on my desk, do you?"

"Of course not," I said. "I don't think Miss Jaloqua would mind." It was, I found, rather pleasant to share the largess.

After she was gone, I rested my head on the back of the chair and let my thoughts drift in Christina's direction. I had to admit that she was such a vision of loveliness that she simply took my breath away. And she had certainly brought excitement into my life.

What if it could work? I wondered. Could I allow myself to go through it all again? Could I really open up my heart and let someone into my world? Would I be able to go all the way this time and not become apprehensive when my feelings became too strong . . . ? *No.* I couldn't go through all that anguish and hurt again. Once bitten, twice shy. Still, had I really become morose since the departure of my first love?

Which one of these arguments was valid? Was my life really that bereft of passion? Had I really replaced love and zest for life, with all its trials and tribulations, for a life of complacency? When a man takes a hard look at his life and asks these kinds of questions, he is seldom pleased with the answers that come from within. He may be able to fool the world that he enjoys his solitary existence, but how does he go about lying to his mirror?

Saddened, I left the office and drove to the marina again. This time, sitting on a cluster of rocks, I listened to the roar of the ocean and watched the waves come crashing in. How peaceful the water had seemed earlier, and, in just a few hours, everything had changed.

I looked at the stars as the tempest released its fury, and my thoughts turned to a past I seldom allowed myself to remember.

Why were you taken from me? Why was I left to suffer? Everything had been so right with our world. I have never known any two people as happy as we . . .

But have I grown cynical about all women? I thought. I measured each one against the essence of you, deluding myself that I could recapture what we had with someone else, and when the façade faded, so did I, leaving them to wonder if they did something wrong, when in reality it was me.

How many women did I hurt before I realized that no one could take your place? I shut down emotionally in order to protect them and devote all my time to work, hoping and praying that the memory of you is all I need.

Such a simple plan: close my heart and avoid all situations that would allow anyone to enter again. So dark were the recesses of my heart that there is no way it will ever see the light of love.

For five years, I have been able to put that plan into action, building an empire that, I told myself, is being built in your honor.

So why, when I am so close to the pinnacle of success, has this woman come into my life? Crying out in anger, I didn't notice an old man on the dock, wearing a ragged coat and torn sneakers. With his long, unkempt gray hair and beard, he was a pitiful sight.

When he asked me for change, my first impulse was to refuse on the grounds that, given the way he smelled, he would probably spend it on something to drink. And later, when I found out that a fifty-dollar bill was gone, I wondered if somehow, as absorbed as I had been in my thoughts, I had actually given it to him.

As quickly as it had come, the fury of the ocean dissipated. Suddenly, as I watched the waves receding, I felt an overwhelming peace. Would Christina's presence make a change in my life? I thought to myself. And if it did, would I be wise enough to embrace it?

Chapter 5

Wednesday morning found me in a chipper mood. I was up an hour earlier than usual, listening to Maggie's station and singing along with the music while preparing to go to the office. It wasn't long after going through Lady's ritual that I was out the door.

Arriving early at the office meant I would have time to plan my special evening with Christina. As I walked in the door, it occurred to me that my waiting room was singularly drab with its black sofas and non-descript tables. I had wanted a conservative look, and had somehow managed to create an atmosphere that reflected my own mood.

After pausing by Maggie's desk to smell a single rosebud, I went to my office and jumped on the computer to make plans for the evening I had in mind. It took no more than fifteen minutes to find the Web sites I needed to complete my reservations. The ringing of the phone startled me.

"Dearest, I needed to hear your voice," Christina told me. "I couldn't sleep last night. I kept tossing and turning, thinking about you."

"Now, princess," I admonished her, "you know you have to perform tonight. You have a long career to think of, after all. And I have a lot to do as well. That's why I am here earlier than usual."

"I'll be fine," she assured me. "Particularly since the next night will be devoted solely to you."

"I'm glad of that," I told her. "I wouldn't want you not to be at your absolute best."

"I know you're right," she said with a sigh. "I must go and practice. I wish I could spend the entire day talking with you, my love."

"I know, princess," I said, "I feel the same way. But we're both busy people."

It would do us no good to be derelict in our duties, I thought to myself. But she had said "my love." Those words had triggered an upsurge of emotions, but before I could give it any further thought, Maggie appeared with notepad and pen in hand. I told her to put them away.

"I want to explain something," I told her.

"Something personal?"

"Yes, sit down and listen. You see, I woke up in a most peculiar mood this morning. I actually found myself listening to your favorite station on my way to work. I stopped to smell the roses on your desk. And when I went through the foyer, I suddenly realized how drab everything is here. Drab and utilitarian."

"I can take care of it," she told me. "Just leave everything to me."

All morning Maggie was on the phone talking to decorators. I kept overhearing bits and pieces of her conversations as I hurried between my office and the conference room, putting the final touches on John's new campaign blitz.

"You are to spare no expense," I heard her say once. "Everything must be changed. I want the very earliest appointment."

Thursday, overanxious about my arrangements

for the evening, I left the office around one, and, since it was still early, went back to the marina. There was nothing ominous about the park in the daytime. Joggers were running, mothers pushed their children in carriages, and couples held hands and watched the boats sail by. It occurred to me that it was ironic that a place to which so many people swarmed during the day should be a spot where drunks and addicts gathered at night.

I saw a father wheeling his son on a bike and I thought about what a wonderful experience fatherhood must be, passing on your knowledge and wisdom, preparing your children for life. What makes some men such good and loving fathers, I wondered, while others like me have been cheated out of our opportunity?

No longer able to watch them, I left the park, troubled and a bit resentful, dismissing the past from my mind. I had to get ready for a lovely evening and didn't need anything dampening my mood.

At five o'clock precisely, the driver from Royalty Limousine arrived. His name was Matt. He was around five feet, six inches tall with a bodybuilder's build, surprisingly soft eyes, and a nose that must have been broken a few times.

"I'll be waiting by the car whenever you're ready," he told me.

After I attended to Lady's needs, I was ready. As Matt held the door open for me, I told him that I was indeed fortunate tonight.

"How is that, sir?"

"I have to thank the people at Royalty, for they not only sent me a driver, but a bodyguard as well."

"That is one way to look at it, sir."

"Ever done any boxing?"

"Yes, sir. Is it that obvious?"

"I couldn't help noticing that your nose seems to have been broken," I told him. "The only thing I didn't know was whether it was due to boxing matches or barroom brawls."

He laughed aloud. "I would say a little of both, sir."

"Can we come to an agreement tonight, Matt? 'Sir' makes me feel as if I am an old man."

"Okay, boss," he replied. "How's that? We are trained to provide excellent service, and it wouldn't look good if I called you by your first name."

"Very well," I replied. "Far be it from me to tell you how to do your job."

When we pulled up at the Waldorf, Matt remained in the car while the doorman opened my door. To my surprise, Christina was waiting in the lobby, a sight to behold. She wore a lovely, black slip-dress studded with a rhinestone neckline and a matching popover shrug, a combination which accentuated her cleavage. Her black pumps featured a unique strap formation that wrapped around her slim ankles. Her earrings were diamond studs, and a Louis Vuitton evening purse completed the outfit.

"I hope I haven't been guilty of keeping you waiting, pretty lady," I said, guiding her to the door. "Your chariot awaits."

I introduced her to Matt, and off we went to the World Yacht Marina from which our yacht was scheduled to depart at seven, with boarding to begin promptly at six from Pier 81.

"I'll be back at ten to pick you up, boss," Matt assured me as he held the door for us.

"Make sure that my other arrangements are confirmed," I said in a low voice, gratified to see Christina's eyes grow wide as she realized what was in store.

I had chosen a cruise on the yacht because it made for such a luxurious setting, with panoramic windows that allow one an unobstructed view of the world-famous skyline, plus a sundeck that was perfect for lounging over dessert or for a simple stroll after dinner. Style, class, and comfort were what the World Yacht was famous for, and their representative had assured me that they would do everything in their power to make the night a memorable one.

I had even added "ambassador service" which included a number of extras such as preferred seating, caviar, a glass of champagne, and personalized service. As soon as we were seated, our waitress came by and handed Christina a bouquet of long-stemmed roses.

Christina cradled the roses and then excused herself. I saw that her eyes had welled up with tears.

"Are you all right, princess?" I asked when she returned.

"Yes, dearest, I am perfectly fine," she told me "It's just that I've never had anyone treat me so special before, with their thoughts only of my happiness. I had to leave for a few moments, otherwise I would be crying uncontrollably."

"I'm sorry," I whispered. "I didn't mean to make you cry."

"Dearest," she said, "there's nothing to be sorry about. The tears I shed were from happiness. You don't realize how you've changed my life."

Have I really? I thought to myself. My God, she is a lovely woman. How do I break her heart? How can

I convince her that she is better off with someone else, and not with some basket case who can't let go of the past?

But, for the time being, the ambiance was incredible with the view of the skyline. The combination of soft lights and music added to an amorous mood which I was certain both of us were feeling.

Five years is a long time to have held on to the past, but how could I forget? All I had done since that tragic day was live my life in her memory.

The waitress approached as Christina finished her strawberry daiquiri, and I, realizing that I had fallen behind, quickly drank the remainder of my usual piña colada. Christina ordered a shrimp cocktail for an appetizer and I the seafood ceviche.

The band was playing something soft that I immediately recognized. It was a Steve Cole track from his latest album, entitled *Our Love*.

Christina took my hand. "I love the way you look at me," she said, "as though there were no one else in the room!"

Was I looking at her or reminiscing about the past? Perhaps, they are one and the same. What purpose had meeting Christina served? Had she helped me to forget, or set me on a course of repeating history? Whichever it was, I had to forget all of that and follow through with my plan. But somehow my heart betrayed me.

"I can't help myself, princess," I told her, brushing back her hair with one hand. "You're a sight to behold. It seems that when God was making you, he told his angels, 'On this one, spend a little more time.'"

When she smiled at me, it was as if the radiance from her smile reached down to the darkest recesses of my heart and illuminated it, but Kenny G's "Innocence" brought me back to reality.

And yet our worlds were so different. She has a talent that deserves to be shared, I thought. Her music could touch the lives of so many and inspire others to develop their gifts. I had always believed that music is the beacon of hope that there is still beauty and good in the world. And then I told myself I must not lose sight of why I was there.

"Tony, what is wrong?" she asked me.

"What do you mean?" I said, genuinely puzzled. "What could possibly be wrong on a night like this?"

Christina squeezed my hand a little tighter. "I know we're together," she said, "but I sense that you're far away. What has made you so sad? Can't you at least share your thoughts with me?"

How can I share? I thought to myself. There was no way I was going to relive that hell again. But Christina's declaration had touched my heart in a way that I thought was lost to me forever. She told me that, from the first moment she had set eyes on me, she had fallen in love.

She went on to say that she thought about me all day, and dreamed about our being together when she went to sleep at night. But what she was trying to understand, she said, was why I seemed so sad. She believed that somehow I must have been hurt in the past, and she said that she would do anything to ensure my happiness.

"All that I am," she said, "all I will ever be, is centered on loving you for the rest of my life."

It must have been the music, but this time I had to leave. I went onto the sundeck and gazed at the Hudson River. I felt the breeze brush against my face, and then the tears that I had held in for so long began to overflow.

I couldn't help myself. Such innocence. Such passion. Such outward and inward beauty. My world would never be the same again.

I didn't realize that Christina had joined me on the deck until I turned to find her standing behind me, hugging herself against the chill. Taking off my sports coat, I wrapped it around her shoulders, and we embraced without saying a word. "You're The One" was playing. I didn't know what happened to me, but suddenly I had to confide in her.

I told her about the war that raged within me because of what she was: innocent, youthful, gifted, with all the attributes that would take her in a direction different from my own. How I had tried to avoid her due to the obstacles that threatened our being together, and how my heart had betrayed me because of the beauty and excitement she had brought back into my world.

I tried to make her understand that I couldn't justify the way I was feeling, that cooler heads must prevail, but I was afraid that, just as she had done, I too had fallen in love.

"Dearest, there is no need to be afraid," she said, putting her fingers to my lips. "Please, no more words."

She inched closer and our eyes met. Hesitantly, we moved toward one another. Awkwardly at first, I tried to trace the outline of her lips with mine. Somehow I felt safer on the perimeter, but Christina was entirely different.

With each retreating trace of my lips, her kisses became more passionate. Moving in unison, we took turns receiving each other until I realized that if we continued, we would never make it back to the table. I tried to pull away, but she clutched me tighter. As our passions overflowed, I gave into her.

I could have gone on kissing her forever, but I remembered the chorus from the song that was playing and I began to shudder.

You're the one I've searched for all my life,
Loving you, girl, just feels so right,
You're the one I needed in my life,
I'll be blessed to have you as my wife.

"Dearest," she said, "is anything wrong?"

"No, no," I was swift to reply. "I guess it's a lot colder out here than I thought."

We held hands on our way to the dining room. I felt my resolve wavering, but I was intent on seeing the night through the way I had planned.

Dinner was a struggle for me since my thoughts were back on the sundeck. I noticed that Christina picked at her food, but I never questioned her, afraid of what she might say was the cause.

Luckily for me, the photographer that had taken our picture when we boarded interrupted us for another, and we purchased both at the end of the cruise.

We arrived in port at our scheduled time to find Matt waiting with the limo. Christina's eyes widened when Matt pointed to a magnificent white steed harnessed to an emerald-green carriage. I felt warm again when Christina rested her head on my shoulder.

"I wish this night would never end," she whispered. "Promise that you'll stay by my side forever."

I didn't know how to answer, so I kissed her as

the carriage headed to our final destination, the Empire State Building, where we were greeted by a guard who was waiting to escort us to the observation tower on the 102nd floor. It was difficult to imagine that we were 1,224 feet in the air with the entire city glittering below us. Indeed, we could see the lights from neighboring states.

Christina leaned back against me when we were alone, and I wrapped my arms about her. The green light that illuminated the tower enveloped us both. It was as if we were transported to another world. Suddenly, all my defenses seemed to disappear. This was not what I had planned and I realized that I was treading on dangerous ground, but I could not hold back what I felt any longer.

"Christina," I said, "I thought that I locked all possible entries to my heart." And if that wasn't enough, I exposed myself further by telling her that somehow she had found a chink in my armor and feelings that I thought I had buried forever were starting to resurface.

I wish I would have stopped there, but I rambled on. I told her that I hadn't made a contingency plan for falling in love and how it warmed my foolish heart to know that her thoughts were always of me. I also explained that I had brought her to the Empire State Building to illuminate our different paths in life, but how it all seemed so insignificant in that moment, surrounded by the majesty of the city's lights.

I couldn't believe what was coming out of my mouth. It was as if someone else had taken over my vocal chords and I was powerless to stop them. At that moment I wanted so much to be with her, but I knew the ghosts of my past would impede my desire to be with her.

"Princess," I concluded, "not an hour, minute, or second passes that my thoughts are not of you. But the lives we have chosen to lead present an obstacle and draw us in different directions."

She held on to me tighter and placed her fingers on my lips. She told me not to worry, for whatever obstacles came our way, we would face them and conquer them together.

"No one has made me feel the way you made feel tonight," she said. "I will not live my life without you. Hold me, Tony. Never will I be far from your loving arms!"

It wasn't long before we were again locked in a passionate embrace. I didn't want to let her go, and yet I knew it would be a struggle to ignore the differences of our worlds. But between her ardent embrace and the glitter of the city's lights, I tried to dismiss those thoughts, opting to enjoy the magic of the moment, at least for one night, if the ghosts of my past would let me.

Back in the limo, I asked Matt to turn on the radio, hoping for some romantic music, and, indeed, the song that played during our short ride back to the Waldorf seemed to be saying all the things I could not. I don't remember all the words, but the ones that stuck in my mind were these: *"Beyond my control . . . "*

"She the one who was in the papers?" Matt asked when I returned from seeing Christina to her elevator bank. "When the fight broke out in this hotel?"
Trying to decide what I should do, I didn't give his question much thought.

"I remember reading how she spellbound the audience," he said, "and that a lot of children are now taking up the violin because of her. Not that I wonder.

The way she looked at you tonight, you can't help but notice how passionate she is."

Caught up in the emotions of the night, I had almost forgotten what I was trying to show her. But it had come back to me when I kissed her by the elevator. I felt the passion from her kisses and realized then that the obstacles were too great. She had to go on and illuminate the world through her music, and I had to continue on my desolate path, to fulfill the promise I had made to another.

At least we would have the memory of tonight and what could have been, I had told Christina. But the road I was traveling on was one I had to walk alone. I had fought the emotions that had welled up inside me and kissed her as fervently as I could before letting the elevator door close.

As I told Matt to take me home, the last words to the song kept playing in my head. How prophetic they had been. Everything was definitely beyond my . . . yet I foolishly struggled to maintain some form of control.

Maybe it is all for the best, I told myself. There had been too much anguish and suffering in my life to subject her to. What kind of future could she and I have if I was unable and unwilling to let go of the past? I rolled down the window. The breeze blew through the limo, perhaps taking my only chance at happiness with it. I wished it would take me away. I slumped in the seat as Matt drove me home in silence.

Chapter 6

Arriving at my office the next morning, I found myself hoping Maggie wouldn't question me. And indeed she did not, greeting me instead with the remodeling designs. Sitting in the conference room, we ate bagels and drank Earl Grey tea while I pored over the proposed figures.

"Everything seems to be in order."

"Yes," she said. "The cost to redecorate the office did not go over budget."

"Maggie, where is the *Times*?" I asked. "I need to take a look at the market."

"It hasn't come yet," she said. "Why don't you look at it on your PC?"

"Never mind," I told her. "What's on today's agenda?"

At a little past noon, she came into my office holding a copy of the *New York Times*. In the arts section of the paper was a picture of Christina and me with a caption that read: "World-Renowned Violinist to Marry Business Mogul."

"I am so sorry, Tony," Maggie said. "I didn't know how to tell you."

I became enraged. What was the meaning of all this? After all, I had explained everything to Christina.

I had made it abundantly clear why we could not be together. I was sure that I had illuminated the obstacles and our differences, and why a union between us could never be possible. Why would she do this to me? Why had she gone along with me through the marvel of last night only to humiliate me in the morning? Was that why she never uttered a word when I kissed her good-bye at the elevator, since she knew that this charade was anything but over?

"Maggie," I asked, genuinely puzzled, "what are you sorry about?"

She crumpled up the paper. "I should have never agreed to her little charade. What woman sends a man she hardly knows flowers?"

"One that thinks that she's in love," I said with a shrug.

Perhaps Matt was right when he had told me how passionate she had looked. Could I have underestimated her feelings?

"Maggie," I said joyfully, "I'm making a big deal over nothing."

"Nothing," she protested. "How can you call your privacy being invaded *nothing*?"

I asked her to hand me the crumpled newspaper. Surely the picture taken of us was the one from the cruise. But Maggie dashed all my hopes when she pointed to the part in the article stating that Ms. Jaloqua neither confirmed nor denied the rumors.

I could find no reasonable explanation as to why Christina would want the world to think something contrary to the truth. I would have kept trying to reason it out, but Maggie interrupted to say that Harry was on the line.

"Listen, son," he said, "the reason why I'm calling is that I need your help. I need to sail my yacht this weekend, and I'd appreciate it if you could join me. I know it's short notice, but if it weren't important, I wouldn't ask."

I wasn't in the mood for sailing, but Harry had sounded urgent, so I agreed to meet him at the marina the next morning at 6:00 a.m. There was so much work to be done that Maggie and I pushed on ahead in silence. Before leaving, though, she checked in on me to see what I wanted done with the flowers.

If we hadn't been on the twentieth floor, I would have told her to toss them out the window. But I wanted them left where they were to rot. They would serve as a reminder that my life, since suffering that tragic loss, should remain forever and always devoid of happiness.

"Leave them where they are," I told her. "Let's proceed as planned with the remodeling."

"I know you like to keep to yourself," she said, "and I am not going to pry. But whenever you need someone to talk to, remember I am here."

I reminded Maggie that I was quite capable of handling my emotions and that I did not intend to let anything get to me. I pointed out the fact that the plan was to dissuade Christina from any notion she had had of being with me, so that I could resume my work in peace and move unobstructed toward my goal. And, although it seemed that my plan had gone awry, I was more determined than ever to rid myself of her.

"I know it was part of the plan," she said, "but I can't help noticing how Christina brought about a change in you. Are you sure you're doing the right thing? That is a very special young lady, and I wish there was some way it would have worked out for you both. Good night, Tony. I'll see you on Monday."

Sleep didn't come easily that night, not with all the tossing and turning I did. I kept telling myself that I should have never let Christina enter my world, while, at the same time, I tried to find a logical explanation for what she had done. I had even let the thought creep in of calling Christina and saying how alone in this world I was without her. Finally, however, I decided that my original plan was my best course of action.

Up at four, I quickly showered, shaved, and dressed in a teal-colored Tommy Bahama sweatshirt, stone khaki pants, and a pair of Amaretto Sperry Topsiders. I made myself a cup of Earl Grey and stared at the crumpled newspaper. Why didn't she deny the rumors? I thought to myself. Could she have misunderstood our last kiss? I was quite sure my explanation had not left any room for doubt, but there it was: "World-Renowned Violinist to Marry Business Mogul."

There was no time to feel sorry for myself. Lady jumped into my lap, and, as she did, it reminded me that I had better get moving in order to meet Harry at the marina by six.

I arrived there half an hour early.

"Howdy, son," Harry greeted me, sporting his usual navy-blue captain's hat.

"What has you in such a chipper mood this morning?" I replied. "And what's this help you need, anyway?"

"Now hold on there," he protested. "How many questions are you going to ask without giving me a chance to answer?"

Harry was stalling and I knew it. What was so

important that he needed to see me? I tried to press him before he could think of a plausible reason.

"You know Bob, my skipper?" he asked, grinning.

"Well, he had this weekend off to spend with his family, and I wanted to sail, so I invited you to keep me company."

"Where's that wonderful wife of yours?"

"She has an appointment with the hairdresser. I couldn't ask her to break that, now could I?"

Somehow I knew that these weren't the real reasons he had dragged me all the way out here. But he had sounded so urgent on the phone that I decided to play along to find out the real reason why he had asked me to join him.

"I'll go with you as long as this unplanned excursion is not an attempt to find out if there is any truth to the story that appeared in yesterday's *New York Times*."

He looked at me incredulously. "You mean to tell me that Christina and you actually made the papers?"

"Like you didn't know," I scoffed. "I understand what you're trying to do. And perhaps you're right. Maybe I do need to get away. The open sea air has always helped me to think and put things in proper perspective. Just give me your word that you won't question me about her."

"Son, the only one that has brought her up is you. Now take a look at this new yacht of mine. Helen's named her *Sea Breeze* and she's powered by twin 1200hp MANs. You should see her under full fuel and water. I swear she's topped out at twenty-five knots and cruises about twenty."

An hour later, with our fishing rods leaning against the rails, we lazily sat back and started talking about a variety of topics. True to his word, Harry never brought up Christina. But in the end, I did, primarily because, no matter how much Harry tried to distract me, I couldn't forget what she had said to me on the observation tower of the Empire State Building, with the sea of glittering lights below us.

Dearest, there's no need to worry. For whatever obstacles come our way, we will face them and conquer them together. No one has made me feel the way you made me feel tonight. I will not live my life without you. Hold me, Tony. Never will I be far from your loving arms.

How had it been, I wondered, that with those words, she had made me lose sight of what I had intended to show her, made me want nothing more than to share my world with her? How was it, then, that the next morning she had chosen not to deny the rumors of our engagement?

I must have been thinking out loud because Harry began questioning me about something he had missed. I contemplated whether to tell him or not, but decided that I needed to get this subject off my chest.

I told him about the evening and how I had struggled as I walked Christina to the elevator bank, part of me enjoying the warmth that had evolved between us, while at the same time pondering how cold-blooded I would have to be to let her go.

I went on to tell him that, for the first time in a very long while, I was no longer able to control my emotions, that I couldn't get Christina off my mind, that I was tempted to run to her and tell her that I must have her in my world—all while rationalizing my decision. She had too long and illustrious a career before her to be saddled with a man who couldn't forget his past. What life would that be for a woman who could be spreading her gift of music throughout the entire world?

Harry let me ramble on. The only indication I had that I wasn't talking to myself were his intermittent grunts.

"Why are you giving me that look?" I said when I was finally all talked out.

"I'm wondering what you're going to do next," he said, tossing me a life jacket. "I sat here and listened to you try to make sense of what she did, and I am wondering if you can live with yourself with those questions unanswered. If you can go through life trying to second-guess your decision as to whether you were right in leaving it alone or that maybe you should have gone after her and found a way to make both of your worlds compatible. But I guess you know best. It's your decision. From the looks of it, you've decided to let her wander through this world alone, and I understand your reasoning for that, too.

"I suppose," he continued, shaking his head disapprovingly, "you can look back later and be proud of yourself for having done the noble thing: letting Christina go so she can find happiness with someone else, and, as you said, spread her gift of music to the entire world."

I was reeling from his stinging criticism, but before I could ask him why he was so angry, he yelled for me to grab my rod.

I lunged at it and started reeling in the line.

"No, son, don't reel it in. Let the line out. Give her more play. Keep her head up or you will pop the line. She is a big one! We'll be the talk of the marina when we bag this one."

I kept my eye on the line. It spun out quickly.

How long did he want me to let the line go before pulling it back in? I started rocking side to side. Harry quickly strapped a belt on me. The fish was putting up one heck of a fight. My abdominal muscles tightened, and my arms ached, but I was determined to keep the fish in front of us.

"Keep a firm hold on her," Harry yelled.

"Harry," I said when the line that had been spinning out of control suddenly stopped, "I think I lost her."

"Nonsense, she's playing with you. Keep her head up! Reel her in, son. Don't let her turn her back on you."

Why don't you take over? I thought. You're far better at fishing than I am.

"Don't crowd the line. Bring her in. Hurry! Do what I tell you!"

"I'm trying! I don't feel anything, Harry! I've lost her!"

Harry ran to start the yacht. "Nonsense, I tell you. She's still with you. We're going to drag her all the way to the shore."

I couldn't see very clearly, but I thought I saw the fish's head bobbing in and out of the water. The line felt slack, but I kept reeling it in.

"No, son, you're doing it too fast. Let the line out!"

The rod bent. I struggled to hold it as close as possible. "Harry, why don't you take it?"

"You're doing fine," Harry said. "We're almost to the shore. Just hold on a minute longer then I'll hook her with the gaff."

But our elusive prize was not to be had that day. The line jammed and I could no longer hold it. I flew back into the seat as the rod shattered.

My hands trembled as I clutched the rod. I didn't know what to do, and, worst of all, I didn't know what to say. Although my eyes rested on the floor, I felt Harry staring at me.

"Son, we all have things get away from us sometimes," Harry said, patting me on the back. "It's not losing that bothers us, though; it's when we haven't done our very best to secure what is rightfully ours. You fought a hell of a fight just now, but today that fish's will to stay alive was stronger than your will to possess her. When you want something as bad as that fish wanted to live, nothing in the world can prevent you from getting it."

It was bleak that Sunday afternoon when we docked at the marina, with dark clouds towering overhead. Perfect, I thought to myself. The murkiness matched the mood I was in. Even though he didn't show it, I felt that Harry was disappointed in me for losing the fish.

We secured the yacht in silence and started walking to our cars. How was I to thank him for being a friend without appearing weak? Men are not supposed to show emotions, especially in the company of other men. But I had to say something.

"Harry."

"We're in for one hell of a storm."

"I want to—"

"Son, I've been meaning—"

I had wanted to thank him for allowing me to escape to the open sea, but when an onslaught of rain made us scramble to our cars, I settled for just saying thanks as I rolled up the window, letting him know that this time the fox got outwitted.

Watching the wiper clear the rain from the windshield, I found myself, wishing it could wipe away my indecisiveness as well. It had been in the palm of my hand. All I had to do was reach out and grab it. But something had always gotten in the way. If only I had taken the time to understand what was really important.

Harry had been so right. I should have put in more effort to secure what should have been mine. A lackluster effort cost me a fish that day, but I could no longer suppress the fact that it had cost me much, much more. After all, all Christina wanted was me to be happy. But I had been too blinded by ambition to see that.

There had been a time that I had fought Harry. With every ounce of breath in me, I had fought as valiantly as that fish had today to keep my world from falling apart. However, fortune had not smiled on me that day, for I had lost it all.

Was I going to take a trip down that road again? I should think not. I had said good-bye to Christina and perhaps to any chance of future happiness. Yes, Harry, I thought to myself, I lost the fish. But I would always keep the promise I had made to my dear, departed one, even if it meant that I would never be truly happy again.

Chapter 7

THE FOLLOWING MONTH WAS FRAUGHT WITH A BUZZ OF activities. John's campaign, in full swing, was a huge success, and other companies were soliciting us to market their businesses. More work than I anticipated had me back to those sixteen-hour workdays, often arriving at the office at eight and leaving at midnight, only to repeat the process the next day. Working twelve hours a day herself, Maggie tried her level best to keep pace until, finally, I decided to hire additional staff and an assistant to help her.

But when the day was over, alone, trying to unwind from the rigors of work, I could not stop thinking of Christina. I was tempted to go to one of her performances, but with my busy schedule I could not even find time for that. I was even working on Saturdays and sometimes Sundays to keep up with the abundance of work. The month was almost at an end and I had begun to accept life without Christina, when Maggie burst into my office with news of an upcoming wedding.

"I am so glad it's over," she said, slamming a few tabloid publications on the desk. "One month you're in love, and the next month you marry someone else."

"Maggie, what are you carrying on about?"

"This," she said, thrusting one of the papers at me. "She is no good, I tell you. She caused you all this trouble—for what?"

It didn't take me long to find out what she was so upset about. The tabloid depicted a picture of Christina and a silhouetted figure holding hands before the altar. I quickly flipped through the pages, but could find no mention of who the gentleman was. "Maggie," I chuckled, "you're making a fuss over this? Since when do you pay attention to anything written in the tabloids?"

"Nothing!" she demanded. "How can you call this nothing?"

"Because they're known to print lies to hook their unsuspecting readers."

"That may be true," she said, "but all lies and rumors start off with some basis of truth."

"I still don't see why you're upset."

"And you're not?"

"Should I be?"

"Yes," she protested. "She almost soiled your reputation and destroyed what you've worked so hard to create. She probably never loved you. You were just a toy, a sort of amusement to pass the time. Why am I surprised? Those celebrities have no morals, changing marriage partners as one would change their socks."

"But Maggie," I said, shocked in her depiction of Christina, "you know as well as I do that Christina is nothing like—"

"Have it your way, then," she said, pointing at the paper. "It's all a bunch of lies . . . Hmm, whose hand is she holding, and why the wedding gown?"

I was taken aback when Maggie left my office.

Why had she brought this up? She had always scoffed at the headlines on the tabloids before.

And also, since we were inundated with work, what purpose would it serve to tell me anything about Christina? After all, wasn't that the real reason for such an elaborate charade?

Why was I wasting time with this? So what if she had married or was going to marry? She was sure to find happiness and continue her outstanding career. With the final piece of the puzzle in place, I was determined to move forward. But curiosity got the better of me.

The tabloids lay in front of me. Several times I had disposed of them in the garbage can and paced around the room only to smooth them out on the desk again. There was no sense in trying to deny it; I had to find out what was going on. An hour elapsed before I was hit with a brainstorm. If I was not too late and Christina hadn't married, then surely preparations were under way. I wondered what famous designer she had contracted to design her gown.

"Maggie!"

"I've canceled and rescheduled all your appointments for today," she responded briskly over the intercom. "You'd better hurry if you plan on catching her." Sometimes it was scary how well that woman knew me. She had not only found out who the designer was, but also when Christina would be going in for her next fitting.

It was ironic, I thought, that the site of the designer's boutique was on Madison Avenue.

I arrived five minutes after the appointed time of three o'clock, parked my car, and sat momentarily, contemplating my best course of action and knowing that this might be my only chance. Finally, I decided to appeal to her emotions and to remind her of all that we had said to each other on that magical night. I used the ruse of being her driver to get by the receptionist. So far, so good. There was only one thing left to do, which was to figure out how to get to talk to her. I passed several rooms and found one with the door slightly ajar. An elderly woman was talking to someone behind a partition, so I went forward to take a closer look just as Christina emerged from behind it.

Startled by a voice asking if I needed assistance, I swung around and stood face-to- face with a designer whose photograph I had seen many times in fashion magazines. Telling her that I was Ms. Jaloqua's driver and that I had an important message to give to her, I followed her into the room. Christina, seeing me, rushed into my arms.

All I wanted to do at that moment was to hug her back, but I fought off the temptation. After all, I needed answers to some puzzling questions.

"What on earth are you doing here?" she exclaimed.

"What does it look like?" I retorted, holding her at length. "I need answers. Are you really going through with this marriage? Was all that you told me just lies made up in the heat of the moment? Just tell me what changed your mind about wanting to spend the rest of your life with me."

"Dearest, nothing I said that night was a lie," she told me in sotto voce, "but I distinctly remember that you were the one who told me good-bye."

"I did it to protect you."

"So why are you here?" she cried. "Who are you protecting me from now?"

How could I tell her that it was me? But she was

right about one thing. If I had let her go, then why was I here?

She asked me if I knew how much I had hurt her. That, after our good-night kiss, she had gone upstairs with tears streaming down her face and had found her mother and father waiting up. There had been a quarrel, and she had succumbed to the argument that she could not forget all the sacrifices they had made, that she owed it to the world to share her artistry, even if it meant never marrying, never having children. It tore my heart in two to see tears streaming down her face as she told me this.

"The three of us were very sad that night," she continued. "They, because they had forced me into a life of loneliness, and I, because my music was about to take the only man I ever loved away from me."

Why had so much beauty been so tormented? I thought to myself. And then suddenly I came to my senses. She asked me why I was there. Wasn't she the one getting married?

"I can't believe what you're telling me!" I exploded, managing to keep my voice down with some effort. "You're marrying a man you don't love just to not be lonely. I guess I misjudged you when I thought you had a fiery spirit, that even though our paths were strewn with obstacles, you were willing to overcome them with me. I really believed you when you said that you couldn't imagine life without me."

Coming here to find her had been a drastic mistake, I realized. How foolish I must have seemed. I had come hoping to find a way to marry her, to alter my five-year plan for financial independence to include her in my world.

"Well, I hope that you're happy!" I told her angrily.

"Be sure and send me an invitation to the wedding so I can wish you and your new husband all the best in life!"

And with that I stormed out of the room, aware of nothing except the need to put as much distance as possible between us.

Why had I gone there? Such impulsiveness was ridiculous. What had I hoped to gain? I must remain calm and methodical. My plan had succeeded. By her own admission, Christina had realized that it was over between us. But if that was so, why had she rushed into my arms? Why had there been such a look of happiness on her face? If this was the woman who was supposed to complete me, she had a funny way of showing it. I hoped she would send me an invitation so that I could actually watch her marry another man and put an end to this ordeal forever.

Several days later, when Maggie came in with her invitation to Christina's wedding, I asked her what she had done with mine.

"Whatever do you mean?" she said. "Only one was sent."

Jumping up from behind the desk, I snatched the invitation out of her hand. "Tell me that you're not trying to spare my feelings by not giving me mine!"

"Now, Tony," she said soothingly, "you know I wouldn't do that. Honestly, though, did you really expect her to invite you? I'm surprised that she even sent me this, particularly since she must have realized that, given what's happened, I have absolutely no intention of attending."

"Oh, you're going to attend," I said grimly.

"Why would I want to go to her wedding?"

"It says here that you are invited along with a

guest. Well, since I didn't get an invitation, I am going to accompany you."

"Tony," she exclaimed, "you're not going to do anything rash, are you?"

"Would I do something as silly as that?" I demanded. "I just want to wish the couple all the happiness in the world and let whomever she is marrying know that the better man won. After that, my conscience will be clear, and we can go back to focusing on business as usual."

Maggie took a deep breath. Is it a sigh of relief, I wondered, or is she hiding something? I still couldn't figure out why she would let me know about Christina's wedding plans. Surely it would have been easier to tell me after she was married? What was Maggie up to?

"I will agree to attend on one condition," she said. "Promise me that you won't say or do anything foolish to disrupt her wedding."

"Maggie, there's absolutely no need to worry," I assured her, crossing my fingers behind my back. "In fact, I'll do everything I can to make sure that the twenty-sixth of June goes according to plan."

The only thing that I neglected to mention to Maggie was whose *plan* I was thinking of.

The next three weeks were very busy with the addition of the new staff quickly transforming us into an operation bustling with energy. The remodeling added even more panache. Every day some new project needed my attention.

Maggie's assistant, a very capable young woman, made it possible for her to spend more time supervising the remodeling of the office. Consumed with all that was going on, I was able to put the thought of

Christina's upcoming wedding at the back of my mind, or as close as possible.

Now that I had more time away from the office to close deals in an informal setting, I was afforded the opportunity to play eighteen holes with John and his cronies from time to time, all of which allowed me to network in a way calculated to increase business. John often had a hard time keeping a straight face when I again and again revealed my true game on the back nine.

A week before the blessed event, Maggie called me on the car phone on my way home from a round of golf.

"I wanted to know if you made arrangements for what you're going to wear to the wedding," she said. "You do realize that it's only a week away, right?"

Suddenly I was overwhelmed with guilt. "It was wrong of me to force you to accept the invitation, Maggie," I said. "I was being vindictive. I'm sorry."

For some reason Christina brought out that nasty trait in me. In my uncontrollable rage, I had needed to exact my revenge and the only way was to gain entry to the affair, even if it meant taking advantage of someone to whom I owed so much.

"Oh, no, you don't!" she told me. "Not after I sent my acceptance. And not to mention the small fortune I spent on a gown for the evening. I've even booked an appointment for you to be fitted for a new tuxedo."

As usual, Maggie's sound reasoning made me change my mind, particularly when she pointed out the fact that my old tux was a bit shabby since I had used it for so many business functions and that, since my tailor kept my measurements on file, it would be far easier to have another one made. What was there left for me to do but comply?

The week went by quickly, and, before I knew it, the day itself was upon us. I had made sure that Matt was available to drive us and so, after picking up Maggie, we headed for Fox Hollow where Christina and her intended were to exchange nuptials at five. Matt picked us up in a stretch limousine, claiming, when I protested, that it had been the only car available.

Arriving at Fox Hollow an hour early, I escorted Maggie inside so she could mingle with the other guests. I chose to walk the grounds to admire the wide variety of daffodils, roses, and tulips that were in bloom. It was so peaceful walking and observing all of nature's beauty that I began thinking about all my inner turmoil since I had met Christina.

I had told myself repeatedly that my inability to deal with my past was why Christina and I couldn't be together. But I couldn't get her out of my mind. She had rekindled a part of me that I thought was lost forever, but her career—what would become of it? Surely I couldn't be that selfish. No, I had to do the right thing. Even if that meant that her future happiness would be in the arms of another man.

It was going to be tough enough to see Christina in her maiden state, but to hear her promise to love another forever might be more than I could stomach. I might have missed the whole proceeding if one of the groundskeepers hadn't inquired if I was lost.

I arrived in time to see Christina emerging from a side door on the arm of an elderly gentleman wearing a cutaway with pants, an ascot, and, although it was difficult to believe, spats.

With no way to get ahead of them, I stood by the door in full view. I wanted to say something to her, but the words would not come. What does someone say at a time like this? Besides, I had given Maggie my word.

As I slipped into a seat beside Maggie, who gave me a reproachful look, I told myself that soon all this would be a distant memory and I could chalk it up as another love I lost. I could have strangled the clown who had first made the observation that "it is far better to have loved and lost, than not to have loved at all."

Christina was standing beside her future husband. Most of what was being said was a blur to me, but I did hear the man say that he would take her to be his lawfully wedded wife, to love, honor, and cherish her till death did they part.

The priest asked the same of Christina.

No answer. The priest reiterated the question. Dead silence. I didn't want to believe what was happening.

Had I caused all of this with my appearance?

Suddenly, Christina dashed from the room, her veil floating behind her. Everyone, clearly stunned, was trying to get a grasp on what had happened.

"We'd better get out of here," I heard Maggie say. "In fact, I want to leave right now!"

The limousine darted from around the back of the building with the door already open. Maggie pushed me in. Off balance, I tried to hold on, but not before banging my head.

"Matt, what the—Matt, what are you doing?"

"Dearest, are you all right?" Christina was already inside.

"What are you doing here?" I demanded. "Where's Maggie?"

"Are you hurt?"

"What is going on here, princess?" I insisted.

"Matt, have you taken leave of your senses?" I looked at Christina. "Who's the maniac driving? It can't be Matt. Where are we headed? Will you be so kind as to bring me up to speed with what is going on?"

"You'll see Maggie and Matt shortly," she told me. "We're headed to Crest Hollow."

"Crest Hollow?"

"Yes."

"Why? What for?"

"So we can be married."

As the limo sped along Jericho Turnpike, Christina began to fill in the missing pieces.

"I tried to tell you that day in the designer's boutique," she said, folding up her train, "but you wouldn't listen. I was so happy to see you, but I was also shocked as to why you were there. I needed to know whether you loved me or not, and that explains my little ruse."

I had lauded myself for being able to size up anyone or any situation, no matter how few facts I had, but after the story Christina told me, nothing could have been further from the truth.

Christina began by explaining that she couldn't understand my insistence on her getting married. It wasn't until I stormed out of the boutique that one of the designer's workers, coming back from lunch, had showed her the picture in the paper.

It had been then that she realized that I must have had feelings for her. Why else would I go out of my way to make a fool of myself at the boutique? And if I had acted that way because I thought she was going to marry someone else, why not let me go on thinking that and use it to her advantage?

She was well acquainted with the designer—so well, in fact, that she had been asked to help promote a new line of bridal gowns for a series of commercials.

That was when the marketing people had had the idea of using our picture from the cruise along with one of her modeling the bridal gowns and cropped them together, slipping them to the tabloids to drum up some free publicity.

With the help of others, whom she refused to name, she had used the set from one of the commercials shot at Fox Hollow to complete the ruse.

"You mean to tell me," I demanded, embarrassed at being outsmarted, "that the whole thing was staged?"

"Yes."

"I don't believe it!"

"And why not?" she asked, with a huge smile on her face.

I told her that, for starters, there was no way she could be that devious. In order for her plan to have worked, she had to be absolutely sure I would show up. And if I did, how could she be certain that I would not decide to remain among the grounds as opposed to ruining her day?

She laughed aloud, and I realized that the person closest to me had to have had a hand in this.

"Why would Maggie, who has worked intimately with me for years, betray my trust for you?" I demanded.

"Whether she rendered aid or not," Christina said, leaning forward, as if taking me into her confidence, "is not for me to say. And whatever her reason, if she did, you will have to get it from her."

I was incensed, but not for the reason I should have been. What bothered me was that this young woman had had the courage to go after what she wanted, while I, hurt from the tragedy that had befallen me, chose to shun life completely unless it was tied to my work.

And there was more. How could I go through with this? I would be the laughingstock of everyone who knew about this little charade. And what of Momma? My God, how she would berate me when she knew that her son, legendary for his practicality, could have been manipulated into marrying someone?

Maggie had a lot to answer for if she indeed had had a hand in this. And Matt, too. Besides Maggie, he was the last person I had thought would betray me.

While all these thoughts were swirling around in my head, Christina displayed the coolest demeanor in the world. In fact, she acted as if she were performing on stage.

You couldn't begin to understand the life I've led, I thought to myself. And as lovely as you look today, deep within your heart, you should have known I was trying to spare you all my anguish.

How I longed to be the source of her happiness. But unable to let go of my past, I knew that our union would bring her nothing but pain.

I decided to tell her exactly how I felt, to put an end to this masquerade once and for all, but just as I opened my mouth to speak, we arrived at the Crest Hollow Country Club.

Getting out of the limo, I was glad to see Maggie and Matt.

Maggie rushed toward me. "Mr. Richardson! Are you okay?"

"Yes, but I'm a little confused as to how all this came together. But I guess you can fill me in on your part in this later. You won't be taking off anytime soon, will you, Matt?"

"No, boss," he said with a chuckle. "I'm not going anywhere at the moment."

I snuck a peek at Christina. What could she have said to enlist Maggie and Matt's help? She might be more devious than I had first thought. I realized that I had to make sure that I did not underestimate that face of innocence. Imagine being manipulated like this! But sensing that I needed to give the illusion that I had not, in fact, become a milquetoast, I took charge of the situation by asking Christina and Maggie to join me under a nearby tree.

"Okay, ladies," I said, "It seems that you two have gone to a lot of trouble to put this together. Now, how am I going to get married? I didn't pick out a ring, and I have no family members present."

With a mischievous smile, Maggie told me not to worry, that all the details had been covered. And sure enough, when Matt led me through a side door of the chapel, there was my cousin Andrew, replete in a tuxedo like my own and wearing a Cheshire cat's grin.

"I see that you finally decided to show up for your own wedding," he said, clapping me on the back. "I thought you might have canceled, citing business concerns, and that I'd have to marry that pretty lady for you."

Andrew and I were more like brothers than cousins. A scruffy old teddy bear of a man who, along with his wife, possessed a voracious appetite, he was always on hand whenever any member of the family needed assistance. But somehow, perhaps because of what I could then see was a nearly manic determination to grow my business and his affection for family life, we had drifted apart.

"Tony," he said, looking puzzled, "what are you doing?"

I'm trying to figure that out myself. I must be crazy. How can I marry a woman I know absolutely nothing about? Is he in on the plot? And if he isn't, do I dare tell him?

"Here's the ring," he told me, taking a black-velvet box out of his pocket. "I see that you spared no expense."

He meant that Maggie had spared no expense. It all made sense. She had to be the one behind all of this, but why? Hadn't Christina said that if Maggie did help, she might have had a good reason?

"I know this is a big step," Andrew said, shaking me, "but do you think you can stop daydreaming until after the ceremony?"

Shaking my hand, Andrew wished me good luck. And then, uncharacteristically, he hugged me before pushing me out the door to take our places, awaiting the arrival of Christina.

Looking around the chapel laden with people sitting in pews on both sides, I spied Momma in the front row, accompanied by my two sisters and my brother, and wondered how Maggie could have invited them without them spilling the beans—especially my younger sister, the psychologist, who regarded me as her own and who had spent her teenage years analyzing my dates to see if they were worthy of me. But there she was, smiling approvingly with the rest of the family. With a limited view and only a second more to go before the ceremony began, I looked to my right to see my old friends Harry and Helen. I really had to admire the way all of this had been planned out, even though I was becoming increasingly concerned about how manipulative Christina could be.

The wedding march was playing, and Christina, a vision of loveliness, had started her walk down the aisle accompanied by her father, while her mother sat proudly.

When Christina stood beside me, the song that played in the background was "Together," and I couldn't help but wonder if we always would be. There were so many thoughts going through my head that I had to force myself to pay attention, otherwise I would have missed what the minister was saying.

The minister, a portly man with a beard as white as snow, had a most reverent look about him when he smiled at us, as though he had never conducted such a ceremony before.

"Do you, Tony, take Christina to be your lawfully wedded wife, to have and to hold, to honor and cherish, forsaking all others, as long as you both shall live?"

I wanted to with all my heart, but my thoughts were about my past possibly ruining our future. There was no time to tell this to Christina, so I settled for saying, "I do."

"Do you, Christina, take Tony to be your lawfully wedded husband, to have and to hold, to honor and cherish, forsaking all others, as long as you both shall live?"

"I do," Christina said emphatically.

"If you two have anything to say before I unite you in holy matrimony, you may do so now."

There was so much that I had wanted to say. How had she and Maggie managed all of this? Was she really sure about the man she was about to marry? It was true that I loved her, but how our paths differed . . . I wanted her to be free to find happiness and she, through her unwavering love, had imprisoned me to undertake the same journey on which tragedy had befallen me before. But all of these musings were lost to me when she expressed how much she loved me.

"Dearest, from the first time that fate intervened and I laid eyes on you," she said, "I began to wonder if you were the answer to my dreams."

She continued by telling how Georgio had pushed her forward, and about all the warm feelings engendered as we dined together, how she felt a sense of loss when she left the restaurant and had realized that she must see me again.

Her outpouring of affection became evident as she recalled our magical night on the yacht and the carriage ride to the Empire State Building. She said I had made her feel like a princess and like nothing mattered to me but her happiness.

"All that I am," she cried, "all that I will ever be, is wrapped up with loving you. I will spend the rest of my life making you as happy as I possibly can. I will love you today, tomorrow, and forever!"

Her words moved me as deeply as if they had reached down and shone a light on the darkest recesses of my heart. What was I going to say in response? Did I really love her that much, or was I caught up in the moment? And then I remembered Maggie teasing me about doodling Christina's name on my notepads. Had she flipped through the pages and saw how I tried to coalesce my thoughts about Christina in a poem? I recalled the one I penned while I thought it was best to let her go but secretly wished that I could love her forever.

If there were one thing I could ask for in this world,
That you and you alone would be my girl,
That you would be forever by my side
At night as I lay sleeping and in the morning
when I arise.

You have broken all the barriers and released the seal,
Showing me how good true love can really feel.
Forever is all I ask, dear; you are indeed a special girl.
Your love serves as a beacon, shedding light on my
darkened world.

I have searched for so long, to find one
as special as you,
Praying at night that Cupid's aim was true,
That he didn't miss the mark, and let you finally see
That who loves you most will always be me.

You have answered all my prayers,
Agreeing to share my world,
It will be now and forever,
Yes, now and forever, girl.

A hush came over the room and I wondered if I
had taken too long to express my feelings for her. The
minister's smile seemed frozen on his face. And then,
finally, he spoke.

"If there be any man who can show just cause
why these two should not be married, let him speak
now or forever hold his peace."

I held my breath and waited. Why must that
question be asked? I wondered. How many people
actually objected or would have the courage to let

their voice be heard? I stared at Christina as I held her hand. I could not detect any signs of nervousness.

"With the powers vested in me, I now pronounce you man and wife. Tony, you may kiss your bride."

He didn't have to tell me twice. When I lifted her veil and looked deep into her eyes, the rest of the world, along with my worries, seemed to disappear.

Before she could utter a word, I put my hand up to her lips. At that moment, all I wanted to do was seal the fact that she was indeed my wife with a kiss.

Passion erupted when our lips met. Heaven knows how long our embrace would have continued had it not been for the minister's clearing his throat and Andrew's patting me on the back more violently than necessary.

We ran out of the chapel to the strains of "Always and Forever" to be greeted outside by an onslaught of well-wishers throwing birdseed.

Photographers were ready and waiting to take pictures of us, as well as members of both our families and our friends. I was somewhat surprised when Christina introduced her father to me to find that he was diminutive in stature, with piercing eyes and a very powerful handshake. I wondered if he was trying to send a message by shaking my hand so hard.

"Tony, she really is a lovely girl," my mother interrupted, giving me a hug. "From what I've seen so far, she simply adores you. So you be sure that you don't do anything to make her unhappy. Otherwise you'll have me to answer to. I wish you and her all the happiness in the world."

"Momma," I said jokingly, "shouldn't her parents be the ones warning me about causing their daughter grief? You're supposed to be on my side, remember?"

"Son, from what I've heard, she is a strong woman filled with ideals. She has a mind of her own. She knows what she wants and has the tenacity to go after it."

My mother had done it. She had launched the first salvo under the auspices of being concerned. I had often seen that look, so often, in fact, that I knew what she was going to say before she said it. She told me how I sometimes overpower people by my way of thinking and that I handle my relationships the same way as I do my business transactions.

"Don't make that mistake with a woman like Christina," she warned me, "or your marriage life will be filled with more unpleasant moments than you can even begin to imagine now."

But Momma, if only you knew how hard I tried to avoid that from happening. How could I tell her without her finding out that I had been manipulated? My mother has always been an opinionated woman, which was, perhaps, one of the reasons we had never seen eye to eye. Whenever I was in her presence, I somehow felt inadequate, as though the tragedy was my fault. Gray-haired and carrying more weight than was good for her, she was pontificating on my good fortune of being married to Christina and how she should be treated, particularly since there were so many women that were "no good."

It reminded me of all the lectures I had had to endure in my adolescence when she had repeatedly reminded me that "one night of pleasure could lead to a lifetime of pain."

Momma, what happened was not my fault, I wanted to say. There was no way it could have been avoided. I'd done everything possible to honor her memory. I was content living a desolate life, but the woman she was so obviously fond of threatened to take me down that road again.

But history wouldn't be repeated, not if I could help it. Christina may have manipulated her way into marriage, but not even she is crafty enough to duplicate the events that had caused me five years of hell.

Chapter 8

THE EVENTS HAD ENGULFED ME AND SO I DECIDED TO SIT
by the pond to think things through. I had enlisted
Matt's help in locating Maggie, but she had remained
tight-lipped as usual. The only information she had
given me was that I needed to ask the Fosdricks where
Christina and I would be honeymooning, and so I
asked Matt for his help once again.

I couldn't believe that this was really happening.
My orderly life had been turned upside down. I decided that our honeymoon would be the perfect venue to
put an end to Christina and Maggie's meddling once
and for all.

"What are you doing out here?" Harry asked.
"You should be inside enjoying yourself."

I would be if I had had a hand in planning this,
I wanted to tell him. But I settled for thanking him and
Helen for the part they had played in making this a
magical day for Christina and me. They all must have
rehearsed their parts, because the only thing that
Harry told me was how he and Helen wouldn't have
missed being involved for the world.

He went on to say that Helen had gotten carried
away and had wanted to book Christina and me all
over the world for our honeymoon, but he had finally

convinced her that two weeks in Bermuda were more than sufficient.

"I wanted to enjoy my last moment of solitude," I muttered, "since I am now a married man."

Harry laughed aloud and motioned for us to start making our way to the reception. We were halfway there when he stopped abruptly.

"Aw, hell, son," he said, hugging me. "I should have told you this that day at the marina. I couldn't be any prouder if you were my own flesh and blood. I've watched you struggle and fight every step of the way. And with each challenge, you have come through with flying colors. Any man worth his salt would be proud to have a son like you."

Now why couldn't Momma have said that? This was perhaps my last chance to find happiness, and she had chosen to chastise me.

Every man aspires to become like the man he admires and respects, and if I could be half the man Harry was, I would be very fortunate.

"Sure got windy out here all of a sudden," Harry said, releasing me.

"Mm . . . hmm," I agreed, "blew something right into my eye."

We laughed at each other and continued to the reception hall. The ballroom was magnificent. Towering crystal chandeliers scattered glittering light over a dance floor surrounded by tables set with peach and white cloth, each adorned with white roses.

I spotted Maggie supervising the catering staff. "Madam," I said, "will you be kind enough to let the staff do their work and enjoy yourself?"

"Where have you been?" she demanded, grabbing my hand and leading me to my seat. "Honestly, Tony, you know the bride cannot enter until you are in the room. No. Don't give me any buts. Have a seat while I get the rest of the wedding party."

I knew better than to tease her, given her temperament. She seated me in one of two white wicker chairs at a long table set on a dais, only to reappear with my mother, whom, along with the rest of my family, she seated to my left. Leaving the chair to my right empty for Christina, she saw to the seating of Christina's mother and father, both of whom gave the impression of beaming broadly even while they stared askance at me.

They can't be happy about this marriage, I thought to myself. But why go along with the charade? If Christina's comments were true and they were indeed saddened to have forced their daughter into a life of loneliness, why had they changed their minds? They were trying awfully hard to conceal their displeasure from everyone else, but it had become evident to me. Why else would her father have squeezed my hand so tightly and her mother had looked upon me with disdain?

"Where does Maggie get all that energy from?" my mother whispered.

"I've been asking myself that for years," I told her, adding facetiously, "She reminds me of another special lady who always refuses to take my advice."

My mother's intrusion disturbed me. Had she picked up on the malevolent vibes?

Suddenly the lights grew dim and Christina entered the room, more beautiful than ever. The train of her wedding dress had been removed, and she was the epitome of elegance in her sheath of white satin.

"Dearest, I love you," she murmured as I rose to greet her.

Holding out my hand, I led her to the dance floor. As the band played "Our Love," I whispered this poem in her ear:

Our love is indeed a precious thing,
I can recall all the warm moments that it brings,
Remember when we danced the night away on that summer cruise,
When I held you close and whispered those tender words, I love you?

Did I do something wrong, uttering words you didn't want to hear?
Since from your captivating eyes came a flow of tears.
You held me that much tighter, as a child clutches their favorite toy,
Saying those were tears of happiness, you brought me so much joy.

I never thought I would hear you say those words to me,
I am so happy now; it's the way I envisioned it would always be,
There is only one thing left to say, and dearest please know it's true,
For the rest of my life, I will love only you.

"I wonder if I will ever find the words to explain how much I love you," Christina told me when the dance was over and others had joined us while the band played "Giving You the Best That I've Got." "Sometimes I get the feeling that I am not showing you how much I do. I know that I've told you this before, but I need to say it again. All that I am, all I ever hope to be, is wrapped up in loving you for the rest of my life. May you never know to what extent I will go to ensure your happiness."

What a strange statement, I thought. An eerie feeling had gone through me when she said, "May you never know to what extent I will go to ensure your happiness." Certainly it started me thinking about what I really knew about Christina.

But they were playing "(I Love You) For Sentimental Reasons," and I must confess that I was arrested by those loving eyes and her captivating smile.

"Princess," I asked, holding her tighter, "why would you ever think that you have to prove your love to me?"

"Pardon me," Christina's father said, tapping me on the shoulder, "but may I have the privilege of dancing with my daughter?"

"Only if you give her back to me when you're done," I said and smiled, although I didn't much feel like it, which was absurd. After all, he had every right to dance with his daughter, but I couldn't shake the feeling that he had deliberately interrupted us as I was about to tell her what the song suggested: *that I had given her my heart.*

"As long as you promise to keep her as happy as she is tonight," he told me.

Strange how much it sounded like a threat. I had just started for the terrace, thinking that perhaps the fresh air would clear my head, when Helen stopped me.

"What does a woman have to do to get a chance to dance with you?" she said playfully. "Why, Tony, is anything wrong?"

"No. Why do you ask?"

"Oh, it's probably nothing."

"Now, Helen, I've never known you to make a statement without any reason behind it."

"Well, you have this faraway look on your face."

I knew that I should exchange pleasantries, but all I could think of was what Christina had said and what I would have said. "You may never know to what extent I will go to ensure your happiness."

"It's really nothing, Helen," I told her. "I was just analyzing something Christina said."

"Everything isn't always black and white, Tony," she said, frowning. "There are a lot of gray areas in life, and sometimes you need to put that analytical mind of yours to the side and let your heart tell you what you should do. When you get a chance, really take a look at the woman you've married. She simply adores you, and through the course of your life together, you will come to find out how much. There's only one piece of advice I can give you, if you'll accept it, that is."

"You know I always value your and Harry's wisdom."

"Do yourself a favor, then. Stop analyzing everything and enjoy the gift of love God has bestowed upon you. Love Christina . . . and more important, allow her to love you."

The rest of the evening went smoothly enough. Taking Helen's advice, I turned my thoughts to making Christina happy by being the perfect bridegroom, which meant dancing with Christina's mother, along with numerous other ladies, while Christina was busy doing the same with my family. From time to time our eyes met, and I knew we were both thinking of the moment when we would board the plane to Bermuda. But, I suspected, for entirely different reasons: she not able to wait for our wedded life to begin, and I, on the other hand, eager to be alone with her so that I could put my foot down and take control. Otherwise, Christina might think she could manipulate me for the rest of my life.

I decided, before we danced our last dance, before we cut the cake and Christina threw the ceremonial wedding bouquet and garter, that there had been someone who was so busy putting all this together that she hadn't stopped long enough for me to ask her to dance. Not wanting to wait any longer, I sought out Maggie.

I found her as she was giving instructions to the staff on when to bring out the cake.

"Tony, I can't," she protested when I put my arm around her. "Not now."

"Maggie," I said, guiding her to the dance floor, "you have done a wonderful job putting all this together for Christina and me. When are you going to rest and enjoy it all yourself?"

"I am," she assured me. "Seeing you and Christina happy is all the enjoyment I want. Anyway, my night won't be over until Matt takes the two of you to the airport."

"Listen to me," I told her as we glided around the dance floor. "I've cherished every moment we have spent together. I see you as more than my executive assistant. You're one of my family and my dearest friend. For all you have done to make sure that this day was happy for Christina and me, I am, and will always be, in your debt."

But she didn't seem to be listening to me. The orchestra launched into "Too Young" and Maggie began to sob. I led her onto the balcony.

"Maggie," I said, "what's the matter? Did I say or do something to upset you?"

"No, dear," she assured me, mopping up her tears with the handkerchief I offered her, "but now is not a good time to talk about it."

"Now is as good a time as any," I protested. "It must be something serious. How can I go away on my honeymoon wondering what's wrong? You're like the Rock of Gibraltar. Not once have I seen you shed a tear in the five years I've known you. And now on the happiest day of my life, you're crying uncontrollably. Please tell me; what's the matter?"

"I guess this is as good a time as any, since I let my emotions get the better of me," she told me, looking away, clearly determined to compose herself. "When I first came to see you that day in your office . . . I had an unfair advantage that you didn't know about."

"What was that?"

"If you remember, I told you that I worked with a stockbroker. Well, what I neglected to tell you was that he was my husband."

What was this? Suddenly I was being besieged by revelations from every side. How had dancing with me made her think of her dear departed husband?

"We were a good team," Maggie told me. "You and he would have gotten along swimmingly. He was a workaholic like you, so obsessed with being a success that I couldn't get him to slow down for anything. We would continuously argue about him taking a vacation. He'd always promise that he would go after he secured the next big account. The problem was that there would always be another. One day, during a furious row, he had a heart attack. I blamed myself, though the doctor said it had only been a matter of time. I spent the better part of that year taking care of him. The stroke paralyzed him . . . "

She started trembling and I put my arms around her. "It's all right," I told her. But I wasn't at all sure that it was. What had, after all, brought this on?

"Tony—please let me finish," she said, taking my hand. She placed the handkerchief back into my pocket, smoothing it out as if it had never left. "I want to remember you this way, complete and unfettered, as you begin . . . "

"Maggie?"

She smiled and touched my face. "Thank God for Harry and Helen."

"What do they have to do with it?"

"My husband was Harry's broker," she told me. "Over the years they developed a close friendship and spent many weekends fishing. That's how Helen and I met. Harry had just purchased his yacht and invited us to be his first guests.

"When he heard about what had happened to Sam, he handled the sale of the business. I was in no condition to look after any of the financial affairs. When Sam passed away, I locked myself in the house for months, living in the memory of him and what we had had. I must have played that song a thousand times."

So it had been the song that had done it. "Is that what started you down memory lane?"

"Yes," she nodded, "it was our song. We heard it on our very first date. I asked them to play it tonight as I watched you and Christina. But . . . oh, Tony. Life without memories is unbearable. But sometimes memories are just as unbearable.

"Sam had given me a gun for protection, since

he worked late nights and was frequently away on business trips. One Sunday morning, no longer able to live without him, I had decided I would join him."

I realized for the first time that Maggie and I were haunted by the same ordeal and had chosen to deal with our loss in a similar fashion. How silly of me not to have known this after all these years.

"As fate would have it, Harry and Helen decided to visit me that day," she continued. "I pretended not to be home, hoping they would leave. But you know how Harry is. He knocked on every door, tried to open every window. I thought he had given up and was about to leave when I heard him tell Helen he was going to break the back window. I quickly shoved the gun in a drawer and rushed to open the patio doors."

She sighed deeply and went on to tell me that she had made some excuse of being in the basement putting away some of Sam's things and not hearing them. She said that Harry had barged in and told her that the reason why they had stopped by was that he needed her help. Maggie had explained to Harry that she was not in a position to help anyone and only wanted to be left alone. But he hadn't listened to a word she had said and kept on about some young man that she could help.

"Helen stood near me," she said, forcing herself to continue. "When I became adamant, refusing to help, she told Harry that he was making me so upset that I might have a stroke."

I wanted to reach out and comfort her, tell her that there was no need to continue, but I had to hear the rest of the story. Maggie said that Harry had told Helen that she was probably right. They should go. He must have been crazy thinking that Maggie could help.

Maggie, he said, had outlived her usefulness. "Let's get out of here," he had told Helen, "so she can go back to killing herself."

"I wanted to know what he meant," she said, staring intently at the fountain. "But you know his stubbornness. I turned to Helen. She told me that he was trying to prevent this young man from ending up like my husband."

"And I am this young man to whom you keep referring?"

"Yes, dear," Maggie told me. "Harry told me that you were in need of a secretary and that you were very meticulous. He would offer no help. I had to secure the position on my own. I told him that I couldn't promise anything, but I would go and take a look at your office."

So that's the reason why you were so bold the day I first met you, I thought. Harry, what else have you helped me with without my knowledge?

Maggie told me that all Harry wanted was for her to take a look. He briefed her on what to expect and on how he and I met.

"One thing still puzzles me about that day," I said. "You made the statement, 'It would have been a great loss.' What did you mean?"

She hugged me. I could scarcely remember being so touched. How many years of sorrow could have been avoided if Momma would have hugged me this way as a child?

It finally dawned on me that the reason Maggie had taken the initiative of clearing out my office of applicants was because of Harry. But somewhere along the way, Maggie seemed to have developed a maternal affection toward me, and in an effort to prevent me from suffering the same fate as her husband, she had collaborated with Christina on our marriage.

Maggie and Christina were two of a kind, I decided. Both, obstinate in their conviction to ensure my happiness, had gotten what they wanted.

"If it were not for you and the Fosdricks," she said, "I wouldn't be here today. Now go to your wife and have your last dance. The cake should already be in place, and soon it will be time for you and Christina to start for the airport."

I wanted to stay, to let Maggie know how much she meant to me at that moment, but I figured I had done enough and felt it was best to allow her to revel in her memories in solitude.

Doing as Maggie had suggested, I took Christina to the center of the dance floor. I asked that three songs be played to end the evening, all sung by Nat King Cole: "The Very Thought of You," "Our Love Is Here To Stay," and "Unforgettable." As I held her close, she became misty-eyed. Suddenly a great fear overtook me, but I couldn't imagine life without her, and so, not wanting to spoil the moment with inadequate words, I just held her tighter.

Halfway through the last song, I started kissing her, as if by doing that, I could seal our union by shutting out the rest of the world and she would be by my side forever.

Soon it was time to cut the cake—and what a magnificent cake it was, consisting of two layers, four tiers high, connected by a bridge overlooking a waterfall on which stood a miniature bride and groom. Sealing the moment with a kiss, we cut into our respective cakes and handed out a few slices before the waiters took over.

The only thing left to do was for my lovely bride to throw her garter and flowers so we could depart. As I hugged Harry and thanked him once again, he told me that he had one more surprise for Christina and me.

"What is it, Harry? You've done so much for us already."

"If I told you now," he told me with a grin, "it wouldn't be a surprise, would it?"

"I'm never going to be able to repay you for all that you've done."

"Son, just make sure you and Christina have fun," he said, placing his hand on my shoulder. "The happiness you two share is sufficient repayment for me."

"How do I begin to express how grateful I am for everything that you've done?" I said when we reached Maggie.

"Tony, nothing more needs to be said," she replied. "The happiness I've been able to share with you and Christina means the world to me. You deserve to be happy. If my humble efforts have helped achieve that, then I am happy. Now get moving or you'll miss your flight."

"I would definitely be lost without you," I told her. "I am so glad you're part of my family."

Christina hugged Maggie. These two women are really something else. Perhaps I should be grateful, that each, in her own way, loves me so much. But I couldn't, no matter how hard I tried, shake the feeling that this wouldn't be the last of their Machiavellian efforts, at least where my life is concerned.

We were pelted with birdseed again as we ran from the reception hall to the limo.

"Wow, that was really special, princess," I said

as we waved from the moon roof. "You and Maggie outdid yourselves in planning this wonderful day."

"I told you that I'd do anything to ensure your happiness. Dearest, I've waited so long for a man to love me the way you do. This is just the beginning. I'll spend the rest of my life making you happy."

What would she do? How far would she go? This was my opportunity to let her know that I wasn't going to tolerate anyone interfering in my life. But when she smiled at me and took my hand in hers, I was moved to the point where I couldn't bring myself to chastise her.

"You did that already, princess, when you chose me," I said. "I am privileged that, out of all the men in this world, I am the one you chose to share your life with. It is *I* who has to spend the rest of my life ensuring your happiness."

Thanks to Matt honking his horn and the cans someone had attached to the back bumper, it wasn't long before we were at Teeterboro airport where, to my surprise, we were escorted to Harry's private plane, a beautiful Lear Jet which was to take us to Bermuda. It occurred to me that I would soon be in a position to have my own corporate jet, complete, like this one, with swivel chairs, a shower, and sleeping accommodations.

The pilot told us that our flight would be slightly over two hours, and we should relax, since when we landed it would be 11:00 p.m. in Bermuda.

Carpe diem went through my mind as we followed the pilot's suggestion. I was going to put an end to Christina's manipulation once and for all, but then the conversation that I dreaded came up. She started so innocently that I did not have a chance to evade it.

"Dearest, your mother is very sweet. You must have had a happy childhood."

If only she knew, I thought to myself. Don't let that sweet charm of hers fool you. My mother could be as tough as nails when she wants to. As I looked back, however, I had to admit that all her toughness had been for my own good, since she had been both mother and father to me.

"Mm, yes," I told her, pretending that the apple at the bottom of the fruit basket Harry gave us had captured my attention. "I would say you're right. I did have an interesting—"

Christina interrupted by asking if I knew my neighbors and if any of them had any children. I had a strange feeling about where the conversation was headed and became more preoccupied with removing the apple without disturbing the entire basket. I didn't want to tell an outright lie, so I settled on letting her know that I wasn't the sociable type.

"When I move in, all of that will change," she said, beaming a lovely smile. "We can have a barbecue in our backyard and invite them to meet your new wife. I asked about them because I want to know how many children would be present in order to have something to amuse them with."

I became irritated by the prospect of my home being invaded by all those people. How could I let her know that I preferred to live my life in seclusion? How could I say something without starting an argument?

"Dearest, you don't mind, do you? I've never heard you speak of children."

And there's a good reason for that, I thought to myself; one which I will probably never share with her. I had realized then, and perhaps even as far back as that night in the restaurant, that Christina, somehow, by entering my life, would put me on the same path where tragedy had befallen me before.

Chapter 9

"Princess," I said, when we were cruising at twenty thousand feet, "I really hadn't thought about having children right now. You have your career and I—well, my business is just beginning to take off . . . "

"You don't want children?"

Now I've done it, I thought to myself. I had never seen that look on Christina's face before. No way could an argument be avoided now. I had to think of something to appease her. But how could I tell her that I had never thought I'd encounter another lovely lady who would steal my heart and show me that the world is indeed a lonely place without someone to love?

"Princess," I said, "let me finish. I was thinking that, what with our busy schedules, we should wait a couple of years before planning our family. Besides, I'm just getting myself acclimated to having a wife. I never gave any thought to starting a family right away. Certainly, you never mentioned it."

"Whose interest would it be good for?" she demanded, and there was a clear edge to her voice. "Were you going to discuss it with me, or just assume that I felt as you do?"

A sad expression spread over her face and I could see no way out of the conversation. I was tempted to try another ploy to see if I could find a way to make her understand my point of view, but then I thought better of it and decided to tell her the truth.

"Princess," I said, taking both of her hands in mine, "I love you more than words could ever explain. I would move heaven and earth to make you happy. But you must listen to me. I've never shared what I'm going to tell you with anyone."

I thought I had buried all the unpleasant memories, but they came raging back. I had to begin somewhere, but as Maggie had said, some memories are just unbearable. I had thought it was going to be more difficult, but once I had started, I went on to bare my heart to her, telling her I was apprehensive when it came to kids.

"Oh, they like me all right," I explained, "but I feel awkward around them. It was fun to watch one of my cousin's offspring for a day, but it was always more fun giving the child back. I believe that my greatest fear is that they look at everything you do. You must be on constant guard to set the right example.

"This may be the strangest thing you have ever heard anyone say, but sometimes I feel that I am incapable of loving anyone. Perhaps I know what love is supposed to be and act accordingly, or maybe I am looking for something more tangible to hold on to."

What she must be thinking! One minute I tell her how much I love her, and the next that I can't love anyone. How could I make her comprehend what I don't understand myself?

I told her that, when she is with me, my world feels complete. And when I thought I had lost her, there was an emptiness that I could not explain. I stopped talking, since I felt like I wasn't explaining what I meant, but she held my hands close to her heart and asked me to continue.

So I forged ahead, letting her know how I envied other fathers having fun with their children. I told her of the man I saw crying on television's *Family Court*, having just lost custody of his son, and how I knew that I would never have cried like that.

"If you love someone and he or she is taken from you, aren't you supposed to feel a sense of loss? Aren't you supposed to shed tears and mourn for that lost love? Well, there have been times that I haven't been able to do either. I just took the loss in stride and went on with my life."

I had never wanted it to come to this. She is too precious to be saddled with an emotional basket case like me, I thought to myself. Why hadn't she seen that it couldn't work between us? And why couldn't she have understood why I had kept bringing up the obstacles that would prevent us from being together?

I told her how all my relationships had lasted an average of five years, and that for no apparent reason, the person and I would just drift apart, and how I would do nothing to save the relationship, resigned to the fact that the lady would be better off with someone else.

"Then you entered my life and overcame all the barriers that I had set up," I told her. "Your tenacity and faith in us is why we now sit together here as man and wife."

I kept trying to gauge her response by watching her face, but she remained expressionless and silent, although clearly drinking in every word. But to what effect?

Had Momma's warning about our marriage being

fraught with unpleasantness been a harbinger of things to come? I began to feel as if our marriage was over before it had had a chance to begin. Had I, after all, in trying to make her understand without revealing the real source of my fear concerning children, done something completely rash?

"It's just that I'm terrified that the same thing will happen again," I told her. "Ever since I lost . . ."

I broke off. I could not tell her about the tragedy. Not then. Perhaps never. But something had to be said. What could I tell her that was close enough to the truth to be believable? I did not want the foundation of our love to be based on lies.

"The point is, I was terribly hurt, once, and I made a vow that I would never let that happen again," I went on. "That was when I locked my heart and buried myself in my business. If—if we were to have a child, all those feelings might resurface. Perhaps I wouldn't be able to love a son or daughter the way I should. Christina, I'm a wreck. An emotional wreck who can't let go of his past. What if I'm a failure?"

"I have faith that you will be a wonderful father," she told me, placing her hand over my lips. "You'll open up your heart to our child just the way you did to me. Remember, I'm here to help you through this."

She was there with me, that I knew. But for what purpose? I thought to myself. Was she there to rescue me from what I had passed through before, or to send me on another torturous journey to the depths of despair?

As the plane made its descent, Christina looked straight ahead. She was quite calm, and I sensed her determination. Momma had been right. She was a strong woman with a mind of her own and her own set of ideals. I found myself wondering how far she would go to uphold them, and then those words came back to haunt me: "May you never know to what extent I will go to ensure your happiness."

When we arrived in Bermuda a little after ten, a minivan was waiting to take us to Cambridge Beaches, located near Somerset Village in the West End. Luckily, it was not a long ride, since we were both exhausted from the day's activities. All I wanted to do was shower and go to sleep, holding Christina in my arms.

Our cottage was delightful, in a typical English garden setting, with antique furnishings and a fireplace and masses of chintz, not to mention baskets of flowers everywhere.

Christina had asked me to shower and shave first, since she wanted to spend some time lounging in the whirlpool. I quickly agreed, since I needed time to think.

What am I going to do? I thought to myself. It has been so long. It should be like riding a bike. What a fix I was in No man wants to be a dud on his wedding night. I found myself hoping that perhaps the day's activities had overwhelmed her and that she would fall asleep before me.

However, when I came out of the shower, I found the bedroom dimly lit. It was a lovely, romantic setting, with soft music playing in the background.

"Dearest," she said, putting her arms around my neck, "can you please ring room service and ask them to bring us something to drink?"

As I hung up the phone, I noticed a brightly gift-wrapped package on the bed. Curious, I went to take a closer look. An envelope was attached to the package with these few scribbled lines: "To my dearest husband with all my love, Christina."

I contemplated what to do. Open the envelope and the gift, or wait until she emerged from the whirlpool? I figured that she would be in there for a while, so I decided to at least open what turned out to be a sentimental card depicting a man and woman enjoying a happy moment.

Inside she had written these precious lines:

"To the man that I have waited all my life for,
Thank you for fulfilling all my dreams.
Let this gift be a small token of more to come.
I will spend the rest of my life
Making you as happy as you have made me."

What is it with me? I thought to myself. How come every time she professed her love for me, it haunted me? This was supposed to be my wedding night, and yet I was riddled with guilt. And worst of all, when I had had the chance to explain, I had told her the superficial truth, and there was no way I could rescind my story without being labeled a liar.

I carefully untied the bow and wrapping paper to find an opulent robe made from the finest silks and embroidered with wonderful Oriental designs. So much had happened today that I couldn't have imagined being here with her tonight. But what kept haunting me was how calculating she had to have been. As I stood in the mirror, admiring myself in the regal gift she had given me, I felt as if I had been trapped.

At that moment, I wanted to lie down only to be awakened to discover that all that had transpired was nothing but a bad dream. But I heard her singing in the whirlpool, and found myself thinking that she was a siren luring me to my eternal doom. And so I decided that I had better do something to stay awake, so we could enjoy our drinks. Going over to the couch, I picked up a magazine showing places to visit while we were there. And then, suddenly, there she was, wearing an enticing, navy-burnout, floral, velvet gown, with a sensual low-cut back finished with French seams, twinned satin straps, and a high slit. She wore a matching G-string and black high-heeled pumps. Clearly this was not going to be a night for sleeping.

"Do you like what you see?" she asked, in a very seductive voice. "I hope that I didn't keep you waiting too long."

All I could do was stare at the incredibly beautiful woman who stood before me. I could have waited an eternity just to see her the way she looked that night. And yet, at the same time, I wondered how many men she had enticed and led to . . .

"The way you look tonight, it was well worth the wait, but I thought you were exhausted and wanted to make it an early night."

"Tony," she said, "I've waited for you all my life and dreamt of this very special moment."

I wondered what she had meant. Had she been waiting for me? Or was I merely a pawn in this game of cat and mouse?

"I hope you weren't planning on sleeping," she said in a low voice. "That will be the least of what we'll be doing tonight."

All the barriers I had carefully constructed broke, then. Once I had taken the first step, everything else followed, no matter what came of it. My only hope was that I could make the night as memorable as she had imagined it would be.

"May this be the beginning of a life filled with joy and happiness," Christina toasted me. "You've made me the happiest woman in the world tonight, and I never want this to end. Dearest, do you like your robe?"

"Yes, it's lovely. I'm only sorry that I don't have a gift for you."

"Don't worry," she told me. "You've given me the best gift any woman could ask for. Keep looking at me with those loving eyes. Keep getting excited when I enter a room, and notice no one but me. Keep showering me with words of affection and adoration. Keep doing all those things, my love, and you'll have supplied me with all the gifts I need."

I embraced her as she put her hands inside my robe and pushed it off my shoulders, beginning to tease me with her lips. When I tried to join in, she pulled away playfully. Shivers of delight shot through my body as she ran her fingernails up and down the small of my back. Then she pushed me backward onto the couch.

"I've waited for this moment all my life," she said. "At last, I can show the man I married how much I love him."

It occurred to me that this was supposed to be the night where the man took charge. Still, who was I to stop her?

"I already know how much you love me, princess," I told her. "You don't have anything to prove."

She started kissing me again, very slowly and softly. Each kiss revealed the mounting passion rising within her. As she used the tip of her tongue to trace the contour of my outer ear, I became aroused.

"Dearest," she whispered, "tonight I will share all that I am with you."

She continued stroking my back with her fingernails. The upward and downward motion sent a chill throughout my body. She moved from my ear and started kissing me softly on the neck, continuing in this fashion until she reached my chest. Moving her hands from my back, she started stroking my face. From my face, she continued outlining my body. Stroking my neck and running her fingernails against my ribs, she bit on my pecs while making an S design on the lower part of my abdominals.

I found myself wondering where this young woman could have learned these tricks of eroticism. She titillated me with such simple movements that I couldn't believe I was so aroused. She continued kissing me, moving slowly downward, all the time massaging that part of me that had gone from a dwarf banana to the size of a giant Cavendish. Kissing me on my belly button and continuing on to my lower abdominals, she began to pull the fruit out of its sheath. Apparently surprised at its size, she looked up smiling.

"I told you that this is my night," she told me rather more firmly than I would have thought necessary under the circumstances. "I have dreamt of what I was going to be doing to you and with you. So please, dearest, relax and allow this night to be the way I dreamt it would be."

Not wanting to spoil her night, I allowed her to continue, anxiously waiting my turn to show her how much I loved her.

Holding my Cavendish carefully in her hand, she eyed it from different angles. Starting from the tip, going all the way to the base, her slow movements and intermittent pauses at various places along the way had me totally inflamed. I began squirming on the couch as she increased the speed at which she was fondling me. When she cupped my two kiwis at the same time, I found myself fighting hard not to erupt. It was a good thing that I had practiced those PC muscle exercises. Still enjoying everything she was doing, I waited for my opportunity to return the pleasure she was giving me.

Finally, however, it occurred to me that she had no intention of stopping. Clearly her mind was obstinately set on accomplishing her goal. The heat generated by her actions had me so excited that I tried to focus on something else by running my fingers through her hair. I wanted to do anything to delay the eruption I felt was on its way. No longer able to stem the tide and completely enraptured by her actions, I moaned in ecstasy and told her what was forthcoming. She ceased caressing but held on firmly to my Cavendish and milked it of all its protein. I was titillated and exhausted from the loss, but it was my turn to return the pleasure and show her how much I loved her.

Pulling her slowly to me, I sat her on the couch and lovingly kissed her neck. Pushing back the straps of her gown, I exposed two cantaloupe-sized melons, a perfect description, in my estimation, of what some might have considered her overripe breasts. As I caressed one while fondling the other, she began to moan softly.

Suckling rhythmically, I let myself be guided by her moans until, removing the rest of her gown, she laid before me wearing only her G-string. This garment, once removed, would allow me to peel the grape, so to speak, unencumbered.

But I had wanted to add to the suspense of the moment, so I started working my way around the contour of the design.

"Dearest, what is it that you're doing to me?" she demanded. It was, I think, a rhetorical question. "In my wildest dreams," she moaned, "it was never like this."

Not wanting to break stride, I continued what I was doing until I felt the moistness at the base of the G-string. Removing it with the most delicate care, I was about to, when she pulled me toward her and whispered, "Dearest, I love you. I really do. You have stolen my heart, satiated my spirit. I share with you tonight the most precious gift a wife can give to her husband."

What was she talking about? I wondered to myself. I was not going to spoil the moment by asking silly questions. I decided to just smile at her. My only thought was to get back to where I had been before her interruption.

Opening her legs as one opens a peach, I had become overanxious to drink from its nectar, only to discover that the seal had not yet been broken.

Where was I going to get condoms at this time of night? She'd never been touched. So where had she learned all this? How was I going to touch her without going down that same road again?

I wanted to stop, but I should have known that I could not. She had entrusted me with her most prized possession, and, no matter what came of the night, I was determined to reciprocate the pleasure she had given to me.

Throwing caution to the wind, I started kissing her while preparing myself for entry into that unexplored region. Her kisses held so much warmth, and those trusting eyes kept enticing me as I nudged against the seal. I was apprehensive about causing her any pain, but she kept assuring me that everything would be all right. I could feel the moistness of it, and started to exert a little more pressure, when she placed her hand on my back. I had thought that she wanted me to stop, so I started to pull back, but she grabbed me from behind and pushed me forward. And with that final push, the seal was broken and she let out a high-pitched squeal.

Fearful of causing her more pain, I started to withdraw, but she wrapped her willowy legs around me. The warmness of being inside her and the tightness of it . . . the pleasure was indescribable. The only thing I could think of was that that was how a nail must feel when held between a vise.

She kept pleading for me to take and share all that she had. Her moaning became increasingly louder, and she began calling out my name when I slipped a pillow underneath her. Wrapping her long legs tighter around my back, she cried out instructions at the top of her lungs. The only way I could silence her was to kiss her, kisses which she returned ardently, all the while digging her nails into my back and rocking back and forth so vigorously that I thought I was back on Harry's yacht.

Caught up with the excitement, I continued as she requested, with no more concern about how much pressure I was exerting. My Cavendish, as thick as ever, was trying to pave a path where none could have possibly existed.

She squealed in ecstasy and shouted for me to join her, but I couldn't, not as long as her legs were wrapped around me. She told me not to be afraid, that there was no need to fight it; she had been waiting to receive it, so I needn't struggle anymore.

What has she known of my struggle? I asked myself. I knew so little about her, and wondered how much she knew about me.

But then she began to massage my two kiwis. Weary from the physical and mental struggle, I ceded my Cavendish, which spurted out so violently that I thought it would continue to no end.

"I love you so much, Tony," she said. "Thank you for sharing all that you are with me. You've made me the happiest woman in the world tonight. I love being your wife. I'm going to spend the rest of my life loving you."

Trepidation shook me. My only thought at that moment was if our first night of romance had led me down that torturous road of despair again. And if it had not, how was I going to avoid it?

I was about to echo her sentiment of love when I took notice of the song playing softly in the background. How different those words had seemed on our first date. Placing my hands on each side of her, I hovered over her and started singing along.

> *You're the one I've searched for all my life,*
> *Loving you, girl, just feels so right,*
> *You're the one I needed in my life,*
> *I'll be blessed to have you as my wife.*

As the song came to an end, I slowly descended and kissed her passionately.

"Every one of those words reveals how much I love you," I told her. "I wouldn't want to spend one night away from your loving arms."

"Dearest, I love you, too," she said, hugging me tightly. "I will let nothing come between us. I finally have the man of my dreams."

She finally had her man, but to me, it sounded more like she had meant *possessed*. She told me that she had waited so long to say this to me, and then she quoted the first line of the chorus, before reiterating that I would never know how far she would go to ensure my happiness.

The entire day had been too much for me, and, overcome by sheer exhaustion, I fell beside her and drifted off to sleep. I don't know how much time had passed, but I remember dreaming that she was fondling me. Realizing that it wasn't a dream, I woke up to find her washing me with a small oblong towel.

It was, I realized, a very loving gesture, probably natural for women of Far Eastern descent. But I couldn't see it for what it was. What suffused my thoughts was that I was losing control. After all, I was a grown man, far removed from needing a mother's care.

The tepid water felt nice, and the way she fondled the sleeping giant woke him up. Atop me, she started riding in a slow and deliberate motion, teasing me with her tongue. Cupping her breasts in my hands, I began to massage them. Every time I rubbed her nipples, she moaned with delight. Pulling her to me, I began suckling one and then the other, finally bringing them together so I could suckle both without pausing.

"Oh, Tony, that feels so nice," she moaned. "Please keep doing that."

"Talk to me, princess," I said, no longer able to control myself. "Let me know what pleases you."

"Oh, oh—Tony, that feels so good. But it hurts so."

"Am I causing you pain again? Do you want me to get on top?"

"No! It feels so damn good. I can't believe making love to you is this good."

Pulling away from me, she began to ride more violently. I held her hands to steady her. She started screaming when I pushed her down on me while, at the same time, I thrust upward. Grabbing my pecs, she dug her nails in again. The pain that shot through my body forced me to thrust even harder. I could feel my Cavendish getting bigger each time she pushed herself down on it. She begged me not to stop.

As if I really had a choice. I was really in a tight spot. It had been so long since I had felt myself being carried away like this. I was frightened.

"Damn, Tony, it's happening again," she cried. "I can't—I can't hold it back any longer. Please, please—join me."

How could I possibly join her? I wondered. I squeezed my PC muscles tightly for fear of my seeds gushing out. How was I going to get away before my Cavendish exploded?

I was close, but once again, she came first. Her body trembled but I could see that she had no intention of stopping. She was determined that we would come together.

She was covered with sweat and oil. Her body had a radiant glow. Her hair was all over her face. I got turned on watching her breasts bounce up and down. I was so hard. And she was so tight. I felt the final push and the heat from being deep inside her. "Princess," I shouted, trying to lift her off of me, "I can't. I just can't."

"I love you," she said, pushing down harder. "I

can feel it. Don't hold any of it back. I want to feel it all. You said it was all mine, did you not?"

I had pledged my love to her that was true. But my love and nothing else. Surely, if I had known that meeting her would have paralleled the events of my tragic past and that this night would set me upon that very same course, I would have formulated a defense against it. But as it stood, there was no comfort I could seek except to wrap my arms around her, so that she would be warm and stop trembling.

"I love you, Tony, I love you," she whispered. "I thank God that you're my husband. I love you, dearest, truly I do. Oh, God, I love my husband. Thank you, thank you."

I didn't know what time it was when I woke up, but I found my beautiful wife in the same position that she had been in when we had fallen asleep, secure in my arms, her head on my chest. The fire had gone out and the room was totally dark. I eased her off of me and groped for the light. After locating my robe, I went out to the terrace. I felt so serene sitting out there. I took a deep breath to drink in as much fresh air as possible, and couldn't help feeling as if the water was calling me.

Under the magical stars of a lavender Bermuda sky, I sat and wondered whether it was a blessing or a curse that had been set upon me. I should have felt blessed that Christina loved me so much. I had never known that she had so much passion locked deep inside her. But before I had a chance to decide what she really meant to me, I heard her voice.

"Dearest," she said, "is anything the matter?"

I couldn't tell her that she had intruded upon my thoughts, that, on what should have been a memorable night for the both of us, I was wrestling with demons from my past. So I merely told her that the starry sky, the swaying palm trees, and the smell of the fresh air had beckoned me outside.

"Makes one realize what is really important in life," she said, kneeling beside me.

"I guess paradise has a way of doing that."

"Paradise is wherever you make it," she said. "When we get back to start our married life, to me that is where paradise begins. This is merely a preview of the finer things to come."

"I guess you're right," I said, though filled with reservations about the outcome. "I would consider anywhere a paradise so long as it contained you."

"Dearest, I'm ready to go back to bed," she said, as she got up and extended her arms to me. "We still have time before the sun comes up."

"Princess, what am I going to do with you?" I said, mindful of the fact that I had to conceal the weariness in my voice.

"That should be easy to figure out," she told me with a satisfied smile. "Make love to me again."

And that's the way it went for two days and nights, with a few intermissions for nourishment and sleep. It seemed to me that my new bride was going to let out all her suppressed passion. No sooner had we finished eating, she became amorous.

"Dearest, I'm going back to bed," she'd say, while letting her negligee fall to the floor. "Are you coming?"

I must admit that I can't be totally absolved from blame, since I initiated some of the action. Waking up from a torrid session, I found her peacefully asleep, lying on her stomach with the sheet partly covering her legs. I was about to pull the sheet to cover her, but

I changed my mind and went behind her and started blowing softly in her ear. That led to another fiery session that led to another, and we continued that way for most of the night.

I had taken the strangest position that somehow my fears of intimacy were without merit. Christina, knowing my apprehension about children, must have taken some precautionary method to ensure we didn't have one.

The morning of the third day, I was awakened by my wife nipping on my ear and whispering endearments, followed by a suggestion that we have lunch.

"Lunch?" I groaned. "What time is it?"

"Eleven o'clock."

"Then you must mean brunch."

"As you wish," she replied, tossing her tangled mane of hair over one bare shoulder. "I told them to have it here in an hour's time. That should give us time for a quickie out in the jacuzzi."

From the look in her eyes, however, I was fairly sure that a quickie was not precisely what she had in mind.

"They were instructed to call before coming," she teased. "I wouldn't want them disturbing . . . "

Needless to say, they weren't able to serve us until a little after three, when we were served tea, complete with a fine silver tea service, Spode china, and, ironically enough, an impressive variety of fruits including strawberries, Surinam cherries, bananas, guavas, and, my favorite, avocados.

For the first time since our arrival, we engaged in a desultory conversation and actually noticed the splendor that surrounded our cabin.

"Out here is so peaceful," Christina sighed, "is it not? Dearest, the gentleness of the wind, and look how the water sparkles . . . "

I had to agree with her. Surrounded by so much beauty, I had become determined to shut out the demons of my past. She had asked me what I wanted to do after lunch. I indicated shopping, since I had nothing to wear.

"But dearest, you do. In fact you have a whole suitcase of clothes."

"What do you mean?" I protested. "I only came with the clothes on my back."

"Maggie's surprise and gift," she beamed. "When you went to get fitted . . ."

So that's why my tailor had insisted on taking all those extra measurements. I had thought it strange that a man as meticulous as him would lose them.

"You and Maggie should be commended," I said. "The two of you act like the cast from *Mission Impossible*. It's amazing the things you ladies can do when you put your minds to it."

"This tea is wonderful," Christina observed. "What is the name of it?"

She was dressed in a ribbon-trimmed, sequin-laced camisole and a pair of skin-tight jeans. Her hair was pushed back behind her ears, with a few baby strands remaining at the front on both sides. I couldn't help staring at what Wordsworth indubitably would have characterized as "a vision of delight" if he had had the pleasure to gaze upon Christina.

"I thought you would like it," I replied, immersed in the essence of her beauty. "It's called Lady Grey. It has a nice citrus taste, doesn't it?"

"Yes, it does. Is it the same that you drink?"

"No, precious, I'm drinking Earl Grey."

"Then it is as it should be."

"What do you mean?"

"The earl and his lady enjoying afternoon tea in this paradise." Getting up from her chair, she proceeded to sit on my lap. "I love you so much," she said. "I will do everything I can to make you happy."

There was an echo there that I found disturbing, but I was replete in so many ways that I did not pursue it.

After eating, we decided to check out some of the amenities our cottage colony had to offer, beginning with a visit to the Aquarium Baths, a magnificent white-columned site that sheltered a large indoor Olympic-sized pool. A solarium ceiling emitted sunlight, adding to the ambiance of the room. Lounge chairs nestled in among miniature palm trees gave an excellent view of the ocean, sparkling like a giant sapphire in the sun.

A muscular damsel named Tatiana welcomed us to what she referred to as the finest European health and beauty spa on the island.

"Would you care to use our facilities, Miss?"

"Mrs. Richardson," Christina snapped.

"Excuse me—Mrs. Richardson."

"I believe that my wife would like to visit your beauty spa," I announced, sensing the tension in the air.

"Very good, sir, would you like to visit our fitness center? It has every imaginable piece of exercise equipment, and, after your strenuous workout, I'll be pleased to give you a massage."

Christina tugged my arm, and, turning, I saw that she was scowling, a most unusual expression for her to assume, and one that did very little to enhance her natural beauty.

"I *do not* want anyone touching you," she said in

a whisper. "That woman is too eager to get her hands on you. Look at her eyes. See how she stares at you. Would you want a strange man touching me?"

"Sweetness," I said patiently, "this is a European spa. If you want to get a massage as part of your treatment, then so be it. I love you, but most of all, I trust you."

"And I trust you, dearest. It's that woman I don't trust."

"Okay, princess," I said. "If it will ease your mind, no massage. I'll wait for your loving hands."

She kissed me and departed in the direction of the spa, leaving me to wonder what could have upset her so. Perhaps, I thought, it might be a result of her lack of sleep.

"Sir? Sir, could you please step this way?" Tatiana asked. "If you could please step this way, I'll give you a quick tour of the fitness center. I take it that the two of you are newlyweds?"

"Yes," I admitted, "we are. Is it that obvious?"

"Your wife is very . . . protective," she hedged. "Can't say that I blame her."

"Blame her for what?"

"You're a very—in her shoes, I would do the exact same thing."

"Well, Tatiana, if a marriage is to survive, there must be a matter of trust. I love my wife dearly, and more than that, I trust her."

"I have no doubt of her love for you. She may even trust you. Still, that doesn't stop a woman from feeling the way she does."

"I don't seem to follow you."

"When a woman has a handsome man, she begins to measure herself against every woman he meets, wondering if one of them is capable of taking him from her. She begins to feel uneasy that someone may be attempting to steal her happiness. I know I have been—I've seen it happen to so many of my friends' marriages."

I hadn't known what to think, and yet I had felt it. Could Tatiana have seen what I was too blind to see? Perhaps it had been my imagination, but it seemed as if Christina wanted to control every facet of my life, and to exclude everyone else. But it couldn't be, I thought. Was Tatiana coming on to me, and had Christina seen through her hospitable façade? I decided to remain quiet and see how it would play out, hoping that Tatiana's comment wasn't another omen concerning my marital bliss.

"Sometimes you won't be aware of it," she continued, ushering me into the weight room. "It could be something as simple as paying another woman a compliment. It doesn't take much to trigger it, but once triggered, it becomes hard to change a woman's thoughts. Good luck with your marriage, Mr. Richardson."

I think that was all she said and yet "you're going to need it" seemed to echo throughout the room.

Chapter 10

"Yes, RIGHT THERE," I SAID WITH A GROAN, EXTENDING myself full length on our king-sized bed. "I shouldn't have attempted to lift so much on my first day."

"Which of your muscles aches the most?" Christina asked nervously.

"My shoulder, mostly," I told her. "I think I did too many military presses. Right there, that's the spot."

"Dearest, are you sure it's all right with you if I give you a massage? I hope you are not saying it is okay to spare my feelings."

"Where are all these doubts coming from all of a sudden?" I asked her, my voice muffled by the pillow. I could remember all too clearly what Tatiana had told me.

"It's just that if I had allowed one of the masseuses to massage you, you probably wouldn't be sore."

"Whether they massaged me or not, I would still be sore from trying . . ."

"I'm sorry," she said, relieving the pressure she was applying to a particularly painful corner of my lower back. "I don't know why I'm acting this way." She stopped massaging me and sat on the edge of the bed. "It's just that it took so long to find you. I never want to lose you."

"Princess, I don't know how else to reassure you," I said, sitting beside her. "All I can say is that you won't." Feeling amorous, I started nibbling on her ear. "Dearest, that feels so nice," she purred. "But if you keep it up we won't have dinner out tonight."

She was right, of course. Two days of sharing our love had sapped her energy, but a visit to the spa had returned her to me ruddy with health and so beautifully coiffed that she deserved a night out. The only thing that disturbed me though, was how her fingernails, which had been French manicured, were painted a shade of red that was singularly like fresh blood.

Why the change? I wondered. What had the color been when we first met? If I had taken notice, I probably wouldn't be here tonight. Could it be that she had concealed it from me? Was it possible that now that she possessed me, she felt comfortable in revealing the true color of her character?

While she went to dress for the evening, I dismissed those thoughts by making several calls and leaving a message for Maggie to call me if she had any luck with my realtor. I intended to buy a new house to celebrate Christina's and my union and was eager to look at some properties once we returned home.

Subsequently, when I emerged from my shower, Christina was waiting for me, a bowl of shaving cream in one hand and a razor in the other. As I wrapped my towel around me, she indicated that I should take a seat.

"You're actually planning on shaving me?" I asked her, trying to disguise my chagrin. From the time I was first able to scrape a few hairs off my chin with grandfather's old-fashioned straight-edge razor, I had prided myself on my ability to shave without a single nick.

"Yes, my king," she replied. She was, I might mention, wearing nothing but a bra and thong.

She began lathering my face. It was difficult to remain perfectly still. If a man ever needed to trust his wife, this was it. Amazingly enough, she gave me a very close shave.

"Princess," I said when she was finished and I dared to speak, "where did you learn to shave with a single-edge razor?"

"I learned from Mother," Christina told me. "She used to shave Father. She made me practice on balloons first."

"Balloons? Whatever for?"

"She told me that once I could shave the lather off the balloon without popping it, I could shave Father. I started shaving him at the age of eleven."

But I am not your father, I thought. Surely, she hadn't thought that that ritual would be passed on to me?

"Well, you're very good," I said, instead of voicing my concerns. "I guess from now on you would like to shave me . . . ?"

"Yes, if that is what you wish," she said simply, patting my face dry. "I will do whatever it takes to please my husband."

The way she was attired certainly made me want to abandon our plans for dining out. But I needed some fresh air. I refused to let myself harbor any ill thoughts toward her, so I pulled Christina onto my lap and kissed her fervently.

"Do you want me to cancel our dinner reservations?" she said gleefully.

"No, princess," I told her. "There'll be time for this later. Just remember . . . "

"It will be my pleasure," she assured me.

Going into the bedroom, I saw that she had laid out my white dinner jacket and black trousers, my French-cuffed white shirt, black bow tie, and patent-leather shoes. Neatly arranged on the nightstand were my money clip, my Omega Deville, and a new set of cuff links, made from onyx and surrounded by diamond baguettes. I was amazed to see that she had somehow obtained a red boutonniere.

"Princess!" I exclaimed, feeling overwhelmed. "You treat me as if I am royalty or something. You make me feel like I'm a king."

"That is exactly what you are," she told me. "You're my king. You made me feel like a princess on our first date."

Ten minutes later Christina came out of the bedroom and asked me to zip her up. She was wearing an alluring stretch sheath with a sexy scalloped neckline. She wore no jewelry that night. There was no need for any. She was so elegant that she took my breath away. One final kiss and we were finally ready to dine in the Tamarisk Room.

The Tamarisk Room was impressive with its limed-wood columns and beam ceilings. We requested to dine on a rambling terrace that overlooked the bay. Christina was a vision of simple elegance—so elegant that I noticed, as we were led to a table set with a lavender cloth and candles, that most of the guests had turned to admire her.

"Dearest, this place is lovely," Christina crooned. "I love the view of the water."

"Princess, all this beauty pales in comparison with you," I assured her.

"That is so sweet of you to say."

"Sweet nothing! Didn't you see all those men staring at you? I thought a few of them were going to fall out of their chairs."

She frowned. "Doesn't that bother you?"

"Not at all," I reassured her. "I always judge the beauty of my date by how other men react to her. Most men take offense to this, especially the insecure ones who are always hovering over their women. But they should face the fact that if their companion is truly lovely, then she will command attention. That's why I said earlier that I love you, but more importantly I trust you."

"I think I am beginning to understand," she said, but it seemed clear to me, from the expression in her bewitching green eyes, that she did not.

"If I couldn't trust, I wouldn't stay married to you," I explained. "Trust must always come first. How can love exist when there is no trust?"

"I wish I could be as confident as you," she told me—playing with her napkin rather nervously, I thought. "I trust you. It's those women I do not."

"It will take time, princess," I warned her. "Keep in mind that it takes two to start anything. I've listened to those hypocrites when they get caught. 'She seduced me.' Poppycock! They knew what they were getting into."

"The thought of another woman taking you . . . well, it disturbs me," she said in a low voice, staring out to sea. "I don't know what I would do."

I shivered at the thought of what she had already done, her obsession to please me. How would it be if all that love was to turn to hate?

"That is something you needn't worry about," I assured her. "Even though I am surrounded by all these women, I still have eyes for you and you alone."

As she stroked my face, Christina told me that she would always love me. Somehow I seemed to recall that she had repeated her undying love for me, in a soft, reverent tone, "Oh, God, I love you so much."

Had she really been waiting for me or were there others who had seen through the innocent façade and decided that her obsessive nature was too high a price to pay for breaking the seal?

I had given it some thought and decided to risk ruining the night when the waiter approached us. We ordered shrimp for an appetizer, followed by a cushion of lamb served with a Stilton mousse soufflé and a red wine sauce and lentils for Christina. And for me, the roasted monkfish flavored with thyme and garlic, floating on a bed of ratatouille.

As soon as the waiter departed, I changed my mind and started discussing plans for the next day. "I'll tell you what, princess," I suggested. "Tomorrow let's take a ride to Hamilton Parish. We can do some shopping and find an Italian restaurant."

"That sounds like a wonderful idea."

"I thought it would be. Then you can get some shopping done. I am quite sure there are many gifts that you would like to take home."

"Now that you mention it, I saw something in the catalog in our room that I wanted us to have in our new home."

"Princess, I told you before that when I married you, I would have two obligations: to provide and protect. If you want to purchase something while we're here, then go ahead and do so. We can clear it through customs and take it back with us or let the store ship it home."

For some unapparent reason, Christina seemed

to be afraid that I would become angry. I had become curious about what she thought would happen if I did.

"Then that is what I wish to do tomorrow," she said, grabbing my hand. "I want to shop and enjoy being with you."

"Princess, can I ask you something?"

"Yes, dearest. What is it?"

"It's probably nothing."

"It must be important for you to ask. Please share your thoughts with me."

"Perhaps it's my overactive imagination, but I sense that you're afraid of my becoming angry. Our marriage must have moments when we will be cross with one another."

"Why would you say that?" she demanded.

"Because sometimes it can't be helped," I said, trying to choose the right words to salvage the night. "When you have two individuals both striving to accomplish their goals, there are bound to be moments of disagreement. Half the fun of fighting is the making up part."

"But I don't want to fight with you," she said petulantly. This explanation was beginning to be more difficult than I had thought.

"Princess, maybe other men would love to have a woman who caters to their every whim, but not me."

"Did I do something wrong earlier?" she demanded. "By shaving or . . . "

We paused when the waiter brought a delectable tray of shrimps arranged in a circular design and resting on a shell mold, accompanied by a lobster tail garnished with lemon wedges and mussels.

He told us to enjoy and that our main course would be out shortly, and I told him that neither of us had imagined that the appetizer would be so much and to check with us before bringing out the entrée. "Very good, sir. Let me know when you're ready." Relieved by this momentary intrusion, I reached for one of the lemon wedges, hoping that we could start eating and avoid this conversation. "It looks good, doesn't it?" I said.

"Yes, it's lovely," Christina replied, scarcely glancing at the tray. "Will you finish, please? I'm afraid that until I know what you're talking about, I can't eat a thing."

Sensing that it would serve no purpose in trying to convince her otherwise, I searched again for the right words to phrase what I had to say, uncomfortably aware that, if I did not, the whole night and possibly the rest of our honeymoon would be ruined. I really needed to learn to keep my big mouth shut, even though it might mean putting a cap on my inquisitive mind.

I went on to explain that, although beauty was enough for some men, I wanted a woman who was intelligent and her own person as well.

"I enjoyed everything you did for me today," I told her. "Shaving me was a very loving gesture. I just want to make sure you did it out of love and not out of fear of losing me. I don't want you to simply do and say what you think will please me."

"Is that so wrong?"

"Yes, very much so, if it causes you to lose your identity," I told her. "Being submissive doesn't mean that I should treat you as a doormat or a sex object. It means that I should always put your needs far above my own. All this I do, not out of fear, but out of my unquenchable love for you."

"But isn't a wife's duty to follow the directions of her husband?"

"Yes, it is, so long as it doesn't suppress the talent she has. You're a woman with strong ideals. No matter how upset I was when we started, I admired your tenacity in going after what—"

"You seemed angry with me."

"Yes, princess, at the beginning I admit that I was, but then I began to admire your resolve that we should be together. That was the woman I fell in love with. I hope that now you don't allow the fear of losing me to turn you into a doormat, allowing me to trample all over your ambitions."

"What if what I want prevented you from getting what you wanted? Mother taught us that a husband should be respected and his word is law. I could do all those things to get you, since you weren't my husband, but our marriage changes all that."

"I'm not asking you to abandon your mother's teachings," I told her. "I'm asking you to be the fiery woman I fell in love with. Believe me, when you do something to anger me, you will be the very first to know it."

"I will try to do as you ask," she said, kissing me. "But please be patient. I hope you can truly forgive me when—"

"Is something wrong with the appetizer?" the waiter interrupted, with a look of dismay.

"No, everything is fine. We started talking and forgot that we were having dinner. Bring out the main course in a few minutes."

I couldn't wait for him to leave so I could ask Christina to finish what she had wanted to say.

"I hope, I—I can truly be the woman you've dreamt of. I love you so much. I will do my best to let nothing ever come between us."

That's not what she had intended to say, I thought. What is she hiding from me? What could it be that she was afraid might anger me? Should I dare pursue this? No, my point had been made, the night salvaged, and so I thought it best to enjoy the rest of the evening.

The meal that followed was simply scrumptious, the monkfish exquisite. The soft, flaky whitefish had a most pleasing effect on my delicate palate. Christina had nothing but high praises for her meal as well.

"That was the most delicious piece of fish I have ever eaten," I told the waiter. "Please give my compliments to the chef."

"Yes, the lamb was so moist and tender," Christina chimed in. "I hope we get a chance to return here before we leave."

"Thank you, miss. I hope the Tamarisk Room will be honored with your presence again. And if I might say so, you're a very fortunate man, sir."

I stared at Christina. Was I indeed fortunate? The waiter had addressed her as *miss*, but there hadn't been the quick retort as I had seen with Tatiana.

"Every day that passes I am finding out just how fortunate," I told him, although I had reservations. "Can you suggest some form of entertainment? Is there anything happening after dark?"

When it came to deciding where to go, the waiter, clearly a party animal, first suggested a pub called the Frog and Onion, because, he explained, it was operated by a Frenchman for the pleasure of Bermudians. Christina tentatively vetoed that suggestion in what I appreciated was an attempt to demonstrate that she intended to maintain her independence. Instead, she suggested a walk on the beach.

"Are you sure?" I asked her. "I thought you wanted to see some of the nightlife."

"I'd rather spend the time alone with you."

"Thanks for all your help," I said, as I tipped the waiter. "Your courtesy and professionalism are greatly appreciated. My wife and I were very impressed."

"Dearest, I love when you say *my wife*. I think that after I do, those are the loveliest words. I'm having so much fun being your wife."

Would I have the same pleasure? I thought to myself. Did she really want to be alone with me, or was she, as Tatiana had said, afraid that another woman would steal her happiness?

"You know what my two favorite words after those are?"

It must, I thought, have something to do with obsess or possess.

"*My husband*," she said proudly. "It feels good to look at you and say—"

"I see it doesn't take much to make you happy," I said, fighting hard to hide my displeasure.

"I don't require much. Sometimes the simplest things in life are best. Tonight, you wanted to take me to some fancy nightclub. But I prefer a quiet walk on the beach."

I was ashamed of myself for what I had thought. Why was there anything the matter with her wanting to share a quiet moment with me, as opposed to being jostled in an overcrowded nightclub? Tatiana had been wrong, I decided. And for the remainder of the evening, I was going to let her omen, like the receding waves, drift quietly out to sea.

It felt lovely holding my princess's hand and walking on the powdery, white sand in my bare feet. I couldn't have asked for a more perfect setting. It was a beautiful starry night, the moon silhouetted against a bluish-purple sky, the gentle breeze blowing softly against our faces. And to top it all off, the prettiest woman on earth was sharing it with me. No man could ask for anything more. Christina was right. Sometimes the best things in life are the simplest.

"A penny for your thoughts," she asked me, clinging to my arm and trying to let the receding waves wash over her feet.

So many women had been in the Tamarisk Room tonight, both young and old, wearing exorbitant amounts of jewelry, no doubt trying to impress each other. But Christina had walked in with a simple but elegant dress, with no jewelry, and left there the envy of them all.

She loved me so much that she was afraid of losing me. But how could I explain to her that I loved her just as much, that my world would be empty without her? And worst of all, how I couldn't bear a day seeing her unhappy, how I would give up all that I had to ensure that she stayed as lovely as she was that night.

"I don't feel as though you are really with me," she said plaintively. "What are you thinking about?"

I heard her, but how could I answer? How could I let her know that the demons of my past walked with us at that very moment? Noticing that she was trembling, I took off my jacket and wrapped it around her.

"We'd better start heading back now," I said, looking at my watch. "Eleven o'clock—I can't believe we spent almost two hours walking out here."

"You've been so deep in thought that I didn't want to disturb you," she said.

"What I should have been doing," I said, "was paying attention to you. If I hadn't been daydreaming, I might have realized you were getting cold."

"No, dearest, the night air and the walk on the beach relaxes you."

She had been right about that, but why couldn't she have simply told me she was cold? This being-a-perfect-wife thing quite definitely had its limitations.

"I like long walks on a solitary beach," I told her. "In the past, I would get up in the middle of the night and drive for miles to the most secluded one. There I would build my sandcastle and dream of the day when my princess would turn that lonely castle into a loving home."

"Will you still need to take those walks alone?" she asked me. "Or may I join you? I wouldn't want to be left in the house alone, not knowing where you were."

"Of course you can accompany me," I told her, wishing she wouldn't. I tried to make it sound as dull as possible. "If you don't mind walking or sitting amongst the rocks with me in silence." But my ploy hadn't worked. Christina said that, from what she had seen tonight, it really didn't matter what I did, as long as she was there with me.

She kept trying to reassure me that she understood, but there was something about Christina's expression that warned me that perhaps she did not.

"What woman wouldn't feel strange," she said, vehemently, "to awaken in the middle of the night and find that her husband has gone for a walk on a cold and lonely beach. Crazy thoughts run through a woman's mind at that time of night."

"So if we hadn't taken this walk, if you hadn't seen how I lose track of time, I'd have had a lot of explaining to do when I got back home," I said. "Is that what you mean?"

"You'd find me waiting by the door," Christina assured me. "It's not that I don't trust you, but it would be very hard for any woman to believe you at that point."

It seems as if I have no escape, I thought to myself as we returned to our cottage. I had married a woman who was intent on being with me every waking moment. I could have put a stop to the marriage, and her meddling, but she had become, in a way I found hard to explain, very special and dear to me.

I turned on the radio and it wasn't long before we heard Kim Water's "Easy Going." I took her in my arms as we stood on the terrace, admiring the beautiful scenery.

"I never said this to anyone before," I told her, "but I wouldn't want to go on living if anything ever happened to you. I love you too much. You'll never know what I passed through to find you. It took so long. Just know that I love you."

"Please, please, please, forgive me," Christina said, as her body trembled and she pressed tighter against me. "Oh, God, I love you, I love you so much, please forgive . . ."

What had she done that needed my forgiveness? After all, it was I that had needed hers. Perhaps her mother's teachings were the reason for her compulsion to please me, but I should have been truthful with her when I had had the opportunity.

I could have told her about the tragedy that had plunged me into the world of the abyss and had left me with a morose outlook on life. But unable to relive past events, I had taken the easy way out and committed the most unpardonable of sins by building the foundation of our marriage on lies.

And so, as Christina begged for my forgiveness, I, instead of simply asking her what she meant, wrapped her in my arms and tried to drown out the voices of the past from a world that had been suddenly torn away from me.

The next morning the ferry took us from Sandy Parish to Somerset Bridge and into Hamilton Harbour. At the insistence of my wife, I didn't wear my watch; I guess my habit of constantly looking at it as if I were running late for an appointment had finally gotten to her. Dressed in the clothes she had laid out for me—khaki shorts, blue polo shirt, and skippers—I did my level best to hide my discomfort.

Christina—dressed in stone-colored shorts, a mustard tee shirt, and canvas tennis shoes—was so beautiful that she simply took my breath away. It was amazing how she found comfort in the simplest of things. On the other hand, I, if not for her, would have worn full-length slacks and a sports coat.

Perhaps a change was inevitable. After all, what woman marries without trying to change her husband? I could tell that Christina was definitely going to try and remake my life in a good many ways. But how could I accept the changes without losing my identity? And worse, if what she proposed had no merit, how could I tell her without hurting her feelings?

I had been contemplating what to do when a little boy interrupted my thoughts by tugging on Christina's shorts. Despite my protests, she scooped him up in her arms just as a frantic woman approached us, dragging an oversized basket.

"I took my eyes off him for a second," she said, trying to steady the basket, "and he was gone. I thought maybe he fell overboard."

An awkward scene ensued with the little boy clinging to Christina. To make the best of the situation, I helped the woman with her basket while Christina held the sleepy lad until we arrived in Hamilton Parish.

What was with the young boy? I wondered. It was strange that of all the women on the ferry, he had become attached to my wife. Memories of my world being torn apart came raging back as Christina cradled him.

This is the last thing I need, I thought to myself. I haven't adjusted to being married and now this child may have ignited Christina's maternal instinct. I decided to ignore it and to try to persuade her that what had happened wasn't an uncommon occurrence. But the damage had already been done, since she was smitten with the little fella.

"Isn't he cute?" Christina asked, waving the flower the little boy had given her under her nose. "Did you notice that he didn't want to go back to his mother?"

I had noticed a great many things that afternoon, and none of them helped to ease my fears where children were concerned.

Hamilton Parish, I thought, would help me forget the demons of my past. There were so many restaurants and stores that we didn't know where to begin. The largest formed a cluster on Front Street, and we elected to go to Mark & Spencer—a store of mammoth proportions that carried a vast assortment of quality merchandise—first.

"Since this is our first time shopping together, princess," I said as we looked at the store directory, "how would you like to proceed? Do you want me to accompany you, or do you prefer to look around on your own?"

"I'd like to be with you," she said, holding on tighter to my arm. "Let's go to the men's department first."

"Any particular reason why?"

"I'd like to see how you shop," she told me, as if she had been speaking to a child.

She had shaved me and then wanted to pick out my clothes. Her desire to please me had gone way too far. What man would allow his wife to dress him? I decided that I would reject whatever she picked out for me. In a nice way, of course.

But Christina, much to my dismay, had excellent taste in menswear. She helped me to pick out a blazer, a couple of British-tailored trousers, two dress shirts, bathing shorts, and some toiletries, steering me clear of somber colors with considerable élan.

Satisfied with my purchases, we moved on to the lady's department, where Christina picked out several tailored dresses, shoes and handbags to match, shorts, and a variety of blouses. I was elated as she modeled each outfit for me, but became vaguely uncomfortable when she insisted that nothing would be purchased unless it met with my approval.

"Dearest, do you like this?" she constantly asked. "Do you really like it?"

I told her that she looked simply ravishing and that I needed to leave her momentarily to purchase something for Maggie. If she finished her shopping before I returned, I added, she was to wait in the store for me, since I also needed to secure the services of a minivan.

The excuse, I thought, seemed plausible enough,

since it afforded me the opportunity to not only obtain a minivan but to purchase a box of condoms as well. I had become frightened by the way Christina was taking over my life. And if I was on the same journey that had caused me all my anguish in the first place, then the condoms would help me prevent it.

Christina found me pretending to deliberate over which teas to purchase.

"Dearest, I'm ready to go to the next store," she said, rather impatiently. "Haven't you picked out something for Maggie yet?"

"You're not going to believe this," I said, shoving the box of condoms deeper into my pocket. "I have both of our teas, and sweet biscuits, but I want something especially nice for her. I know Maggie is fond of English and breakfast teas. Should I get her this size or this one?"

"The one with the pretty canister," Christina said at once, proving again that she certainly knew her own mind.

We were hitting the other stores in rapid succession when Christina stopped abruptly and clutched my arm as we passed by Vera P. Card, the window of which was full of Lladro and Hummel figurines.

"Ooh, aren't they lovely?" she exclaimed, dragging me inside. "Isn't that nice? Dearest, look at this! Don't you think they'd look wonderful in our new house?"

I had merely mentioned the prospect of purchasing a new home and already she was intent on taking over that, too. But surely she realized that it would take time to buy a house; where had she intended on putting those figurines?

"Princess, I'll leave the house decorating to you," I said, disguising my chagrin. "Please forgive me if I don't get as excited as you."

And yet, what am I worried about? I asked myself. Once we returned home she was bound to be so busy with her concerts that her incessant meddling would cease.

Needless to say, we spent a small fortune on those figurines, although I didn't mind, because it brought Christina so much happiness. By that time, I would have been content to return to our cottage, but Christina's energy was inexhaustible.

We visited the Irish Linen Shop for tablecloths and then Astwood Dickinson Jewellers, where Christina became enamored with an emerald necklace set with diamonds. When I suggested that she try it on, however, she demurred, saying that it was too expensive.

I, however, was not about to give in that easily and asked the proprietor if I could look at some watches before we left. Once again Christina proved invaluable as she picked out a watch with an unusual moon face.

"I see that madam has excellent taste," the proprietor said, taking the watch out of the case. "This is a Patek Phillipe. Only a few are handcrafted every year."

"Is this the right time?" I said, asking him for a card. "It can't possibly be two o'clock."

"I'm afraid it is, sir."

I jotted down a figure and handed him back the card.

"That price seems equitable enough. Sir, I believe that we can do business."

Christina took a final look at the necklace while I gave the proprietor our hotel information. We then passed Crisson Jewellers where I went in to compare prices, while Christina admired the funny design of a Gucci watch.

"Princess, how do you like it?"

"It's very pretty," she sulked.

"But you would rather have the emerald necklace, right?"

"No dearest, that was—I mean, why spend so much money?"

"We never asked the man the price. How do you know?"

"It was lovely, all those emeralds and diamonds. But I couldn't let you buy . . . "

"Well, maybe in time you will realize that nothing is too good for my wife," I told her, motioning to the clerk that I would purchase the watch.

"Dearest, I already have a . . . "

"Princess, enough! The watch is yours. Ma'am, send it to this hotel."

"I love you so much," Christina said, hugging me affectionately as we went out into the sunshine. "Why did you refuse to haggle?"

"I like to pay as close to wholesale as possible," I told her, looking at the guidebook.

"But what if they won't accept your price?"

"I walk! I'm not trying to kill their profit margin, just decrease it. My price allows them to make a profit, but not fleece me in the process."

"Fleece?"

"Yes, a term where a fool and his money are parted. Going after a deal that is too good to be true."

"I love you so much," she said, taking my arm. "You're going to be a wonderful father."

Those were the very words I was afraid I would hear, I realized. And quickly asked her what she meant.

"You have so much to teach. Imagine what our child will learn from you."

"Well, I'm glad that we don't have to worry about that anytime soon."

"Dearest," she said, "I'm famished. Where are we eating?"

The rapidity with which she changed the subject had not escaped me. But tired and hungry as well, I didn't have the heart to spoil what, up to that moment, had been a marvelous afternoon.

La Trattoria was everything the guidebook had said it would be. Obscure was an understatement, since it was tucked away in a narrow alleyway two blocks north of Hamilton's Waterfront. From the outside there was nothing glamorous about the place, but inside, however, was quite a different story. The décor looked like it came out of a picture book of old Naples, with checkered tablecloths in green, red, and white, and Chianti bottles hanging from the ceiling. Such a homey atmosphere. We felt welcomed at once.

"Dearest," Christina said as we were being seated, "I love this place. It even smells like the restaurant where we first met."

"I know," I said. "Who would have ever imagined that a night on the town would lead me to be married to such a beautiful woman as you?"

When the waiter asked for our orders, I noticed that Christina's attention was fixed on a flower girl coming toward our table.

"Flower for the pretty lady," asked the adorable little angel with hair similar to the waiter's.

"Thank you very much," Christina said, taking the flower and drawing the young girl to her. "What's your name?"

"Bellissima," she answered, as she waited for payment.

I didn't know what to think at that moment, but I was struck by the way Christina had with children. I became frightened that the more she was around them, the more resilient she would be to my arguments about waiting to have our own.

The episode on the ferry and the little flower girl started me thinking. Christina had been quick to change the subject, as if by talking about kids her true feelings would be revealed. What was she trying to hide? What had she done that she was afraid would anger me? What had she been trying to tell me?

There was no way of knowing how long the little girl had been doing it, but I was suddenly aware of a little head popping up from time to time as the staff tried to get out the food.

"I could be wrong," I told Christina, "but I swear that child looks out at you every time the doors swing open."

"Does she really?" she asked excitedly. "She's adorable, isn't she?"

I was wondering where the waiter had disappeared to. At that moment, all I wanted to do was eat and get back to our cottage. But that was not to be. Out of the kitchen, a short man and a sandy blond woman approached.

"Pardon me," the man said, "but my son thinks you are Christina Jaloqua. Is that right?"

"Yes," Christina smiled, grabbing my hand. "But I am Christina Richardson now."

"My wife and I would be honored," the man told us, "if you and your husband would join us at our table."

Christina must have sensed my annoyance because she squeezed my hand tighter. Because of that, I decided to accept their hospitality. I was seated at a large table, while the man's wife took Christina on a tour of the kitchen. I became worried about where she was taking Christina when Poppa, as the family affectionately called him, put his hand on my shoulder and shouted for his son, Nicholo, to bring out the food.

"Just married," he roared, slapping me on the back. "You're a lucky man to have such a pretty wife."

The waiters started bringing out the food. Oversized plates with mussels, scallops, shrimps, calamari, and other mollusks were served with a variety of pastas. The man's wife and Christina came back with the rest of the family, carrying a little baby. All in all, I counted ten kids.

"You're not telling me that's their baby?"

"No, this is Nicholo's baby," Christina told me. "They're proud grandparents. They have fifteen children and ten grandchildren."

How was it that Poppa and his wife were blessed with so many, while others couldn't have one? Christina was an ethereal beauty as she cradled the baby in her arms. Again an overwhelming dread seized me. I loved her so much and was terrified to lose her— but how could I make her understand?

"Eat up," Poppa roared. "There's plenty of food."

We were being treated to an Italian-style meal. You'd eat a little from one dish, and then someone would pass you another plate. That way, everyone had a chance to sample everything on the table, although Poppa seemed intent on pushing every form of mollusk toward me to eat.

Christina was having a great time. She especially liked the calamari.

"Dearest," she asked playfully, "do you know what this is?"

"No, Princess," I said, eyeing her plate with great suspicion. "What is it?"

"Calamari is squid. Do you want to try it?"

"Just this once," I assured her, and then, when I discovered how delicious they were, "I wish you would have told me at the end of dinner."

Everyone's laughter had a pleasing yet adverse effect on me. I was moved by the warmth and expression of love that overspread the table, but at the same time wary, if in trying to reproduce the genuine affection of this family, it would cause me again to lose my own.

Near the conclusion of a wonderful evening, Christina and Nicholo's wife went to put the newborn and Bellisima to bed. When she came back, Christina kissed me and told me how much fun she was having.

"I'm so glad that we came here to eat," she said. "They really are wonderful people."

We had come to Hamilton Parish to shop and ended up making new friends. It was so late when we left that we realized we would have to take a taxi.

"Taxi! Nonsense, Nicholo will drive you home," Poppa roared. "Take care of that pretty wife," he said, winking at me. "Take good care of her."

"Poppa, how you tease him so," said his wife. "He's a good man. He will take care of her," she continued, pushing Poppa away. "Never you mind; they will take care of each other."

She quickly hugged me and kissed me on the cheek. But as she embraced Christina, I noticed that she whispered something to her before heading back inside.

"Nicholo! No fast driving," Poppa shouted. "Good night, my pretty," he told Christina as he kissed her on both cheeks.

As Christina rested her head on my shoulder, I couldn't help but reminisce about the night of our first date. I had tried to send her away, but ironically enough, her pertinacity was why we were now man and wife. She had looked so beautiful that night, a vision of everything I held dear—but would I be cheated again?

There was so much we could teach each other, if we would only listen. But I had seen her motherly instinct starting to bloom. And then her question raced through my mind.

What would our child learn from me? If the condoms in my pocket had any say in the matter, absolutely nothing.

Chapter 11

W E GOT BACK TO OUR COTTAGE SHORTLY AFTER ONE. While Christina, weary from our shopping excursion, was happily soaking in the whirlpool, I was left—gratefully, I might add—to ponder the day's events. As I have done on numerous occasions while trying to discern the pros and cons of a business deal, I took a notepad, drew a line down the center of the page, and began listing the pros and cons of my life with Christina.

Sitting on the terrace dressed in only a robe, I was tallying up the list against her when Christina called me into the bedroom. I was not prepared for the sight that awaited me. She stood in the middle of the room, dressed in an elegant two-piece outfit consisting of a jacket and bikini made of silk so golden that it blended with the color of her skin.

"Dearest, I hope that I'm not taking you away from anything," she said. "I know how you hate to have your thoughts interrupted. But I wanted to show you one of the things I bought today, something that I couldn't model for you earlier. I thought now would be as good a time as any."

I cursed silently to myself for being momentarily annoyed at having been disturbed, not because I didn't want to see her like this. What man wouldn't? But she had admitted that she knew that I did not like to be bothered at such times, and yet she had done it all the same.

Still, she had never looked as ravishing as she did then.

"Do you see now why I had wanted to bring it back with me?" she asked.

"I see. I see."

"Would you have preferred me to model it in the store?"

"Good Lord, no!"

"Perhaps I should have waited until tomorrow. How thoughtless of me. Can you forgive me for disturbing you, Tony?"

Eager to show her that I forgave her, I turned off the light, picked her up, and carried her over to the bed where I began caressing her, kissing her while pulling strands of hair behind the nape of her neck. Starting slowly, I began teasing her by tracing the contour of her lips with my tongue as an artist would trace the outline of a picture, while she shivered in delight. Aroused, she kept trying to bite my lip, but each time I pulled away before she could. I slowly pushed my tongue into her mouth and she responded by sucking on my lips with fiery intensity. I could have gone on kissing her this way all night, but I had other plans to please her.

Becoming an artist again, I began nibbling on her neck and then her ears. She began to moan as I pressed my tongue as far as it could go into her inner ear. At last, I traced her ears a final time and began nibbling on her neck en route to those precious fruits below, which, released from the confines of the jacket, stood firm as if they were at attention, awaiting my tender touch. As I fondled one and suckled the other, her moans became a little louder.

"Tony, ah, Tony," she groaned, "I love what you're doing to me."

Feeling a need to increase her pleasure, I began moving my lips toward her cord of life. Like a consummate painter, I slowly traced an S design around the outer edges of this orifice and then moved slowly toward its center.

"Dearest, ooh," she cooed, "I love when you do that. You know my body so well."

If she thought that was nice, she hadn't felt anything yet. I was content to remain silent for the moment. But confident with the condoms in my possession, I was determined to make this night as memorable for Christina as possible.

Easing her body to the middle of the bed, I admired those willowy legs and then began caressing her feet while sucking each toe in turn.

"Oh, Tony!" she cried, when I ran my tongue across the bottom of her feet, and then exhausting the amount of pleasure that could be derived there, I prepared myself to peel the peach.

I started my slow progression by tracing the contour of one leg with my tongue, while stroking the calf of the other leg with my fingertips and fondling a breast. I traced and nibbled until I had reached her inner thigh. Moving the bikini over slightly, I began to trace the perimeter.

"Tony, Tony, why do you tease me so?"

I heard her pleas, but how could I have answered? What would I have told her? That I was afraid to consummate the marriage for fear of bringing children into the world? But tonight, I needn't fear. The condoms as my allies helped me vanquish all my fears.

"Tony, I'm sorry. Are you getting back at me for teasing you?"

Satisfied that I had teased her enough, I removed her bikini and watched her open those long legs, welcoming me to drink of the fruit's nectar. Slowly tracing the perimeter once again, I listened to her moans, trying to make sure that I knew exactly the spot that gave her the greatest source of pleasure.

Pushing my tongue gently inside, I felt the warmness of her body. Going as far as I could go, I began to explore until suddenly she shot to an upright position, and grabbing me by the neck, pushed my head toward her.

"Oh, God!" she cried. "Tony that is—right there—ah—the spot! Please, don't stop. I love what you're doing to me. Please, dearest! Don't stop. Right there. Stay right there, please!"

Falling back onto the bed, she began rocking violently back and forth.

"I can't hold back anymore, Tony!" she screamed. "Oh, Tony, I'm com—"

She jerked back violently as the dam broke. Feeling the saltiness of her nectar, I continued as she tried to pull away. But I wasn't about to stop there. I wanted to know my wife's body so well that there would be no trial and error. Going back to exploring, I pushed my way in again.

"Tony, what are you trying to do to me?" she squealed with delight. "Oh, God. Tony—doing it again. Right there! You found it again."

Imagine that. So much pleasure concentrated in such a tiny space. Good things indeed come in small packages.

"Dearest, please!" she moaned. "Give it to me. I want you to. Please, I need you."

I had used the opportunity while she soaked in the whirlpool to remove the condoms from the box and conceal the packages in my robe, but I wondered how to produce them. I disrobed as I approached her and started tearing one of the packages when Christina grabbed my arm.

"There is no need, dearest," she told me. "Please let there be nothing between us."

What had she meant by that? I thought. Was there no need because she had already taken precautions, or because my preventive measure had come too late? But I was turned on by Christina's pleading me to take her and decided that if she had asked that nothing come between us, then she must have safeguarded herself somehow.

I started kissing her again while slowly putting myself in.

"Oh, Tony, it is so hard. Oh, it feels so good."

I was definitely hard. In fact, I couldn't recall myself ever being this hard before.

"Tony," she cried, "I can feel it growing inside me. It's so good. Please don't stop. I want you to give it all to me."

I wondered if she knew what she was asking of me. I was so hard. What if I lost my discipline? I prided myself on always being in control of my emotions. She really didn't know what she was asking of me.

I kept going, but under complete control and still a little apprehensive.

"Dearest, do you love me?" she asked.

"Yes, princess. You know I do."

"Then show me how badly you want me."

"Princess, I don't want to hurt you."

"Please, Tony. I need to know that you want me as much as I want you. I'll let you know if you're hurting me."

"Give me your word," I commanded.

"I promise, but I have to know that you want me—that I'm pleasing to you, that you are not holding anything back."

That was very perceptive of her. I wondered how she knew that I was holding back.

"Stop thinking about pleasing me, Tony. Enjoy yourself. Besides, I'm your wife. It's my right to have it all with nothing held back."

"Princess, you don't know what you're asking."

"Yes I do! You told me to be the woman that you fell in love with. Dearest, I want all of you. It's my right."

It's been so long since I let myself really go. God help me. God help us both.

I started slowly and deliberately. It felt so warm being inside her, my Cavendish hard as ever. Letting myself feel all the sensations, I began picking up speed while she wrapped her legs tightly around me, running her fingernails up and down my back, creating a marvelous tingly sensation that had me shivering.

"Oh, Tony. I can feel it. It's growing. It feels so good. I want it all. Nothing held back."

I continued picking up speed, thrusting it in like a wild man. "Princess, you're so hot. This is really tight."

"Yes, my king. It's all yours. You have the key to unlock it. Open it up. It all belongs to you. All that I have is yours."

It was so hot inside. Her constant moaning and talking turned me on. "Princess, this feels so good," I shouted. "It's so tight. I'm so hard. Wow—so hot."

"Yes, I feel your heat. I want it all. Tony, right there. Yes, right there. It feels so good. Doesn't it feel good to hold nothing back?"

I had become almost barbaric as I drove it deeper. With each push, she screamed out louder.

"Damn you, Tony! I always want it to feel like this. I want it all!"

Her nails cut into my back again as I became a savage, no longer saddled with apprehension. My desire at fever pitch, I rammed as far in as possible.

"Oh, God! Oh, God! That's it. Damn you! Damn you! Why did you hold this back from me?"

Lifting her legs up over my shoulders, I bore down like a man possessed.

"Oh, God. Oh, God. Tony, I can feel it. Oh, God, I can feel it. Tony!"

A change in her facial expression alerted me that this position might have been too much for her, so I decreased my speed slightly and continued without breaking stride.

"Princess, you're really something. I never thought that making love could be this good."

"Oh, that's it. Right there! Keep doing that! Oh, God. I love you so much. Oh, God! Oh, God!" she cried, her legs wrapped tightly around my back. "I can't hold back anymore."

Her nails were cutting into my flesh. She was biting on my lips. There was so much pain and pleasure shooting through my body that I rammed my Cavendish in over and over again.

"Oh, Tony, what are you doing to me? It is growing again! It's getting harder! Please, what are you doing?"

You're asking me? Better ask my friend. What is he doing? It's full, so why won't it come out?

That night we did it every imaginable way: sitting at the edge of the bed with her back to me, facing me, standing up with her in my arms, on the mahogany table, atop a small counter, on the bathroom sink, and still my Cavendish would not erupt. I was beginning to worry that this thing would never go down. She began to caress it and that only made matters worse. We couldn't seem to get enough of each other. We were like two wild animals in heat.

"Dearest, I love you. I wanted to have it all. We will not stop until you come with me."

"At this rate," I replied nervously, "it probably will be tomorrow."

"Then, dearest, the sun will come up with you still making love to me."

There was only one position left, to my knowledge, that we hadn't yet tried. "Princess," I said. "Lie on your stomach, please, and if this position causes you pain as before, tell me immediately."

"Yes, dearest. I promise."

What a remarkable woman! She must be sore and tired. Still, she wouldn't stop until she had pleased me. I knew that there was no use trying to convince her that she had done so already. Then I knew how a woman feels when the man is finished and she hasn't even started. No one would ever believe that this was happening in reverse. Most men would have given up and gone to sleep. But not this woman. She was determined to please me—no matter how long it took.

"Tony," she said, "is anything wrong?"

How could I ever explain that I was in awe of her? Might I never know to what extent she would go to ensure my happiness? I never wanted anything in life as bad as I want this now: to make love to my wife and let her know that, yes, she has pleased me.

"No, precious," I told her. This is my favorite position for the serendipity that it holds. I could gaze upon my lovely wife as she wiggled herself up to me with her derriere slightly elevated, waiting patiently for me to bear down.

"Dearest, I am all yours," she said. "Anytime. Anyplace. I am yours to have. Share all that you are with me."

When I slipped it in, moving slowly and deliberately, her insides grabbed me like a vise, wrapping around me as though they would never let me go. Suddenly, I felt at peace. No longer feeling barbaric, I began thrusting, picking up speed.

"Damn, this feels good," I said, surprising even myself. "You don't know how long I've waited for a woman to love me like this."

"Yes, dearest, I know. You probably spent so much time trying to please them that you forgot that you deserved to be pleased, too. I don't ever want you to do that to me!"

She kept pushing herself up as I bore down. I was being titillated in all kinds of ways: watching her wiggle up to me, listening to her moaning and sweet words of affection, and my Cavendish being wrapped and squeezed. The pleasure was indescribable. As she grabbed the pillows to muffle the sound of her moaning, I grabbed on to the headboard and rammed down as she pushed up.

"Princess," I shouted, "that feels so good! Ah, if you knew how you've made me feel. I never want to hold anything back from you!"

I knew that this was the point of no return. I wanted to slow down to savor the moment, to remember how good it felt to be really loved by a woman. But she was too excited, her juices flowing.

"Oh, God. Oh, that's it. Tony! Tony, damn! It feels so good. Damn you, Tony! Give it all to me!"

She pushed herself up against me as I squeezed my PC muscles for dear life, determined to hold back as long as possible, with her just as determined to have me explode. We were going at an incredible pace with the bed rocking violently with us. It was a test of wills. Holding on to the headboard for support, I bore down like a barbarian. I felt it growing thicker, swelling up within her. And then, finally, my Cavendish spurted out violently, driving her deeper into the bed.

"Oh, God. Oh, God, Tony. Tony I can—I can feel it. It's so hot. Don't stop. Please don't. I want—I want it all. I've waited. Waited all my life for this. It's mine. It's mine, all mine. I love you. I'll never let you go. Never! You're all mine!"

My Cavendish showed no sign of weakness, even as I fell on top of her. Hearing her shallow breath, I realized that she had fallen asleep. Exhausted myself, I could no longer fight off sleep. With Christina wrapped safely in my arms and everything, for the moment at least, right with the world, I closed my eyes and thanked God for sending this woman to me.

"God, how I love her," I prayed. "Thank you, Father, for sending her to me. May I always be worthy of her love. Thank you."

The sunlight peering through the shades woke me up the next morning at a little past eleven o'clock. Christina was still sleeping peacefully, her hair fanned out on the pillow.

My God, what a lovely woman, I thought to myself. Although the tally had gone against her, I couldn't help but love her.

Slipping out of bed, I dressed and went out to play nine quick holes of golf, not because I really wanted to, but because it seemed a pity to leave Bermuda without having done so. I dashed off a quick note and fought the temptation to run my fingers through her hair as I placed the note on the nightstand.

How could the cons have outweighed the pros? I wondered as I watched the angel sleeping. Perhaps I was not worthy of her. She deserved far better, especially from a husband whom she had declared her undying love for.

It was a little after three when I got back to the cottage, in time for afternoon tea, or so I thought.

"Dearest, how I missed you," she said, kissing me repeatedly. "I have great news! Maggie called and—"

"God, you're beautiful. What have you got on?"

She was dressed in a black-floral print bathing suit, with a third piece wrapped around her waist, which she told me was called a *pareo*.

"But, dearest," Christina insisted, "Maggie said the house is on the market."

"That's nice," I said, trying my best to relieve her of the *pareo*. "It's amazing how I don't even know you."

"Why do you say that?" she retorted, as if I had accused her of something.

"It's just that you always seem to amaze me," I replied slowly, hoping to uncover what she had been afraid to tell me. "You look more radiant and gorgeous every time I see you."

But I had no choice other than to admire how quickly she changed the subject by offering to remove the garment as she modeled for me. I was tempted and would have agreed, but I insisted on hearing Maggie's message.

"The house," I said, cutting her off. "Are you sure? She said—the house! Could you have misunderstood her?"

"Tony, is something wrong?"

"Princess," I said, pushing her into a chair. Snatching another, I placed it in front of her. "Nice and slow, tell me everything Maggie said."

"We spoke a little about the weather," she began nervously. "How nice it was here. How she would like to visit here one day."

"No, no, not that part. The house! What about the house?"

"You asked me to tell you everything, didn't you?"

Simply amazing, I thought. Why wasn't she so forthcoming when I had asked her about other things? But it wasn't the time for this, not where the house was concerned. So I brushed it aside, ironically blaming myself, and asked her to continue.

"Your realtor called. The house is on the market. Maggie said you would understand."

"This can't be! After four years of waiting, that house will be mine! I've got to call Maggie!"

"She wants you to call back tomorrow when she has more information," Christina told me. "Besides, I've planned a picnic, unless you want to finish what you started."

"I would love to," I replied, "but a picnic sounds like a wonderful idea. I'll take a quick shower. Where are we having this picnic?"

"The person at the front desk said that Somerset Long Bay is nice. It's not far from here, and I've rented a moped. You can tell me all about this house when we get to the beach. We're so fortunate, darling. I can't believe all this is happening."

Half an hour later, our picnic basket secured to the back of the moped, we were on our way. It didn't take us long to reach the beach, and it was a perfect place, with a quarter mile of crescent-shaped sand ideal for taking long strolls by an area of undeveloped parkland that sheltered Sandy's Parish from the rest of the island. Christina reiterated the clerk's instruction that if we took a certain path, we would find a nature preserve nearby.

They had packed us a nice lunch: a combination of Bermudian and American favorites, including Johnnycakes, fried chicken, snapper, and "Hoppin John," or black-eyed peas and rice.

Christina was attentive, to put it mildly, tucking a napkin under my chin and watching me closely as I sampled everything.

"I need to know everything about you, my love," she said when I chided her for not eating herself. "And that includes knowing what you like to eat."

She wanted to know everything about me. A tall order, I thought to myself. I couldn't deal with the past, let alone tell her about it. She was my wife, and by all accounts she should know everything about me, but what did I really know of her? And worse, with my refusal to entertain thoughts from my past, I was less inclined to learn anything about hers.

When we had finished eating, I was ready and eager to start my tale about the house. I had to wait for Christina to finish tidying up, so I used that time to formulate how to tell my story without her noticing the disparity in time.

She asked me to lay with my head in her lap when she had finished.

"Princess," I said, "don't you think it should be the other way around?"

"You'll find it easier to talk if you lay down," she insisted. "See? This way I can stroke your face while I listen."

"You may have a point there," I said, but I couldn't rid myself of the feeling that she always went overboard to please me. As I looked up into those bewitching eyes, I began my tale.

I told her that, about three years ago, I had made the decision to go into business for myself. What I neglected to tell her was the impetus behind such a rash decision. I continued by letting her know of the three goals I had set: a short-term goal of buying a house, an intermediate goal of purchasing a pre-owned Benz, and the third was to be pursued after the first two were accomplished. I read countless books, I went on, and their underlying theme was that you'd only be as big as your dreams. I pointed out the fact that it was hard for people to do anything great, since most of their dreams were about the size of a pea.

"I wasn't about to have that happen to me," I told her. "The way to combat it: reach for the impossible, stretch oneself beyond self-imposed limits to make a decision, and the path will present itself. That is, depending on how bad you want it. And so I became determined to put my plan into action."

I felt strange as I told my story, for it seemed as if Christina was absorbing my words before they had a chance to escape my lips.

I continued, however, by telling her that I had done what the books suggested and had visited homes in neighborhoods that my financial mettle gave me no right to look at. How foolish I had felt walking through those homes, because my business hadn't gotten off the ground yet, and the only thing in my pockets, beside my hands, had been lint. Armed with scarcely anything but determination, I had gone in pursuit of my dreams.

The first realtor, I went on, had been so much of a cynic that he had warned me, if I didn't intend on buying a house right away, his time would be better spent on someone who was.

"Needless to say, we never went out after that. He taught me a very important lesson. Never—and I mean never—surround yourself with negative people. Their negativity will have a damaging effect. You won't notice it at first, but if allowed to continue, it will lull you into a cesspool of mediocrity while the time clock of life passes you by."

I wondered if she was bored, but when I questioned her, she just smiled and lovingly continued stroking my face.

I explained that the second realtor had understood that I wasn't in the market to purchase right away, but that I still needed to know all the preliminaries involved. She was a great salesperson, since she had taken me to see the most expensive property first. Subsequently, each home decreased in price, but I had become so infatuated with what she had shown me first, albeit undeveloped, that nothing else would do.

"I realized after she left me," I concluded, "that what she had done was to expand my dreams. Do you understand what I mean?"

"Yes, dearest," Christina assured me. "I believe I do. She made you feel that that house could be yours."

"Exactly. I bought the home I'm presently living in now as a stepping stone to bridge the gap between what I could afford at the time and what I would eventually own. But I'd go out and gaze upon this property and dream that one day it would be mine. A couple bought the property and built this magnificent home on it; I would go and look at it twice a month. They noticed me and threatened to send the authorities after me for planning to rob them. I took one last picture and haven't been back there since.

"So imagine my surprise when you told me that Maggie called, stating that that very house is now on the market. I framed the picture I took and placed it on my desk! I wanted a constant reminder of the home I would own one day. Well, princess, that's the whole story."

"Not quite, dearest . . . "

"Did I leave something out?" I asked, worried that perhaps she had noticed I omitted some facts.

"Yes. Is it not the home that we will one day own?"

"Forgive me, honey. Yes, it will be our home," I said, relieved, disguising my chagrin. "Nothing will prevent us from having it!"

I was sure of it then. The fact could not be denied. Had she really been drinking in my every word? Could what I had mistaken for attentiveness merely have been Christina consumed by her own thoughts? Were they thoughts of us being in our new home, or thoughts of a new addition, maternal in nature?

Whichever it was, it seemed to me that Christina's obsession to please me meant that she intended to be involved in every facet of my life, whether I welcomed her or not.

Toward evening we strolled down one of the nature preserve's paths, a winding road flanked by colorful hedges of hibiscus, oleander, and flowering plants. Then we headed for the beach to see the sun set. The water was a picturesque bluish-green, the tide rippling in. Above us, in a sapphire-blue sky, unusual cloud formations appeared to be so close that, had we reached up, we could have touched them. Christina was having fun running near the water's edge, while I, a few paces behind, admired the scenery.

"I love this beach," she said, untying her *pareo*.

I wanted to answer, but found that the words wouldn't come quickly, for I stood in awe of her. I had been no more than a foot away when she opened the pareo and the wind caught it. It was a breathtaking sight as she extended her arms upward and slightly behind, trying to hold on to the garment. With the darkness of the bathing suit contrasting against her skin and the wind blowing her hair behind her left shoulder, she was prettier than any model I'd ever seen.

I wish I had had a camera. The only thing we brought was a radio. I couldn't believe that God had blessed me with one as lovely as her. I never tired of admiring her beauty. Turning on the radio, I placed it on the sand, as far from the water as possible.

"Tony, Tony, is anything the matter?"

How could I tell her that she was the woman I had dreamt of on those lonely nights as I built my sand-castles? That I couldn't recall how many nights I had prayed that God would send her to me? How only faith had kept me going when all appeared bleak and hopeless? And now that she stood before me as my wife, it seemed like the culmination of a dream come true.

"No, nothing at all," I said instead. "I'll never forget how beautiful you look today."

Taking her hand, we continued our walk. The water from the incoming tide felt refreshing, and I felt totally at peace. I didn't want that moment to end.

"Princess," I said, "I love you and I always will."

Christina told me how much she loved me and that her dreams had been answered as well. Countless nights she had prayed that God would send her a man that not only loved her with all his heart, but one who would also possess strength along with tenderness. She had cried herself to sleep, thinking she would never find a man that would be gentle and kind. She had finally found her happiness with me.

"A man that will be a good provider for our family," she said, hugging me. "God answered my prayers. I will let nothing take away what God has given me. Nothing!"

Lifting Christina's chin in order to kiss her, I saw the tears in her eyes. "Honey, what's the matter?"

"I love you so much!" she explained. "I don't ever want to lose you!"

"Why must you persist in thinking that way?" I asked her.

Why couldn't she let me be? Why was it that every time I thought I could find solace in our marriage, her constant fear and doubt of losing me cropped up? She must be hiding something, or could she know about my past? The elaborate ruse that had made us man and wife—surely a woman capable of pulling that off could have dug into my past. No, that couldn't be. It has something to do with her. What could she have possibly done that would make her fearful that, if I found out, she would lose me?

I had to find a way to calm her fears, but how? The poem I had been working on was the first thing that came to mind. Halfway done, I would have to make up the rest. The sun had begun to recede, but unwilling to leave without a fight, lit the sky in a bright glow of fiery red. Against this brilliant backdrop, I began. It was, I told Christina, to be entitled "Know You by Heart."

What is there left for me to say
That the wisest of all sages didn't impart,
The beauty that your love possesses,
Is to love you, to know you by heart?

How do I show how much I love you?
To ease your fears that we will never part?
You're filled with fiery determination,
Vowing that nothing will keep us apart.

I can't take my eyes off you, prettier than any rose.
I've searched the whole world over,
Finally realizing how it goes.
With the passing of time, my love will not diminish.
By leaps and bounds it grows.

There is not much more that I can do
Than to take you, in my arms,
Softly whisper, I love you
While keeping you safe and warm.

Dancing this close to you, I can feel the first drop of tears.
'I don't want anyone to touch you, to look at you,'
That seems to be your greatest fear.
Sweetheart, I have done my best to reassure you
That as long as you need me, I will be here.
Please take a look in any mirror,
Then you will see what I also see,

That the loveliest of God's creations,
Promises always to be in love with me.

I will make you this promise:
This is not the end, but where our journey starts.
I will go on loving you forever,
Since to love you is to know you by heart.

"Dearest, that was beautiful. How can I help but love you? Promise me."

"Promise?"

"Yes, promise that you will keep writing those beautiful words to me."

"I—one day, I will find just the right words to let you know how much you mean to me."

"My precious love," she said, squeezing me tighter, "you have done so already."

The next morning I was up very early, even though we had spent most of the night showing each other how much we loved one another. I really couldn't sleep thinking that ownership of the house I had long thought of as mine was within my grasp. To pass the time, I inventoried all our purchases that I had asked to be sent to our cottage. Satisfied that everything was accounted for, I looked in the guidebook.

It was barely ten o'clock Bermuda time when I placed a call to Maggie.

"Everything is going fine," she told me. "In fact, all your new clients have been raving about what superior work the staff is turning out."

"Good!" I told her. "Perhaps Christina and I and can extend our honeymoon."

"I'm afraid that may not be possible," Maggie said. "The bidding on the house is set for Monday.

Seems that the couple is in serious financial straits and they'll take the first serious offer. I think you ought to be here in person, Tony, just to make sure. I know what this means to you."

"Tell our realtor that we'll be bidding on the house. Inform her that we will top any offer!"

"That's all been taken care of," she quickly reassured me. "I called Harry, advising him of the situation. He understands and will have the jet on standby if you need it."

"I only hope Christina won't be too disappointed," I said. "But you're right. It's important. Thanks for all your help. I'd be lost without you."

"Dearest," she said, hugging me from behind, "what is it that you wish will not disappoint me?"

"We're going to have to interrupt our honeymoon," I told her, hanging up the phone. "They're starting the bidding on the house on Monday."

"I understand," Christina told me. "What could be more important than our new home? That is as it should be. We will go!"

"I'll make it up to you," I assured her.

"You've already given me more than I ever dreamed of," she said, hugging me tighter. "That's why I will always love you."

For our last two days, my wife wanted to relax. As a consequence, we spent a lot of time on beach mats floating at the water's edge. We also rented a boat and went sailing. Our last night, we sat on the terrace and talked.

"Everything is packed," she told me. "I just can't wait to go home."

"You want to go home?" I teased. "But I thought you were having fun!"

"Of course it was fun," she scolded me. "But I want to wake up in our home. I want to cook and clean for you, and be there to greet you when you come home."

"I understand," I said, reaching for her hand, "but with all of our commitments, when will we ever lead a normal family life?"

I was at a loss as to what to do. I had hoped that our busy lifestyles would safeguard us against any desire for starting a family. But the way Christina was carrying on, that wasn't going to be. How could I tell her what I was afraid to confront, that my greatest fear was of losing everything, as I had before? And that history wouldn't have to be repeated if she would only leave this desire for family life, with all it entailed, behind. Why couldn't it be just us two?

"I'll see that we do," she said, vehemently. "I'll be a good wife!"

If she wanted to be a good wife and do all that she could to please me, then why wouldn't she do what I told her? But I knew this wasn't the place to have it out with her, so I changed the subject as adroitly as I could.

"Apple pie!"

"Apple what?"

"I'm sorry, princess," I said, staring out to sea. "Your statement about being a good wife started me thinking of apple pie, my favorite dish."

"Did your mother bake them for you as a child?" she asked, quizzically.

I could tell by her expression that she was trying to figure out if I had been joking or not. But I went on to share the picture I had held in my mind about being in the backyard while my wife made a pitcher of lemonade and baked pies in the kitchen.

"Apple pie and lemonade," she said, coming over to me.

"Strange combination, I know. The man you married has a lot of idiosyncrasies."

"I love him all the more," she said, lying on my chest. "I want you to be happy."

"I have been," I assured her, "since the day you became my wife."

She sat up and stared incredulously at me. I wondered if she realized what I had done. I held my breath and waited for her to chide me about changing the subject.

"I love you with all my heart," she said, fervidly. "You'll have your dreams! I shall see to it!"

"Ladies and gentlemen, this is your captain speaking. This flight will take two hours and fifteen minutes. We should be arriving in New York at . . ."

I was relieved to be finally going home. Although our honeymoon was filled with precious moments, there were frightful ones as well. Taking Christina's hand, I leaned back and closed my eyes.

"Dearest," Christina said, "there's something I've been meaning to tell you."

"Yes, princess, what is it?"

"Please look at me," she insisted. "This is important."

I became apprehensive. What was she going to tell me? Would it be why she had acted so strangely on our honeymoon, or had she seen through my aversion to discussing family life?

"Do you realize how much I love you?" she asked,

squeezing my hand tighter. "And why I shaved you?"

"Yes," I replied, but with a great deal of reservation. "Wasn't I appreciative? I said it was a most loving gesture."

But it was much more than that, she intimated. She went on to explain the time-honored tradition of the women in her family to ensure that their husbands remained faithful.

"What does that have to do with us?" I asked, pressing the button on my chair.

She told me how they would do anything to please their husbands and that their every waking moment was devoted to making the men happy. That what I had characterized as a loving gesture was their way of letting their unsuspecting husbands know what would happen if they were ever unfaithful.

"No man," she said, forcefully, "can sit perfectly still if he has."

I had suspected a great many things, but nothing of this magnitude. I had thought it odd that she would shave me, but never a warning against infidelity. It was true, I had been nervous, but more on account of doubting her skills.

I wanted to let go of her hand, but couldn't. If the plane had broken apart and sucked me out, I wouldn't have minded. I wished someone would pinch me and awaken me from the horrid dream. I couldn't believe what she was saying, yet she had been sitting beside me, unwavering in her conviction of undying love.

She literally meant it, I thought to myself. The walls were closing in on me, sealing off any possible chance of escape. I felt as if I were falling deeper into an abyss. But I had to know. I had to hear those very words uttered from her lips.

"Are you saying what I think?" I asked, in disbelief. "That if I were ever unfaithful . . . "

"Yes, dearest," she said, calmly, "I would cut your throat!"

Chapter 12

I COULDN'T BELIEVE WHAT I HAD HEARD. I KEPT THINKING that maybe I had heard her incorrectly. How could a woman as beautiful as her—a woman who looked so innocent and to whom I had pledged my life and love—demonstrate such a capacity for ruthlessness, all in the name of love? Could she, with that tender hand that was holding mine? Those loving hands that had stroked my face, could those hands just as easily have slit my throat?

I sat there motionless. All I could think of was that I had let her shave me. It had never entered my mind to ask what she was doing with a single edge razor. But that was absurd, of course. Were we not living in modern times? She would never carry out such a threat. What she had said must have been hyperbole. What kind of demented ritual was that to pass on? No one should be that determined to possess someone else, and certainly not to the point of trying to frighten them with an outdated tradition.

No doubt she had seen the appalled expression on my face, because she squeezed my hand a little tighter. I realized that I had better say something. The infantile stage of our marriage was similar to a single thread that could easily be broken.

"Have I lost you?" she asked, clearly agitated. "Is our marriage over before it begins?"

She poured her heart out, letting me know that her love was so strong that she couldn't have followed in the footsteps of the women in her family. But to me, the damage had already been done. Whether she could go through with it or not wasn't really the point, but the fact that she had confided in me left no doubt in my mind that I had married a very strange, and perhaps deranged, woman.

"Princess, dry your tears," I said gently. "You haven't lost me. Your revelation simply took me by surprise, that's all."

"My love, I'm nothing without you. God sent you to me! He answered all my prayers! Nothing and no one will ever take you from me! Remember your promise."

I frowned. What was she talking about? And then I realized what she meant. It was the poem. Of all the verses I might have recited, why did she choose to latch on to that one?

Oh, God, what have I done to deserve this? Have I been blessed or cursed? Why had I started writing poems in the first place? I realized that I had to be careful of what I said going forward. I couldn't be like other husbands, who in a moment of passion rattled off whatever came to mind only to forget the instant the climax of the occasion had been reached. Christina, it seemed, planned on literally living and dying by my words.

"Dearest, will you . . . ?"

I could have simply told her no. Made it clear that a mistake had been made and our marriage should be annulled. But enraptured by her beauty, I could not bring myself to believe, despite what I had seen and heard, that the woman I had pledged my love to could cause me harm.

"I meant every word," I said, forcing my eyes to meet hers. "Perhaps one day I will no longer have to prove it."

"But you needn't," she said, stroking my face. "You already have. In more ways than you'll ever know. Dearest, dearest, there's Matt," she said, pulling on my arm and pointing to the sign he was holding. On a placard, large enough so that it couldn't be missed, he had written "The Richardsons" in big, bold letters.

We waited in the limo while Matt helped the skycap with our luggage. "Princess," I said, "do you want to stop and see your parents?"

"No, I wish to go home. I've waited so long that nothing will keep me from it now!"

"Where to, boss?"

"Uh, take us home."

Traffic was moderate so it didn't take us long to get home. Thanking Matt for his hospitality, we bid him good night. As for me, I was eager to find out what she meant about waiting so long.

"I couldn't wait to get here," she said, extending her arms to me. "I did not feel complete until I fully entered your world. Please show me our home."

I will never forget the eagerness with which Christina examined everything in the house, from the dishes in the cupboards to the boiler room in the basement. Finally, when we entered my bedroom, she began to cry.

"Princess, is there anything wrong?"

"All I ever wanted was to be here," she said, hugging me, "to share the warmness of your bed."

I realized that the woman I married was very sensitive. The simplest things brought her the most joy. Not knowing what to say, I just held her tighter.

"Dearest, I can't help it," she cried. "I love you so much. You don't know how many nights I wished I could be here with you."

"Well, you're going to have to help me," I said, moving toward the window. "It's going to take some getting used to."

"What is that?"

"Your tears of happiness. I'm used to people crying because they're sad, but crying for happiness is new to me."

Christina told me that she was sorry. But I explained that there was no need for her to apologize. She needn't change on my account. I realized that she was a sensitive person, and I had no other choice but to accept it.

"Do you really mean that?" she asked, smoothing out the bedspread. "Even after what I told you?"

"That is water under the bridge," I said, choosing my words carefully. "I will not stand in judgment of you. Let's not hear anymore of it and forget that that conversation ever took place."

"As you wish, my love. Dearest, can we go shopping?"

"Shopping?"

"The refrigerator is nearly empty," she said in an accusatory tone.

"Estelle didn't expect us back until next week," I explained.

"I heard you mention her before. Who is she?"

"She is the woman who cleans the house once a week. I pay her a little extra to shop for me."

"Well, she won't be needed now," Christina said decisively. "Not now that I'm your wife."

"Now hold on a minute!" I told her, startled. "You're not an ordinary, everyday housewife! You're a world-renowned violinist! You can't think those mundane duties are important and that you are going to be the one performing them; I hope the only performing you do is in concert."

"What's so mundane about being a wife and mother?" Christina demanded. "I made a vow to be your wife! I intend to keep that vow, in every sense of the word!"

"Are we to have our first disagreement on our first day home?" I asked her. "I can't believe that we're on opposite sides on this issue. Most women would be glad that I think the way I do. I want you to be all that you can be."

"You are my husband. I'm your wife. Therefore, your word is law in our home. Just answer this one question for me: shall I break the vows I made before God?"

"What on earth are you talking about?" I asked helplessly.

"At the ceremony, the minister asked if I took you as my husband, did he not?"

I knew I was in trouble. Somehow she had sprung the trap again. Clearly, I had to remember not to let that innocent face fool me. Right then, however, too stubborn to quit, I played it out to the bitter end, beginning with a hedge.

"He asked the same of me," I told her.

"Do you intend to keep your vows?"

"You know that I will."

"Then would you have me do any less?"

"Princess," I said, "why didn't you become a lawyer?"

I had to figure out what to do. How could I make her see my point of view? If all else failed, did I dare tell her the truth about my past?

"Have I angered you?" she asked.

Angered wouldn't have aptly described what I was feeling. I was running out of options. It seemed that my world was about to cave in, and I had become helpless to prevent it. As she stood before me, smiling so innocently, I wondered how to explain my fears in a way that she would understand.

"Dearest, I love you. Don't fight with me so. If you want me to be all that you wish I should be, why can't I be a wife and the mother of your children? Is it so wrong for me to want that?"

"No, princess," I said, trying to suppress my anger. "It's rather noble to want to be my wife, to love me so much that your only wish is to see me happy. I love you and only want your happiness. I understand that in a marriage a lot of sacrifices have to be made, but a common housewife's life for a world-renowned violinist is not one that I am willing to make."

"But the choice is not yours," she retorted.

It is no use, I thought to myself. I felt as if I was about to lose it. Why was she so stubborn and couldn't see my point of view? Suddenly, I had to get her out of the house so I could get my bearings.

There were several supermarkets in the area, but I chose to take her to King Kullen, an upscale market that stocked superior products.

We walked around the store, but neither of us placed anything in the cart.

"Princess," I said finally, "I thought you wanted to shop."

"Yes, I do."

"Well, sweetheart, I'm curious as to how you do it."

"What do you mean?"

"You haven't put a single item in the cart. What's the matter?"

"I was hoping that I could watch how."

Now I was in a bit of a pickle. How do I let her know that for a long time life wasn't worth living, in fact, it had become so distasteful that most of my purchases were done for my cat?

"Don't you shop with your mother?"

"No, not really. My father and mother own a laundromat and a small grocery store."

"Oh, I see. But when you were flying around the world, you must remember some foods that you enjoyed."

"Yes, but can I watch you shop?"

She is at it again, I thought. Deliberately suppressing what she wants in order to please me. But surely two can play that game.

"I'll tell you what," I said, "since we are both new at this, let's go down every aisle and pick out what we like."

By the time we left, the car was packed with groceries. Within an hour of getting home, outfitted in a long-forgotten apron, I was playing chef. Washing off the cutting board, I started slicing the things I asked Christina to pass me, slowly at first until I became used to the feel of the knife. Once I became familiar with it, she marveled at my increased speed.

"Sweetheart, there is a wok in the oven. Can you pass it to me?"

"Is there anything else you need?" she asked excitedly.

"Now that I think of it, pass the oil, the rice, and seasonings."

Taking down the steamer from overhead, I asked her to wash it, along with the cooking utensils. It was amazing how much dust had accumulated on them. After seasoning the chicken and adding the vegetables, I placed them to one side. While the rice was steaming, Christina washed the ingredients for the salad. The knife and I made short work of them.

Forty minutes later, when the rice was almost done, I stir-fried the chicken along with the red and green peppers, and when mixed with the onions, it was a feast for the eyes as well as the palate. Christina stood silently near me.

"Princess, I need one favor."

"Yes, dearest?"

"In that drawer behind you, there are some place mats and you know where the knives—"

"I understand," she said, kissing me. "I will set the table."

She returned as I was pouring punch into tall glasses and admired the garnish I placed on top. I got the candlesticks and holders from the closet, while she carried the plates to the table. I held her chair and unfolded her napkin.

"Dinner is served," I said, as I lit the candles.

"I love you," she said. "I love you."

We bowed our heads and I said grace. When I looked up—God, what a beautiful woman. Her hands were still together in—no, she was crying again. I reached across the table, placed my hands on hers, and silently prayed.

How can I ever repay you for sending her to me? Will this time be different? Is it possible for me to find happiness? You and I alone know the contents of my heart. She means the world to me. I couldn't bear to live a moment without her. Thank you, Father. May I always be worthy of her love.

After dinner we conversed while washing and drying the dishes. Although the house had a dishwasher, I felt more at ease talking while we did them.

"Tony, where did you learn to cook like that?"

My thoughts were consumed with my past and so I tried to make light of my culinary skills in hopes that Christina would not ask me any further questions. But how foolish of me to think that I could have gotten away that easily.

"Dearest," she said, placing her hand on mine, "what you did tonight, I will never forget. Please don't joke about it."

I saw no reason not to share how my culinary skills came about. I felt safe talking about it, as long as she never questioned why I had stopped. I told her of my childhood dream to become a bachelor like my uncle. On occasion, my mother would let me stay with him and I admired his lifestyle. But the one thing that had perplexed me, I had explained to my mother, was the fact that we'd eat out every night. She had told me that my uncle couldn't cook, and if I was dead set on being a bachelor, she would remedy that by teaching me.

"When I got to high school," I told her, "classes were being switched due the feminist movement. Women were complaining that their rights were being violated and that they should be given the opportunity to participate in classes that were deemed appropriate only for men."

I went on to explain that, much to my dismay, the switch had taken place in my second semester. And so instead of being in the metal and woodworking workshops, I was forced to learn sewing and cooking. I pointed out the fact that I had managed to pass the sewing class, although I never became proficient at it.

"But whatever skills I lacked in sewing," I told Christina, "I more than made up for in cooking. I was very fond of my Italian cooking teacher. She was simply amazing and taught us to prepare every dish imaginable."

I concluded by telling Christina how my unsuspecting tasters were members of my family, and how my confidence soared after they raved about my lasagna.

"I hope I haven't bored you with all this?" I asked, passing her another plate.

"Dearest, please stop doing that," she said, urging me to continue. "I never find what you say boring. Did she teach you to make the drink and garnish it as well?"

"Remember, you asked me to finish. When I moved out on my own, I saw an advertisement for Time-Life Books, offering to try their recipes for thirty days with the option to return any book you decided not to keep. I can proudly say I am the owner of the whole series."

"Dearest, where are all those books now?"

"I believe that they're in the basement. Why do you ask?"

"Oh, just curious," she replied. "Are the books no longer useful?"

How could I tell her what the books now represented? And that as long as they remained in those boxes, I was shielded from the anguish of my past, which was threatening to destroy my future.

"Sweetness," I said, as the last plate almost slipped from my hand, "don't you think you should call your mother?"

"Tony, is something bothering you?" she demanded.

"I—I need to check my e-mail. And do my homework for Monday's bid. I didn't want you to feel neglected."

"As you wish, my love," she said, petulantly. "I will call mother and let you work."

I felt horrible. A lovely evening could not end like that. I had to do something to put a smile back on her face.

"Before you go," I said, reaching for her hand, "can I admire how beautiful you look?"

She was wearing a lavender jacket with a simple cotton blouse and a matching short skirt.

"You know, all day I've been admiring you in that outfit, and trying to figure out what was missing. You're simply gorgeous, but it needs a touch of something. And I know exactly what it is. I left it on the dining room table. Why don't you go take a look and see if you like it?"

While she did that, I put on some soft music.

"Dearest, when did you have time?" she exclaimed, showing me the open box.

"When I asked Jacque for another of his cards," I said, fastening the clasp. "I simply wrote the number for both items. If he agreed, they were both to be sent to our cottage. I had wanted you to find it while we were there. But I couldn't wait any longer, so I decided that I would surprise you tonight."

"I love you with all my heart," she said, hugging me. "All of me belongs to you. I love you."

"I just wanted you to know that nothing is too good for my wife," I said, taking her in my arms. "Princess, I love you."

As we slowly danced to the music, I whispered:

"As words form verses to complete a rhyme,
Your love has formed the completion to a heart like
mine.
Making me want to shout, making me want to sing,
Your love to me means everything.

I've found my best friend speaking all night on the
phone.
At the end of a hard day, you will find me rushing home
To be close to the one that I hold so dear,
For I love you so much and need to always have you near.

Our love will stand the test of time.
It is amazing what your love has done to a heart like
mine,
Making me live again and teaching me to believe
That in this entire world there was one made especially
for me.

I have always told this, and believe me, it is true,
That of all God's creations, he must have spent a little
more time on you,
For how can it be explained that somehow I got my
wish,
That upon your creation, God made a simply wonderful
dish.

He must have emptied his bag, using everything he
could find,

To create one as lovely as you, to capture a heart like
mine.
I am forever in his debt, and the only way to pay
Is to show how much I love you, each and every day."

When I finished, she hugged and kissed me. "I love you," she said teary-eyed. "That was so beautiful." Suddenly, Christina tore away from me and ran upstairs. I hesitated before going after her. I asked her if everything was okay as I stood outside the door.

"Yes," she cried, "but I need some time alone."

I told her I would be in the den if she needed me and went into the guest room to bathe. It was a good thing I had furnished that room. I never really knew why, since I never had visitors. But it sure came in handy that night. What an emotional woman!

When I finished bathing, I passed by our room and listened at the door. Not hearing a sound, I assumed that Christina had fallen asleep and continued on to the den. I read a few of the work e-mails of the many that Maggie had forwarded to my personal e-mail account. Quickly scrolling through them, I found that most were from companies wanting my firm to do their marketing work, but there were others from associates and friends congratulating me on my marriage. From the few I read, the consensus was the same: disbelief that I, never a great proponent of marriage, had finally been hooked.

Although only a week had passed, the work had already begun piling up. I could only imagine what would have happened if we had completed our honeymoon. The most pressing issue was the bid for the house on Monday. Finding the file Maggie had forwarded, I pored over the details to familiarize myself with the property. I didn't want to lose this golden opportunity by underbidding. The right information was crucial. Knowing what the other fellow was holding would be paramount in a deal of this magnitude. I was lost in my world of figures when Christina knocked on the door.

"I'm going to bed now," she said.

"Princess, I thought you were asleep," I said, without turning to look at her.

"No, I was talking to mother."

Trying to calculate how much I was going to bid, I hadn't paid attention to Christina when she offered to get me a drink.

I couldn't understand this woman. She knew how I hated to be disturbed, especially when I was in front of the computer. Didn't I tell her that I needed to do my homework for the bid on Monday?

"Here you go, dearest."

My attention, fixed on the figure close at hand, had me totally oblivious to her presence in the room.

"Is that all you wish?"

"Yes, princess," I replied, turning to face her. "Thank you. This is . . . "

I couldn't believe my eyes. Looking innocent but seductive as only she could do, Christina stood before me in a red, two-piece outfit with a long-sleeved bolero jacket, so short that it enhanced her bosom.

"Dearest, I'm sorry. I didn't get a chance to thank you properly."

"Thank me properly for what?"

"For buying me this necklace. I think it looks better with this outfit. Don't you agree?"

"Mmhmm."

"I think I ought to be ashamed of myself, running

off like a little schoolgirl after you cooked that wonderful meal. Don't you? Don't you think I should be ashamed, Tony?"

"Uh, yes, little schoolgirl."

I should have been cross with her for interrupting my train of thought, but there was something about Christina when she assumed that childlike persona that I could not resist.

"Can I thank you now or should I come back later when you're not so busy?" she asked, approaching me.

And before I could utter a word, she had answered her own question by turning off the light.

"After all you did for me," she said coyly, "it will take me all night to thank you properly."

And it did.

Chapter 13

I WAS AWAKENED BY THE SWEET SOUND FROM ONE OF Vivaldi's violin concertos, so beautiful that I kept my eyes closed to revel in the richness of the music, only gradually becoming aware of the smell of bacon cooking. Instantly, I was transported back to Sunday mornings when I was a child. Back then, no matter how I had promised myself to sleep late, I had always got up early. But try as I did, I never beat Momma.

Sunday morning had been the time for a big breakfast with mountains of scrambled eggs, along with piles of bacon, and silver stacks of pancakes nestled among sausages. The toast had been lightly buttered, just waiting for me to add orange marmalade. The silver tea set had held the hot water and a variety of tea bags had always been neatly arranged on the tray. How I had rushed to shower to beat my sisters to the table. "Slow down, son," my mother would say. "The food isn't going to run away." I had never paid her any mind, though. I knew she was happy that I enjoyed her cooking.

But I wasn't at Momma's. I was a newly-married man in his own house. Grabbing my robe, I slowly descended the stairs.

Halfway down, I heard voices.

No, it couldn't be. What would she be doing here? The last thing I had ever imagined would be that she would set foot in this house after . . . and then I heard Christina's voice.

"Momma," she said. "What was Tony like as a boy?"

My mother, here! And at this time of the morning! I remained where I was, just outside the doorway to the kitchen.

"Quiet," my mother said. "No, shy. Yes, he was shy. He didn't have many friends. He was always content to spend hours in his room. How that boy liked to read."

"I have seen," Christina said proudly.

"Christina, honey, you can turn the pancake now. There are two things to look for: it should be dry around the edges and bubble in the center."

"I'm sorry." Christina sounded devastated.

"Don't try too hard to learn everything at once," my mother reassured her. "It will take some time. My son is a lucky man. Not many wives would call their husband's mother to ask how to cook for him."

"I only want to please him."

"That's all well and good," my mother warned her, "but be careful. He's stubborn. Too set in his ways, and he is never really content with anything for long. In fact, he usually wants the opposite of what he has. He can do so many things well that he'll pick up one thing, and before you know it, he's off on to something else."

I felt like a heel for listening to their private conversation.

"I knew when I first met you that you were the one for my son. Perhaps you'll have better luck teaching him than I did," Momma was saying.

"Teaching him? What could I possibly teach him?"

"You've already started without knowing it. This is the first time I've ever set foot in my son's house!"

I didn't want to hear any more. I knew what was coming. I trudged back upstairs. Some memories were just too painful to bear.

Flopping down on the bed, I grabbed a pillow and pulled the sheets over my head. But there wasn't going to be any time to wallow in self-pity. I heard my wife bounding up the stairs.

"Wake up!" she cried, pulling the covers from my head. "I have a surprise."

I better play this for all I'm worth. No need to let on that I know what the surprise is after she went through all this trouble. The least I can do was be appreciative.

I opened my eyes. Christina was wearing a gray three-piece, floral-embroidered pajama set, cute, but definitely not for our bedroom. I tried my best to lift the camisole, but she resisted, although I could tell from the gleam in her eyes that she would rather she didn't have to.

"Get up!" she told me. "You need to shower and shave. I have a surprise for you downstairs."

"Yes, my queen," I said, bowing. "Can I just tell you something?"

"Yes," she said, with her hands firmly upon her hips, "but please don't take too long."

"You look so sexy giving orders," I teased her. "I love you."

Christina stared at me, and I thought she was about to say something when she quickly kissed me and dashed out of the room.

I couldn't help but remark to myself as I headed

to shower that, indeed, I had married a very emotional woman.

Ten minutes later, wearing the blue pajama set, slippers, and robe Christina had laid out for me, I walked into the kitchen under the pretense of being astonished when I saw the bowl full of eggs, ready to be scrambled, the stacks of pancakes encircled with bacon and sausages, and slices of bread ready to be popped into the toaster.

My lovely wife stood alone at the table holding a teapot.

"Wow! Princess, this looks great!" I exclaimed. "How did you manage to do all this? This is a wonderful surprise."

"That's not the only surprise," she said, smiling. "I have another. Look who came and helped me this morning."

"Momma!" I exclaimed, thinking that I should have won an Academy Award. "What are you doing here?"

"I'm visiting with my daughter," she said, tightening the apron around her bulky waist. "I wanted to see how you've been treating her."

As usual, why aren't you concerned about me? What you should be asking is how I am being treated. Don't tell me that Christina has you fooled, also?

"Momma, how many times have I invited you here? And each time you refused. How is it that you're here now?"

"I felt the time was right. What are we standing around for?"

I held a chair for each in turn. "Everything looks great," I said. "Reminds me of those wonderful Sunday breakfasts you used to make."

"Still do. Only your brother seems to have time to come and eat them," she observed dryly.

How could he not? I thought to myself. What would he possibly miss, still tied to your apron strings?

"Princess, you're full of surprises."

"I called Momma to find out what you like to eat," Christina muttered, perhaps sensing the tension in the air. "We started talking, and I asked her to come over. I hope you don't mind."

I told Christina that she was full of surprises, which was true enough, but what I should have added was that sometimes her desire to please me went too far.

"Don't worry about it," I said instead. "It's good to see that you like each other."

"She's adorable," Momma insisted. "She lights up the room."

Christina took a plate and prepared it for me. Placing four pancakes in the center, she buttered each one and completed the stack. Cutting the stack into neat squares, she piled on eggs, bacon, and sausages. Placing a cup and saucer next to me, she poured the hot water and steeped my tea.

I wondered what Momma was thinking about all this. It was fine for Christina to go out of her way to please me, but to do it in front of Momma? Well, she was smiling. Was it a smile of happiness? She herself was a hard woman to read. But what would have possessed Christina to invite her over? Or had my mother simply invited herself? That would certainly be like her. It was uncanny how she had apparently taken to Christina. And yet, I could see the genuine affection my mother held for her. But I found it strange nonetheless, since it was unusual for Momma to display any emotion at all, since she had taught me the art of concealing my own.

"Dearest, would you like me to pour the syrup?"

"What—excuse me?"

"Would you like me to pour?"

"I'm sorry, princess. I will do it."

"As you wish," Christina said, taking a plate to serve Momma.

"Christina, honey, just two pancakes," Momma said, "and a small portion of eggs and bacon."

"Very well, Momma."

Before she sat down, Christina placed a napkin in my lap and laid the paper beside me.

I was so glad that my siblings were not there. I could only imagine the ribbing they would have given me about her treating me as if she were an indentured servant. I wondered if she was going to be that way when we visited her parents or went out anywhere. I'd have to talk to her about it later. Maybe Momma would correct her, let her know that was the fastest way to spoil a husband.

Proper etiquette was the last thing on my mind as I gobbled down my food, much to the delight of my wife and mother. Christina was getting up to replenish my plate, but Momma interjected. She was smiling as she handed me the plate.

What was going on I could not tell, but it appeared that both of them were trying hard to conceal devilish grins. I had to know what they were hiding, so I pretended to read the paper while Christina and Momma talked.

My wife was truly remarkable. She had my tough-as-nails mother clearly smitten with her.

They posed a few questions to me, but each time

I managed to revert the conversation to them. All they talked about were matters that would only be of interest to women.

"Ladies, that was simply marvelous," I said, hiding my annoyance. "Would you consider me a poor host if I eat and run, Momma? I have some urgent business to take care of on Monday and I need to go over some figures."

"Go take care of your business," she said, shooing me away with both hands. "It will give my daughter and me more time to talk."

Suddenly I found myself missing Lady. I spent the next three hours in my den. There was no need to, but I went over the figures again. Finally content with the numbers, I tried to read my e-mails, but my heart wasn't in it. As a result, I ended up playing solitaire on the computer. I could hear the two women's laughter as they chatted upstairs and it occurred to me that my mother had never had that much to say to me.

Out of the four of us, I was the only one that called her Momma. Hmm, she even referred to her as *my daughter*. I should be ecstatic that they liked each other—no, that they adored each other.

It was nearly noon when my wife knocked on my door. I had finally found a puzzle on the computer to occupy my time, but then I quickly closed the game and retrieved my list of figures.

"I don't mean to disturb you," Christina said, "but I'm afraid that I've been neglecting you."

I felt lower than a snake. Imagine my wife apologizing to me because she felt guilty about spending time entertaining my mother.

"It's just that your mother is ready to go home now. Come and say good-bye."

Momma was ready to go home, but how much had her little visit cost? What had she told Christina? Why were they smiling? Perhaps I was getting worked up over nothing.

Christina had no sooner left the room to unpack the gifts we had brought home from Bermuda when my mother told me to take a seat. She was sitting erect, her hands folded across her lap, and had a scowl on her face.

I knew that look and tone. A lecture was coming. What had I done to deserve this? I used to be able to quote her verbatim. How did she normally start? "Son, take my foolish advice." That was it. No, there was something before that.

"Tony, although I am only your mother, it would serve you well to take my foolish advice."

How could I ever forget that opening line? At least I got part of it right.

"Son, that is a lovely woman you're married to. I hope you realize that God has blessed you with her. She's trying awfully hard to fulfill her role as your wife. Don't pressure her. Let her love you. For God's sake and for mine, let her! No man could ask for a better wife."

I had to agree with Momma on two things, but everything else she said was totally off the mark. It was true about Christina's loveliness and her desire to please me. But how could I tell her that in trying to fulfill her role as a dutiful wife, Christina had gone way overboard?

When I came back from taking the packages out to my mother's car, she and Christina were hugging each other.

"Remember," Momma said, "don't let him bully you!"

Me, bully her? How could you be so blind to my plight? You never knew how much I suffered then, and worse, you don't even realize how I still am suffering. Can't you see how history wants to repeat itself? Where was God when the first tragedy struck? For his sake, as well as ours, I hope you have counseled Christina on her role as my wife, because if I have to go through that hell again, this time, she won't be the only one buried.

Chapter 14

Sunday night I tossed and turned, anxious to get the bidding over with for our new house. Numbers running through my mind, I played out a solution to every possible scenario. Finally, I decided that it was no use lying in bed. What I needed to do was go for a drive. It was the only way to clear my head, to ease my apprehension. But, given what Christina had told me in Bermuda about being left alone, I was afraid of what might happen if she should wake up and find me gone.

Before, it had been so easy. When I had a problem, I could jump into my car in the middle of the night and drive anywhere, even to the beach. There, I could sit on a rock and listen to the waves until a solution came to mind. But it would, I realized, never be that way again. Even though Christina might say I could go, I would feel funny about leaving her alone, especially on only her second night in this house. Estelle would be keeping Lady for another week, so our nightly talks in my den would have to wait.

I eased off the bed and sat at its edge. She looked so beautiful, sleeping like an angel, that I didn't have the heart to awaken her. I turned the stereo on low and went into the kitchen, hoping that a cup of chamomile tea would provide the same solace that driving did.

While waiting for the water to boil, I reflected on the many changes in my life. Suddenly, there was Christina, her hair tousled, tying her robe around her.

"Are you all right?" she demanded.

"Princess," I exclaimed, "what are you doing up at this time of night?"

"Looking for you," she told me accusingly. "Is anything the matter?"

I could have told her a thousand things, but her intrusiveness no longer seemed to bother me. Even if given a million years, I wouldn't have been able to explain it. I drew her closer and chuckled to myself.

How could I tell her that every day I found myself loving her more and even more afraid to lose her? That what I had been fighting was the very thing I had wanted the most, to have her always by my side?

I listened to Fibich's *Poéme* playing softly in the background and watched the steam escape from the kettle . . . suddenly my world was at peace.

In the end, I never did make that tea. The drive was no longer necessary. Everything I needed was there.

"Dearest, the teakettle."

"I know," I said, as I held her tighter and watched the steam rise. "Yes, *Mrs. Richardson*, I know."

Whatever concerns I had had the night before totally dissipated with the beginning of the day. I felt a quiet inner peace. When I emerged from the shower, Christina greeted me with a towel. My toiletries were all laid out on the sink. It was incredible. Every day she added a new item to the list of things to do. At this, I had mixed emotions. This woman was an accomplished violinist, not my maid. I told myself that when she resumed her concert schedule, everything would work itself out.

I had just reached for my razor when a feeling of anger overtook me.

"Princess," I shouted. "Come here!"

Christina rushed back to me.

"What is this?" I asked, waving the razor.

"Don't you recognize it?" she asked, clearly startled. "It's your—"

"I know what it is," I interrupted. "What is it doing here?"

"I don't know what you mean," she said, dumbfounded.

"The only time I should see this is when I'm going away on a business trip. Now get your razor! I need a shave!"

I shouldn't have been so cruel to her, but what choice did I have? If our marriage was to survive, there had to be a measure of trust. What ideas would she harbor if she thought my fear of letting her shave me was not due to her overzealousness to please me, but to hide the fact that I had been unfaithful? Given her temperament up to this point, not a moment's peace would be realized, I thought to myself, if I allow her to entertain such a notion.

She walked very slowly toward me. When I reached out to her, she shied away.

"Princess, I love you," I said, extending my arms. "When I gave you my heart, I entrusted you with *my life* as well. I'm sorry if I scared you. Just make sure that it never happens again."

"I promise it won't," she said, rushing into my arms.

"The glue that holds this marriage together," I told her, "should always be trust."

Just then the phone rang and she bolted out of the room.

"It's Maggie," she called. And then, when I took the phone, "Is anything the matter?"

"Princess, I'm sorry," I said, slowly putting down the receiver. It hadn't escaped me that she had been trying to tell me something before Maggie's call, so I decided to hedge a little. "You were saying."

"After I shave you, my love," she whispered. "I wanted to know—is there—?"

"I thought that after last night this was settled," I said, disguising my chagrin.

After my conniption about trust, what dark secrets could she be harboring that she felt would result in her losing me?

"Dearest, when will you learn?" she asked, tugging at my towel. "I never grow tired of your making love to me."

She is right, I thought to myself. Perhaps, by the time I learn, it would already be too late.

"Sit, so I may shave you," she said, pushing the door closed with her foot. "We don't have much time."

Traffic was moderate on our way to Glen Cove. I had told Christina to dress casually, since there was no one we needed to impress.

"I don't understand," she said. "Isn't this deal important to you?"

"Very much so," I told her. "That is why I refused Harry's offer on the use of his Bentley."

"May I know why?"

"His car would have brought us unnecessary attention. In a deal like this, we have to be indifferent."

"I don't understand," she said, knitting her brows.

"When we get there," I told her as we approached our exit, "it is very important that under no circumstances do you give them the impression that you like the house. We don't want to show our hand. The price would significantly go up if we did. So keep your thoughts to yourself. I want you to talk to the owner's wife and find out the real reason why they're selling."

The first thing that had always impressed me about this house was the neatly manicured circular driveway. Today there were several cars already parked there: a Jaguar, a Lexus, and two brand new BMWs—which made my Mercedes look appropriately modest.

Christina immediately pulled on my arm. "Dearest, it's lovely."

"I know, but remember what we discussed."

The butler, who had been positioned by the door, led us to where the other participants were.

"These people must be broke," I whispered.

"Tony, how do you know? We haven't met any of them yet."

"The bidding is supposed to start at eleven o'clock. We arrived half an hour early, and they're already here. That must mean they're desperate bargain hunters."

We were led into a very large library, where we joined the others. The shocked expression on our host's face led me to believe that he remembered me. Introductions were performed by my realtor, and then Mrs. Broadhurst took the wives on a tour while their agent explained how the bidding would be conducted.

"A financial disclosure of your net worth will be required," the agent said while looking directly at me, "to ensure that all of today's participants will be able to honor their bids."

I became incensed. That simply would not do.

"Joan, what is this?" I said, drawing her to one side. "Half these fools probably can't afford this house! Must we play these childish games? Does the man want to sell the house or not?"

"I know how you feel," she said, ushering me to take a look at the landscape. "But please try to bear with the proceedings."

I liked Joan. She was as cunning as a fox, even tempered, and had the uncanny ability to remain cool under pressure.

"What did your due diligence on the property reveal?" she asked, pulling out her notebook. "Our researchers came up with a property value of two million."

"I have no intention of paying that," I said flatly. "They're in a financial bind. They can't even afford to pay their property taxes."

"I see that you're very well-informed," she told me, beaming.

"That's why I am irritated about this financial disclosure business," I grumbled. "They're only steps away from foreclosure, and yet they want to know my net worth!"

Seeing Christina's signal, I excused myself and joined her.

"This house is lovely," she said, beaming. "Wouldn't you like to see the upstairs?"

"Perhaps later. Now what did you find out?"

"You were right," she said, squeezing my hand. "Mrs. Broadhurst is very unhappy. She doesn't want to sell her home."

"What about the other wives? What are they saying?"

"They all like the house, especially Mrs. Hatcher. But I don't like her!"

"Why? Did she offend you in some way?"

"Her attitude, that's all. But let's not talk about it now."

"Princess, must I pull it out of you?" I asked, annoyed. "What about her attitude?"

"Well, Mrs. Hatcher said that her husband knows what she wants and that whatever she wants, she gets."

"What's wrong with that? She seems to have faith that her husband will provide for her. That can't be the real reason. You're keeping something from me. Out with it."

"One of the wives recognized me," Christina replied meekly. "She started boasting to everyone about who I was."

I hadn't planned on that contingency. I had hoped Christina's fame wouldn't cause the price of the house to go up.

"We were concluding the tour when I overheard Mrs. Hatcher remark that it was typical for people of my culture to marry beneath them, particularly if they are well-known."

"What! Of course you took issue with that, right?"

"No, dearest," she said, trying to soothe me. "I didn't want to ruin our chances; she knows they can't afford this house, but her husband will do what he must. She wants this house, and no matter my status as an entertainer, he'll have to get it for her."

"How about the other two?" I asked, trying to hide my disappointment about Christina's not taking Mrs. Hatcher to task.

"Ms. Greenfield's fiancée is a doctor. She said something to the effect that the house is too big for them and that she would never encourage him to pay more than he could afford for this house. The woman with Mrs. Hatcher didn't come to buy, only to accompany her, and the man we thought was her husband is the Hatchers' lawyer."

Very interesting. Ms. Greenfield would push her fiancé out and that wretched woman will force her husband to drive the price up. So the only competition seemed to be from the Hatchers.

Christina stopped me as we were about to reenter the house. She voiced her concerns about if we really needed it.

"I thought you liked the house," I said, taking her in my arms.

"I do," she sighed. "But we've just been married. Perhaps we should wait."

Have Mrs. Hatcher's comments born fruit? I asked myself. Did Christina doubt my ability to provide? Why else would she not defend her husband?

"Your concern is duly noted," I said, lifting her chin. "I have the responsibility of providing for you. Would you have me break my vows?"

"No, Tony," she said, emphatically. "I trust that you will always take care of us."

"Then, princess," I said happily, "I am now ready to look at our home." It felt so good to finally win by trapping Christina with her own words.

When we rejoined the other bidders, my worst suspicions surfaced. I have been in too many deals not to know the signs. Our presence here was unwelcome. The owner of the property, Mr. Broadhurst, never made eye contact with me. As for his wife, she sat twisting a handkerchief and looking as though she were about to break into tears.

"I'm sorry, Mr. Richardson," Joan said, finally.

"They have decided not to sell the house after all."

"Joan, how long have we known each other?"

"About four or five years now. Why do you ask?"

"In those years, have we developed a mutual respect for each other?"

"Yes, sir," she replied, fidgeting slightly. "I can say that we—"

"Then don't insult me! I deserve better from someone I trust!"

"Well, actually, they've decided to sell their home—but not to you."

My first acquisition for Christina—our home—and I failed. She probably thought Mrs. Hatcher was right. Bargain-basement hunters, the whole lot of them, yet they had found a way to keep me from my dreams.

Christina never looked up at me. She just extended her arms upward and rested them on mine.

"I'm so sorry," Joan said, scowling at the owner. "It makes me so mad!"

"Don't worry about it. It's their home. They have a right to sell to whoever they want. You did your best. Princess, let's go home."

Christina tried her best to comfort me. "Dearest," she said, "there will be other homes."

"I know," I said, putting my arms around her, hiding my outrage. "But not like this one."

If I had been outbid, that would have been fine, but to lose this way was a bitter pill to swallow. But for Christina's sake, I had to pretend not to care. Otherwise she would worry that I was unhappy. I'd experienced this kind of inequity before, but whether it was the first or the thousandth time, the hurt was the same.

We were silent on the drive back home. I didn't

want to talk because I wouldn't have been able to hide my feelings. Then again, I thought to myself, what does one talk about when one feels like they've been kicked in the teeth?

I recalled my first business deal. I had done all the preliminary work to secure the contract. I was sure that I had come in with the lowest bid, only to watch the contract go to someone else. The good old boy network, they call it. That was the first of so many so-called encounters, but through it all, I still managed to persevere and gain strength.

The look on Christina's face and the way she held my hand so tightly made me realize how fast I had been going. The speedometer was well over a hundred.

"I can't help but think," I said, easing off the pedal, "that we gave up our honeymoon for this."

"Tony, can we stop?"

I pulled over at the pier so we could look at the boats, even though, in my present mood, that was the last thing I wanted to do. It was a euphoric atmosphere, with couples holding hands and kids running about, but I found that I wanted no part in it. Still, to make Christina happy, we walked to the very end of the pier where a group of men were fishing and talking about the "big one" that had gotten away.

What a bunch of hypocrites, I thought to myself, glorifying the past. Don't they realize that life is lived in the present?

And then, just as I might have guessed, it became apparent that Christina had only wanted to stop to comfort me. Clearly, she had determined that, as long as I was her husband, nothing was going to make me unhappy.

"Please don't hide your hurt from me, Tony."

"What makes you think that I'm hurt?" I asked, looking out at the water. "It was a business deal like the others."

"Can't we find another house that would do as well?"

"Yes, we can," I replied. "When one door closes, another opens."

"We can take our time about it," she assured me. "I'll just move my things into *our* house. It is our house, isn't it? I can move in tomorrow. Everything is packed and ready to go."

Everything packed. How could that be? And yet, how could I forget the degree of trickery that got us married in the first place? Perhaps I was being unfair. Was there anything really so strange about a wife preparing to move in with her husband on her return from their honeymoon?

Christina woke me up very early the next morning to say that her family would be arriving with the truck at eight. And by family, it appeared that she meant six or eight people. It transpired that that was a family custom. I must admit that I was appalled at the thought of that many strangers swarming all over my house. But I had to be easygoing about it, or at least I had to pretend to be. I had already seen one so-called custom and wondered what demented ritual this family gathering would bring.

"You welcomed my mother with open arms," I said, hiding my concerns, "and I'll do no less for your family."

One thing I can say about them: they were prompt. The bell rang at eight on the dot and the flood came in. They were very well organized. Christina escorted three women, who were introduced as aunts, into the kitchen. Each one carried a paper shopping bag. Christina's father, mother, and sister came next. After we greeted them, her father signaled to two men standing by the truck, and the avalanche began.

They started bringing in things so fast that I was incredulous. Christina and I agreed for the time being that most of the items were going to be stored in the basement. I let her supervise while I went into my office so as not to get in their way.

It wasn't long before the house was full of the smell of food cooking. Sitting in my den, I had to admire the way her family stuck together, but the truth was that my reclusive life was over.

Two weeks later our life began to take shape. With the help of my lovely wife, I was able to put the Broadhurst incident behind me. Well, not really behind me, but I didn't brood about it as much. After all, I had to always seem to be in control, hiding the war that raged continually inside me, suppressing feelings of doubt and fear. But daily, more and more often, angry thoughts consumed me.

". . . Joan is on line one for you."

"Good morning, sir," she said. "I hope that I'm not disturbing you."

"Joan, what is this 'sir' business? You know that I always have time for you."

"I felt that you were disappointed in me. I didn't want to call you until I could redeem myself."

"I told you before that I respect and admire you. You should know by now the standards I hold people to. Besides, it wasn't your fault. Don't worry about it. What's on your mind?"

"I don't know where to begin," she sighed. "You're going to hate me for this."

"Why would I hate you?"

"I've found you a home," she exclaimed. "It's a colonial, so I know you will like that. There are five bedrooms, bringing the total of rooms to nine. It has an exquisite eat-in kitchen, a library, and two fireplaces, one in the master bedroom, another in the living room. It even has a private driveway so well hidden that unless someone knows that you live there, you won't be seen."

"No need to go any further," I interrupted her. "It sounds like my dream house all right. When can I see it?"

"You already have."

"What are you talking about?"

"It's the Broadhurst's home."

"Never! You've got to be kidding! Are you crazy? But you know me well enough to realize that once a deal falls through, I don't look back."

"Believe me, I had reservations about making this call, Tony. I know that you never return to anything that connects to the past."

"If you know, why are you?"

"I had to make the call. I didn't want you to be upset when you found out that the Hatchers' deal fell through. I didn't want a display of that famous temper."

"Temper! What famous temper are you referring to? I have no temper!"

"Well, I wouldn't want whatever you don't have vented on me. Please accept my apology."

"Apology for what?"

"I called you at home first, thinking you were still enjoying your honeymoon. And I spoke with Christina. I—I'm afraid that I got her excited about the new house."

"Joan, I appreciate everything you've done," I said, struggling to keep myself under control. "But my wife and I are happy where we are. If there is nothing else, I have to get back to work. As always, it's a pleasure talking to you. Don't be a stranger. Keep in touch."

Imagine the nerve of that woman trying to put one over on me. She deliberately called the house knowing that I wouldn't be there so she could have a clear shot at convincing Christina. I'll never go back. I simply won't. No matter how Christina feels.

"Maggie," I shouted over the intercom. "Please hold all my calls unless it's my wife. Also, do me a favor and get Matt on the phone."

"Yes, sir. Will there be anything else?"

"Yes, call our place and order the usual. I've been neglectful."

"Don't give it another thought. I know you've had a lot on your mind."

"No need to make excuses for me. I know when I'm wrong and I can admit it. You've done a lot for me. Your friendship is one that I would hate to lose."

"Thank you, sir."

I pulled out my planner.

"Mr. Richardson, you have Matt on line two."

"Thanks, Maggie. Matt, what are your plans for the day?"

"I have to pick up your wife and bring her into the city by four."

"After that, pick me up here. I want to take a drive."

With Maggie holding my calls for the rest of the afternoon, I was able to get a lot of work accomplished. I enjoyed our talk over bagels and tea, the kind of talk that had become almost nonexistent since my return. After that I held a staff meeting where I handed out assignments that would greatly reduce my workload, while inspiring my new employees to take ownership in the business. I enacted a new company policy after reading Napoleon Hill's book, *The Master Key To Riches*, that would allow my staff to share in the profits they helped build, thus increasing my own.

Prompt as usual, Matt was in front of the building when I had reached the lobby. He waited until I read the note Christina had left.

How could I not love her, I thought to myself, especially when she lets me know how slowly the day passed because I was not with her?

"Where to, boss?"

"Take me to Glen Cove."

"Anywhere in particular? Glen Cove is a big area."

I was hoping that the long drive would ease my apprehension and allow me to look over a few reports. Joan, crafty as ever, had certainly boxed me into a corner. No doubt Christina would bombard me with questions as to when we would move when I returned home.

"Matt, is something wrong?"

"No, boss. Why are you asking?"

It occurred to me that, although Matt had sometimes played an important part in my wife's commute to the city, I knew very little about him. Putting my papers aside, I asked him a few questions to determine whether it would be wise to employ him on a permanent basis.

We moved at a snail's pace due to the usual congestion, which seemed to irritate him more than was customary. When he wasn't readjusting the brim of his hat, he was looking at his watch.

"Matt, am I keeping you from something?"

"No, sir."

"Well then, why are you so jittery?"

"It's my wife," he blurted out. "She's expecting."

"Congratulations! Your first?"

"My third," he said, trying to change lanes.

"You're an old pro at this, then."

He slammed on the brakes and pounded on the steering wheel. "Sorry," he said, honking his horn and swearing as the other drivers tried to cut him off. "She's due any day now."

"Why so nervous?"

"She wanted so badly to give me a son," he lamented. "Now she has nothing but problems."

"Matt, take the next exit."

"We better continue," he said. "Traffic is worse the other way."

What was I doing? I had never gone back once a deal fell through, and yet I had Matt driving me to Glen Cove. Surely, he would never tell about me sitting in front of the Broadhurst's home.

"No, go on home to your wife."

"Back to the city?"

"Yes, my wife and I are having dinner after her performance. By the way, I'm looking for a permanent driver. Know anyone interested in having the job?"

"Boss, you don't have to do that. I didn't mean to tell you my problems. I'm not looking for a handout."

"Matt, are you trying to insult me?"

"No, sir."

"I don't give handouts to anyone! This is strictly a good business decision. My wife is too busy to contend with transportation. She'll be coming home late at night. I can't always be there to pick her up. She knows and trusts you. If you accept my offer, you'll find me very difficult to work for. I'll expect you to take my wife to all her concerts and recitals, and to be at our beck and call twenty-four hours a day. When there's nothing planned, that's your day off. For that dedication, you'll be well paid. You'll be given a leased vehicle and a monthly car allowance. I don't want an answer now. Think about it and get back to me."

Handouts indeed! Imagine me being sentimental.

We weren't able to make it back to the city because Matt's sister-in-law called and said his wife's water had broken, she was already on the way to the hospital, and that he shouldn't worry because she would be staying with his other kids.

I had no choice but to accompany him. He became so unglued when we arrived at the hospital that I parked the limo while he ran like a chicken with its head cut off to the emergency room.

I hated these places. What was I doing here? Maybe I could just sit out here and wait for him. I couldn't do that. He had enough to worry about. Couldn't have him wondering where I was. Reluctantly, I started my slow trek through the doors, swearing that I would never go through them again.

I found Matt in the waiting room, pacing the floor, working up a sweat like he was running a marathon. His eyes never diverted from those double doors. I didn't know what to say. How do you tell a man to keep calm at a time like this? I had better do something, though. He was making the other fathers-to-be nervous.

"Matt, I'm sure everything is okay," I told him, pointing to a seat. "Why don't you sit down and relax? The other fathers are nervous and your incessant pacing isn't helping them any."

"I can't help it," he wailed. "I should be in there with her. She's never going to forgive me."

"Matt, get a hold of yourself! She will be all right." He started pacing again. He got up, sat down, got up again, and then quickly sat back down, gripping his head.

"I should be in there," he kept murmuring. "She's never going to, never. I just know she won't."

I knew what I had to do. I only hoped that it would work. If it didn't, I'd need a lot of help to subdue him. I got him a cup of coffee, slapped him, and ordered him to sit down.

Matt's face turned red. He stared at me and sank into a chair. I had taken an awful chance hitting him, but I had had no choice. If I hadn't, perhaps one of those fathers would have. He took the coffee, spilling half of it on the floor. Clutching the cup with both hands, he took a few sips.

"Matt, I will be right back," I told him, before leaving to arrange transportation for Christina. "Are you listening to me?"

Amazing how a man as tough as nails could turn to putty.

We waited silently for two hours. Every time the double doors swung open, he got up. When the nurse went to one of the other fathers, he'd plop down, dejected. I felt sorry for him. What had he said again? She had wanted to give him a son, but now she had nothing but complications. Was he worried about that? How I would have given everything to be in such a situation. Why had I been cheated out of my chance?

When we first entered, six men were waiting. All six became proud fathers until there was only one.

Sometimes the silence of a moment can seem so loud. The doors finally swung open, but Matt never moved. It was as if his feet were riveted to the floor. I jumped up and helped him to his feet. The nurse approached us and congratulated Matt on the birth of his son.

Matt took the child tenderly in his arms and pressed his face against him and wept. I had to turn away. This was becoming too much for me to bear.

I wanted to run away, make some excuse that I had to leave. But as Matt showed me his son, I found the resolve to stand my ground and congratulate him. Now that the child was in his arms, he didn't want to give him back. The nurse escorted him to see his wife with the baby wrapped tightly in his arms.

What a lucky child, to have a father that loves him so much, I thought. He'll probably never be far from his father's safe and welcoming arms. I sat there with seven men, men from all walks of life, unique in all respects. But no matter their background or stature in life, each of them acted the same way when the nurse brought out their newborn.

One after another, overcome with emotions, each had breathed a sigh of relief and given everyone a hearty handshake to celebrate the new life they had helped bring into the world.

Why couldn't it have been that way for me?

I left the hospital, hoping that I would never have to walk through those doors again.

Will I ever find peace? It's been five years. Why does it still haunt me so?

It was a little after two in the morning when I got home. I entered as quietly as possible, since I didn't want to awaken Christina. Silly me. I should have known she would never have gone to sleep unless I was there. She rushed to greet me at the door and hugged me so tightly that I could feel her trembling.

"Dearest," she said, "I was so worried. The driver explained what happened to Matt and that you called for another driver to take me home."

"I'm sorry, princess," I told her. "I should have called. I just needed some time alone. You could have called me."

"I thought you and Matt were out celebrating, but when he called for you, I began to worry. He is worried also. He asked that you call him, no matter what time."

"Okay, princess," I said, flopping down on the couch. "I'm sorry for keeping you up. Go to bed and I'll join you in a little while."

She paid me no mind at all. Why had I thought she would? She brought the phone and my slippers. She then helped me off with my sports coat and removed my shoes.

"Dearest, what would you like to drink?"

"A tall glass of water would be nice."

She returned with a pitcher of lemonade and two glasses. I told her it was a pleasant surprise and asked what prompted her to make it.

"In this house alone," she said, clutching my hand, "I wondered what to do. It was good that Lady was here, but Tony, no one can take your place. I missed you. I love you so much."

"I love you too, princess," I said, putting my arms around her. "I didn't mean to worry you."

We were both startled when Lady jumped into Christina's lap. She then stretched herself out and curled up like a little ball.

"I see that you and Lady have become good friends."

"Yes, we have. She likes lying in my lap."

"I'll say she does," I replied, trying to avoid the subject of where I'd been. "I guess you're waiting for me to explain where I disappeared to?"

"Only if you want to tell me," she replied, staring intently at me.

"It's hard to explain and would probably take the rest of the night. Can we just sit here? I promise I'll tell you in the morning."

"Yes, dearest," she said, resting her head on my shoulder. "As you wish. You're home now. Our family is . . . complete."

Would it ever really be complete? I had thought so before and look what happened. My world irrevocably altered forever. How could I tell her that the ocean had beckoned me, that voices from my past were drowning me in despair? What could I say that would make her understand how afraid I was of losing her? And if I had to go down that road again, surely, it would be the death of me.

"Tony, it's only a dream. Please, please, wake up."

"Thank God! It was only a dream?"

"Yes, dearest, only a dream."

"It was so real."

"It's over."

"Never do I want to—why now?"

"Nothing will harm you. Tony, I'm here."

"Thank God . . . "

I woke up the next morning and found my wife pressed against the couch with my head in her lap. Christina then told me how I had cried out in my sleep.

"Cried out in my sleep?" I asked. "What did I say?"

"That the dream was real. You thanked God it was only a dream. You asked 'why now?'"

I started pacing the floor, trying hard to remember what would have made me cry out like that.

"Don't worry," Christina said, trying to comfort me. "All will be revealed in time. I expect it was too much excitement with Matt and the baby."

"Wait a minute, being chased. That's it. Someone was chasing me!"

"Who?"

"That's where it gets fuzzy. I was in a hospital. Someone was chasing me! I kept running. Door after door, each one leading nowhere. The more I ran, the deeper I went. I couldn't get out! They were closing in on me, stifling me! Those doors wouldn't let me leave."

"Tony, what does it all mean?"

"I only wish I knew. One thing I'm sure about."

"Yes, my love," Christina said, in a soothing voice, as if comforting a deranged person. "What is it?"

"I'm never going back there again."

"Back where?"

"The hospital. Nothing will ever get me to go through those doors again. Absolutely nothing!"

The rest of the week went by without incident. I was content, and there were no more dreams. I was puzzled by one thing. Joan said that she had told my wife about the house, and yet Christina had never mentioned it. Perhaps it was due to our busy and conflicting schedules. But by the weekend, it began to bother me, and so, as we prepared to make lasagna, I decided to question her.

"Princess," I said, hedging a little, "I spoke with Joan earlier in the week."

"Yes."

"She claims she called here looking for me."

"Hmm."

"And informed you that the Broadhurst's home was available."

"Tony, is there anything else we'll need?" Christina asked, as if the ingredients for the lasagna were the only thing on her mind. "Have I got everything?"

"Princess," I said, grabbing her hands, "are you listening to me?"

She had drawn me in with those bewitching eyes. She never uttered a word, but I knew there was a call to make.

I couldn't fail her a second time. Where would I begin? How could I tell her that she was all I needed? This time was going to be different. Those loving eyes, so warm and tender, I wasn't going to let them shed any more tears. Mr. Broadhurst wasn't going to cheat me a second time. And I knew exactly what to do to make sure of it.

Chapter 15

THE CLOSING WAS THREE WEEKS LATER. I GUESS I HADN'T fooled anyone. Joan knew the day she called Christina that the house was sold. They had both waited patiently, knowing that I would be the new owner. For the aggravation the Broadhursts had put me through, I was not willing to pay more than 1.5 million.

We were driving back to Glen Cove in the Bentley, since this time I had decided to accept Harry's offer. I reasoned that anyone could rent a limo, so to make a grand entrance, nothing but Harry's Bentley would do. Christina was so excited that she could hardly sit still. I, on the other hand, portrayed the same cool demeanor as usual although I was a bundle of nerves, my major apprehension being that I didn't want to fail her twice. She had been such a good sport about our losing the chance to own this house the first time. This time I refused to let anyone spoil the good mood she was in.

As we pulled into the driveway, it seemed as if I was looking at it through someone else's eyes. Even the roses seemed to be more vivid than when we were last there. The entranceway with its white columns added to the majestic look of the place. Stepping out of the Bentley, I inhaled the fresh air. It was as if the house spoke to me, welcoming me home like a long-lost friend. Christina and I held on to each other as we stared at this magnificent edifice, the house I had dreamed of owning for years.

It was Christina who first noticed the gardener. She commented on how lovely the roses were, and he clipped one for her. I finally remarked to the man that he indeed must have a green thumb, given how vibrant the flora was.

"Thank you, sir. They're my pride and joy. I wouldn't enjoy them as much if they all were the same. My mammy use to say, 'A garden can tell a lot about a man. If he plants all of one thing, his mind is closed to the world. If he plants a little of everything, he's open-minded, likes the different hues of life.' Mammy was sure right," he concluded. "Anything grows that stays in the sun long enough."

Perhaps it does, I thought to myself. But I couldn't resist adding to the wisdom of his statement that anything could be attained if one persevered long enough.

And, finally, would I be in possession of it? Was it really to be mine? I had to make sure to keep my wits about me and not let them know how much this meant to me.

The butler greeted us at the door. I wasn't going to make the same mistake and overlook him this time.

"Thank you, Bascom," I said, extending my hand. "My name is Tony and this is my lovely wife, Christina."

"Welcome, sir," he said, unsure of whether to shake my hand. "They're expecting you in the library. This way, if you please."

"Dearest," Christina said, tugging on my arm. "He's so formal."

"I was thinking the very same thing," I told her. "The house and he seem inseparable."

Joan was in the library once again to greet us. She and Christina kissed.

"That's right," I said, "congratulate yourselves on a successful conspiracy."

"Why, Mr. Richardson, what are you insinuating?" Joan exclaimed, grinning.

"Nothing, Joan. I've said it before and it bears repeating—you're the best realtor I have ever met."

"Thank you," she said, "that means a lot coming from you. But let's not celebrate prematurely."

"They're not having cold feet again, are they?"

"No, but they want three hundred thousand more."

"They *what?* Never! Where are they? Let me give Broadhurst a piece of my mind."

It was a good thing that Joan didn't rile easy. If it hadn't been for her, I would have walked on the deal, particularly when Mr. Broadhurst came in strutting like a peacock. His wife, however, was gracious enough, taking Christina to meet the staff and leaving Mr. Broadhurst, his realtor, Joan, and I to close the deal.

I learned a long time ago that you learn a great deal more about a man when you watch him accept defeat as opposed to when he is winning. And so it came as no surprise when Mr. Broadhurst blurted out, "I'm curious about one thing. How could the likes of you afford to buy a home like this?"

"How dare you ask such an impudent question?" Joan said, clearly heated. "Mr. Richardson need not justify that with an answer."

"But Joan, you have to understand that's not what Mr. Broadhurst meant. He wasn't questioning my ability to buy this house inasmuch as his inability to keep it." Seeing his face flushed with anger, I decided to provoke him a bit further, hoping that in his irrational stage I could quickly close the deal.

"Mr. Broadhurst," I said, "there is one thing I want to make absolutely clear: my mother never raised a fool. I have no intention of paying three hundred thousand dollars more for this property. I'll give you two options. You can take my offer of a million-five and it will be wired to your account today. Your other choice is simple. Try to play hardball, and I walk on the deal."

"How dare you speak to me that way!" he exclaimed. "Do you know who I am?"

"All I see is a man who can't pay his bills, a man about to lose his home, a man attempting to pull my chain, a man trying to make me pay for his mistakes."

"I will not budge from my price of one million-eight," he said, pounding his fist on the desk. "That's my final word on the matter."

Not wanting to weaken my position by losing my temper, I counted to ten before replying. "Mr. Broadhurst, I came to buy this house. This asinine stance of yours will force me to lower my bid."

"Are you threatening me?" he demanded. "I will not be intimidated."

"Sir, my bid is now one million-four. Do you wish to test me further?"

"You insolent son of a—"

"One million-three. I'll join my wife and await your decision."

"Dearest, we heard shouting," Christina said, clearly concerned.

"It was nothing," I told her, "just two stubborn men haggling over price."

Joan shook her head in disbelief. "I guess he found that you're a man to be reckoned with."

"Let's hope his common sense prevails," I told her. "He's an ornery old man. I wanted this to be a peaceful transaction."

Fifteen minutes passed before Mr. Broadhurst emerged from the study to tell his agent to close the deal at 1.5 million. I was about to protest when Joan said, "Everything has been set at that price. You've got your house at the price you wanted to pay, and your wife is happy. Congratulations, Mr. and Mrs. Richardson."

"Thanks, Joan," I replied, allowing myself to smile for the first time since we arrived. "There'll be something extra for you. I won't forget how instrumental you were in closing this deal."

"Thank you, Joan," Christina said, hugging her. "Like my husband said: a very successful conspiracy."

We moved into our new home in September, both families assisting with the move. Christina was ecstatic since she would finally be able to have her barbecue in the huge backyard, which could easily accommodate over a hundred people. What intrigued me about it was the marvelous old oak tree that shielded a portion of the yard from the sun. Christina could decorate the house any way that pleased her. All I wanted was a hammock in the backyard.

I like to reward people who have been loyal to me. We hired Estelle as our maid. This made her happy since she no longer had to travel from house to house. Bascom decided to remain with us as our butler and cook, which pleased my wife and me immensely, since we both agreed that he added to the mystique and charm of the place. With Matt and the gardener, that brought our household staff to four.

When Christina wasn't charming the world with her violin, she was engaged in decorating the house. Our weekends were spent moving furniture from one place in a room to the other. Poor Bascom, Matt, and I suffered from her indecisiveness, and although we teased her because of it, we loved every minute of it, because it made her happy.

And then, after a month or two, the business world started interfering with my family time. Ah, the price of success. Suddenly, Christina and I were moving in different worlds, with her playing nearly every evening and me working up to sixteen hours a day. Even with the new staff in place, it wasn't enough to handle the increase in business. We were getting offers from international companies also, wanting my firm to represent them both here and abroad, all of which forced me to be away from home more than I cared to be.

Three months into our marriage, I could feel that we were drifting apart. Christina must have sensed it also and was determined to prevent it. She was working hard to give us a normal family life. I would come home late at night and just sit in the car, staring at the house and thinking of my lovely wife inside. When I finally went inside, I would find a snack and a little note, telling me how much she loved me and missed me, on a tray in the microwave. When I got to the bedroom, Christina would be fast asleep, a cookbook or a home-decorating magazine on the floor beside her. I would sit at the edge of the bed and admire her tenacity for holding our marriage together.

My fears and doubts did not start to rear their

ugly heads until Christina began playing with so much emotion that she received accolades everywhere she went. She would be recording soon and preparing for another tour. Everyone seemed to be talking about her, so young and yet so talented, with a gift that enriched the world. I had international clients as well, and soon I would be flying all over the globe. It would take an entire floor of the office building to house all the staff I'd need.

Sooner or later I knew I was going to have to choose which was more important to me: the love of my wife or the promise I had made to myself to run a successful business. Was there a way to accomplish both? I didn't know.

Why was it that love always forced you to hurt the one you cared about the most?

The last weekend of September was very busy for me. My business concerns forced me to be in six different cities in five days, and I was relieved to be finally going home, particularly since this trip had helped me realize how badly I had missed my wife. When Matt pulled up at the house, I felt at peace, perhaps because this place that I had loved for so long had a way of welcoming me back. Wandering into the backyard, I could see that the falling leaves had made their bed in my hammock.

I went into the house and put my briefcase down on the floor in the foyer. Strange, usually Bascom or Estelle was there to greet me. No one here tonight? No matter how late I got home, one of the two would be up waiting. I took off my shoes, since the mistress of the house didn't allow anyone to enter with them on. I noticed a poster on the wall.

"Dearest, welcome home," it read. "Please don't

enter the dining room. Shower and change and meet me in there when you're done."

I was only too eager to comply. As usual my clothes and toiletries were laid out. Even though I was tired, the water had a way of reviving me. I took a little longer than usual getting dressed so as to not spoil her surprise.

Going downstairs, I noticed the lights were dimmed and that soft music was playing in the background. The dining room table was beautifully set with the linen tablecloth, the Spode china, and the Georgian silver service that we had purchased in Bermuda. Clearly, we were to dine alone by candlelight.

When Christina appeared, she was a sight to behold, wearing a low-cut black dress that revealed the beauty of her bosom. I could not take my eyes off her, especially since the dress had a slit up the back to her lower thigh.

"I'm so glad you're home," she said, walking seductively toward me. "I hope everything is to your liking. I can't wait to show you how badly I needed you home."

My God, what a lovely woman. Could a man ask for anything more? She looks so sexy in high heels. I wonder if she knows how turned on I get seeing her in them.

When Christina reached me, she put her arms around my neck and began kissing me passionately. Before I could reciprocate fully, she pulled away and started heading back to the kitchen.

"Don't worry, you will have a chance later," she said, teasing me with her tongue as she moistened her lips. "You shouldn't have stayed away so long."

After dinner—which I later found out that Bascom and Estelle had helped prepare before she had let them go for the evening—we went upstairs to sit on the balcony outside our bedroom to gaze at the full moon.

"It's lonely here without you," Christina murmured, putting her head on my shoulder. "I miss you so much."

"I thought they were keeping you pretty busy, what with the upcoming tour and your recording commitments."

Turning toward me, Christina touched my face. "Dearest, don't you understand? All that I am, all I will ever be, is centered on loving you. I've been performing since the age of eight. Now I want to start our family."

How could she be bringing up this subject again? Surely, I had made my intentions clear about wanting to wait. Why wouldn't she leave this alone? Finally I'm at peace with the marriage, but if she keeps this up, I'll lose everything again. Why can't the past be buried?

"But, princess, is that fair to me?" I protested. "I hardly have time for you now. My business is about to explode. I was hoping we could spend a few years together . . . alone, enjoying each other's company, before starting a family."

She started to her feet and stood looking down at me, hands on her hips. "Can't you understand how I feel?" she demanded. "Is money more important to you than I am?"

It never ceased to amaze me. Most women I'm sure want to marry men that are financially secure. But I wonder if they realize what it takes to make that happen. How could I make her understand that money isn't more important than her, but it was what had gotten us this house.

"I've done all I can to make this house into a home. I want you to be proud that I'm your wife. Everything of mine, I want you to share. I ask for nothing but to share your love."

I got up and tried to comfort her, but she pulled away. "I've told you a thousand times that I appreciate everything you've done for me."

"What I want is my family. I don't want to wait— that's your plan! Don't you care how I feel? Did you ever think to ask me?"

What brought this on? I thought to myself. How could such a wonderful evening have turned out like this? I was fighting hard to listen and not fly off the handle. "Ask you what?" I said. "What am I supposed to be asking?"

"I wanted this night to be special," she told me. "One that we would always remember."

"Are you saying that I ruined the evening?" I asked her. "I don't know how all this got started. One minute we're sitting out here looking at the moon, and the next minute you're accusing me of not understanding you."

"Why won't you listen to me? I've tried to tell you! You never let me speak!"

"Okay, princess," I said, exasperated, "tell me whatever is on your mind. I'll keep my mouth shut!"

"I had hoped it would be special," she told me. "I wanted to find the best way to tell you. Tony, we're going to have a baby."

All of a sudden I felt like I was on a merry-go-round spinning out of control. Those were the words I had hoped I would never hear again. And I had to say something. But what?

Oh God, I can't believe this. Why now, Lord?

Why must I suffer so? How much pain must I endure? Haven't I paid my penance? How could I be going down this road again?

"Say that again," I said in a low voice.

"I'm going to have a baby," she said with conviction. "Tell me you're as happy as I am, Tony."

She held out her hand. I took it and followed her into the bedroom with as much enthusiasm as a condemned man going to the gallows.

Christina led me to the edge of the bed and then she placed my hand on her stomach. "Our child grows in me," she said. "It's been twelve weeks now. You'll think that I'm a fool, I know, but I didn't tell you because I wasn't sure how you'd take it."

It occurred to me that she should know very well how I would feel about her having a child. Certainly, I had made no secret about wanting to delay this blessed event, if, in fact, it were ever to take place. But clearly, and not surprisingly, this was a very important moment for her. And yet there were so many questions I wanted to ask.

How does one ask those questions and not sound insulting? This was a very joyous moment for her. She would always remember tonight, my every word and facial expression, all my movements since her surprise announcement; I couldn't blow it.

"Princess, I'm happy," I said, while rubbing her stomach. "Surprised, but very happy to know that, inside you, our child is growing."

"Tony, are you truly happy?"

One man's happiness is another's curse, I thought to myself. How could it be that I was traveling down the same road again? She too had wanted to start a family, despite all of the doctor's warnings against it.

No good had come of it then, and I could see nothing but another tragedy disrupting my life again. Only this time, I swore she wouldn't be alone.

"How can I be otherwise?" I told her, as we hugged each other. "I'm married to a very beautiful woman who wants nothing but my happiness. Princess, I love you. And as sure as I am that there is a God up in heaven, I always will."

My words seemed to have comforted and reassured Christina, because she smiled lovingly at me. How I wished I could have believed and found comfort in them as well.

"As for the other surprise," she said, while unbuttoning my shirt, "didn't I promise that you would have your chance? That I needed to show you that you shouldn't have stayed away from me for so long? Later is now! And as usual, it will take me all night to show you."

Chapter 16

EVERY MORNING I WAS RUDELY AWAKENED BY THE SUNLIGHT glaring through our bedroom windows. Since I had given Christina total autonomy to decorate the house, thick, heavy drapes were not permitted. Every curtain was made of a material that allowed light to enter unencumbered, which took some getting used to. On this Saturday in particular, I would have preferred to sleep late, since we had been up most of the night showing each other how bad we missed being together. This, coupled with her surprise announcement, had me emotionally and physically drained.

Fortunately, I had nothing planned for that weekend; all I wanted to do was lay in the hammock. It had been a very trying week and some rest was in order. I pulled the sheet over my head, determined to get at least a half hour to an hour more sleep. But it seemed that my wife would not hear of it that morning.

"Dearest, are you awake?" she asked.

"No, princess," I murmured. "My brain is up, but the rest of me is still sleeping."

"Tomorrow you may sleep late, Tony, but today you simply cannot."

"And why is that?" I asked, still clutching on to the sheet.

"The installers are on their way," she said, pulling at the covers.

"Installers—what installers? Why am I the last to know?"

"You said that I am to decorate the house, didn't you? Then please go and shower. I have another surprise for you."

After last night, I wondered how many more surprises I could take, but I did as she requested, still peeved that I was up this early on a Saturday. In the shower, my thoughts got the better of me. How could she be three months pregnant? I needed a calendar. And yet I trusted my wife. She would never have me believe another man's child was mine. Maybe she was wrong about being with child. Certainly there were no physical signs of pregnancy. I explored every inch of her body last night and she was as petite as ever. There had been no nausea, no vomiting, none of the apparent signs of morning sickness. The doctor must have made a mistake, I told myself. I would have a good laugh over this when the truth was known. But, I reminded myself, I must remember not to show my exuberance.

We were just finishing up breakfast when Bascom announced that the installers had arrived.

"Madam, he is waiting in the foyer," Bascom said, clearly annoyed. "He may be a bit out of sorts. He did not take too kindly to my refusal to allow him entry without first removing his shoes."

"Thank you, Bascom," Christina told him, while reaching for my hand. "Tony, come and see what I've planned for you."

Bascom had been right. The man waiting in the foyer, shoeless, looked annoyed, and I did not blame him. I know I was shocked the first time Christina had met me at the door and asked me to remove mine.

He quickly brought me up to speed with what Christina was planning. She was having a music system put in that would provide music throughout the entire house.

"Princess," I said jubilantly, "that is a marvelous idea."

"I'm so glad that it pleases you," Christina told me. "I want this house always to be filled with music."

When he explained that each room could program its own selection, I was definitely impressed. Aside from the customary annoyance of having the workmen trample all over the house, I was eager for them to get started.

"But dearest, that's not the only surprise," Christina beamed. "You'll have music in the backyard, too."

"You're kidding!" I rejoiced. "That's wonderful. I'll be able to lie in the hammock . . . Sir, what are you waiting for? Do get started right away!"

As he walked out to the van, I had a good laugh. Obviously still upset by the fact that he was asked to remove them, the installer had gone outside without his shoes. I took my lovely wife in my arms. "Princess," I said, "you're full of surprises."

"All done," she said, looking up at me, "in the hope that they please you."

I may have spoken too soon. The next three months were frightening. Morning sickness was the first order of the day. I awoke to the sound of her retching and would rush to the bathroom to find Christina resting on the floor, near the commode, awaiting the next spasm. Her helplessness tore my guts out. With a blanched face and moist eyes, she would push me away so that I could not comfort her; after a while, I just stayed in bed trying to drown out the sound.

I became the victim of so many emotions. I was nervous and scared. Worse, I was growing angrier with each passing day. I didn't know if it was helplessness I felt or irritability at her determination to put us through this. Estelle suggested that, to lift Christina's spirits, we should give her a surprise baby shower. I told her to arrange it and have Bascom assist with whatever she needed.

"But I'll need your help also, sir," Estelle said, clearly puzzled. "You need to be there."

"Whatever for? It's a baby shower. A room full of women talking of things that can only be of interest to them."

"She'll feel better if you're there," Estelle assured me. "It will show her that you—"

"Estelle, I have no intention of spending any time kowtowing to a room full of women. I can think of far better ways to waste an afternoon!"

"Spending an afternoon providing your wife with comfort," she mused. "I'm sorry, sir, I see how that would be a waste of time."

"You know that's not what I meant!" I told her, finally realizing how harsh I had sounded. "They wouldn't be able to speak freely with me in the room."

"I know of one who would," Estelle retorted, as she emptied my wastepaper basket. "But I'm sure you know best. I'll leave you now. I'm sorry to bother you."

My time was being manipulated between my business concerns and attending to my wife's needs. It didn't help matters that I had secured two international accounts that would eventually force me to spend about a month or so away from home, although, not wanting to alarm Christina, I never mentioned it. I was going to Lamaze classes with her. I was being dragged to look at this crib, that stroller. I saw so many baby things that it was becoming increasingly difficult to hide my annoyance, but, smiling hypocritically, I forged on. I knew that my nagging tetchiness was due to fear, of course, but I was too deep in denial to even acknowledge that.

It was two Saturdays later when we put the plan into effect. The ruse had been very simple. After Lamaze class, I had to keep Christina preoccupied until two. And since her favorite activity had become window-shopping, that was what we did.

"Dearest, isn't this bassinet cute?" she said. "And look! Look at the little swing."

"Now why would they have a swing for a baby?"

"To rock the child to sleep, of course."

Noticing that she was about to become emotional again, I tried to hug her, which was no longer easy, given her beach ball of a stomach.

"Sweetheart," I said, "It's almost one. I have a very important conference call at two. Besides, I think you've walked enough. If there isn't anything else that you want to look at, let's head for home."

It was a forty-five minute drive home. I laid Christina's seat back so she would be more comfortable. About fifteen minutes into the drive, she fell asleep. She looked so serene with her hands resting on her stomach.

Would this time be different? I thought. I didn't think that I could bear to go through it again. All I wanted right then was that feeling to go away. I must be crazy, loving and hating my wife at the same time. But why couldn't she understand that I would continue to love her whether she gave me a child or not?

Why was this all so important?

Meanwhile, every morning she grew paler and paler. And she was so big that she could hardly walk. Even her violin playing suffered. Certainly she didn't have the stamina to play for very long. There had been so many complications. Every time we visited the doctor, he had concerns about one thing or another. Although he had been reassuring us that Christina was healthy and everything was fine, I didn't trust him.

Matter of fact, I had little confidence in the medical profession. Hadn't the other obstetrician assured me of the very same thing? And look what happened. Why was it important for her to drag me through this? Perhaps it was all my fault. If I had only had the courage to tell her the truth, just maybe this so-called blessed event could have been delayed. For all our sakes, I hoped he was right. I would never be able to forgive him—worst of all, I couldn't stay married . . .

"Princess, wake up, we're home," I said, as I parked along the driveway to be closer to the back of the house.

"I'm sorry," Christina told me, as she struggled to raise the seat. "I wanted to keep you company."

"Believe me, you did," I replied, while reaching over to assist her. "Even though you were asleep, my thoughts were of nothing but you."

I continued the ruse by telling Christina that since there were a few minutes remaining before my conference call, would she mind if we sat in the backyard and admired the roses? Pushing on the wooden gate, I let her enter first to a chorus of "Surprise!" The backyard was inundated with people; more than I'd thought would have been invited.

"It was Estelle's idea," I told Christina when she turned and thanked me. "I can't take any of the credit. I just had to keep you away long enough for them to pull it off."

Estelle motioned for me to escort Christina to the wicker chairs. She had done a marvelous job. The garden's tables and chairs were arranged in a circular fashion so that Christina and I would be the center of attention, with the gifts piled to one side on a long rectangular table. Bascom was directing the serving of refreshments, while Matt and Christina's father seemed to be in competition, each handling one of the huge grills.

"Princess, I will be right back," I said, as I helped her into one of the wicker chairs. "I need to speak with Estelle."

"Please hurry back," she said joyfully.

"I will, princess."

As I joined Estelle, who was checking the table settings, I realized how right she had been. All of our close friends were here. It would have been inconspicuous if I, the most important person in Christina's life, had been absent.

"Thank you, Estelle," I said, as I marveled at the way Maggie orchestrated the seating of the guests. "Why do I get the feeling that another conspiracy went on here?"

"Bascom bought the food, ordered the grilling equipment, and hired the extra help. I decorated the backyard and assisted with setting everything up. Maggie called both of your mothers to help send out the invitations. So you see, sir, there can't be any conspiracy in that."

"Well, I want to thank you," I said, hugging her. "I now see it would have been a terrible mistake not to have been here. Every man needs a woman to show him the folly of his thinking, to stand her ground until he gets her point. I'm blessed to be surrounded by so many."

"Thank you, sir," she said, blushing. "You'd better be getting back to her, sir. Your place is at her side."

Feeling surprisingly at ease, I sat by Christina most of the afternoon, devoting my full attention to her, and never had I seen her so happy. With her father and Matt being old pros on the grills, we ate ourselves silly.

"Well, princess, is this the barbecue you dreamed about?" I asked her as everyone gathered around to watch us open the gifts. There were so many that I couldn't remember them all. I just knew that our child wouldn't want for anything. There were bottles, strollers, clothes, and toys of every conceivable kind. Someone even gave us a magazine subscription to *Parents* magazine. Christina's parents gave us the gift that stood out in my mind the most, something that looked like a walkie-talkie set.

When the party started breaking up around ten, I thanked everyone for coming. I was exhausted and could only imagine how Christina felt.

"Princess," I said, trying to coax her upstairs, "I think you've had enough excitement for one day. It's bedtime for you."

"And you," Christina replied. "Aren't you tired?"

"I am, but I believe that Maggie, Harry and Helen, along with our parents, want to sit around and talk for awhile."

But Christina refused to listen to reason. Although I warned her about overdoing it, she insisted on staying

up with me. I asked Bascom to prop up one of the lawn
chairs, and she rested comfortably against me.

What was I going to do with her? Besieged with
one complication after another, yet she refused to heed
the doctor's advice. How was I going to get her to fall
asleep before me?

I invited Matt and his wife to join us, along with
Estelle and Bascom. Some would say that it's highly
irregular to have one's staff sit among one's guests, but
I didn't care what people thought. These were the people who mattered most to us. And tonight I needed
them to keep talking in hopes that it would lull
Christina to sleep.

Around midnight everyone left. I told Bascom and
Estelle that the backyard could wait until morning, but
neither would hear of it. So Christina and I remained
outside a little while longer, admiring all the gifts.

"Princess, I hope you enjoyed the baby shower."

"Yes, very much, and look at all the gifts our child
will have."

"I'm confused about this one," I said, picking up
the walkie-talkie set. "How do your parents expect a
newborn to talk through this?"

"No, Tony," she chuckled. "It's a monitor to hear
the baby crying. One will be in the crib and the other
with me."

"Hmm, ingenious device," I remarked, helping
Christina to her feet. "What will they think of next?
Come on, it's time for bed. You've been up far too
long."

"Dearest," she said, when we reached our bedroom, "don't you find me attractive anymore?"

"Why would you ask me a question like that?"

"You don't touch me anymore," she said. "I know

that you've been busy. And when you get home, it's so late that I'm usually asleep."

I knew exactly where this was headed. Why couldn't she have fallen asleep? I hoped I could have gotten away with it. Perhaps I still could.

"You don't expect me to wake you, do you?" I asked her, trying to keep from sounding impatient.

"Why haven't you made love to me?" she asked, point blank.

The woman is impossible, I thought. She was not having an easy pregnancy. We had been out half of the day shopping. She had just been given a shower with a cast of what seemed like thousands. And then, when I was nearly asleep on my feet, she wanted to know why I didn't make love to her anymore.

"It's kind of hard to explain," I said, helping her to the bed. "I suppose this isn't a manly thing to say, but I'm afraid."

"Of what?" she snapped.

"Princess, can't we leave it at that?"

"I need to know," she said grimly.

I thought of lying to her, of making her believe that I really didn't find her attractive anymore. But I couldn't hurt her that way. And besides, I had told her that between us there should always be trust.

"It's because of all the complications," I said, determined to be frank. "I know you'll think me crazy for having these thoughts, but I can't help it. I'm afraid that if we make love, I'll get carried away and wind up hurting you or cause the baby to come prematurely. I do most of my work at night so that I can fall asleep in the den, anything to get me through this and not have to face you."

"Thank God," she murmured, stroking my face. "I was afraid you didn't desire me anymore. But this . . .

Well, I understand, my love, I truly do."

I breathed a sigh of relief. Why hadn't I explained this to her before? All that needless worry for nothing. Just three more months to go. Maybe it wasn't going to be the same as before.

When I came back from taking my shower, I thought that she had fallen asleep.

Good, she's asleep. Have to make sure I don't wake her. She's had enough excitement for one day, I thought.

Easing myself into bed, I kissed her gently on the lips, but before I could pull away, she had wrapped her arms about me.

"You didn't think it would be that easy, did you?" she whispered. "I've waited long enough." As usual, Christina had her way.

The last month of my wife's second trimester was December. The world was in a frenzy over Y2K. I, on the other hand, gave it no thought, having purchased computer equipment that was compatible earlier in the year. To me, it was just a way for technology companies to feed on people's paranoia and to make a fast buck. I scoffed while watching these so-called experts try to predict the amount of chaos that would occur. But I had more pressing concerns at that moment than paying attention to those fools.

My wife's listlessness and lack of appetite seemed to have stabilized, but her stomach had gone from the size of a beach ball to that of a baby whale. And there were new complications such as swollen feet and excruciating back pain that kept her bedridden, conditions made even worse by the fact that she couldn't sleep. She became touchy, disagreeable; nothing in the world could please her.

It seemed, to me at least, that the whole world was going through mixed emotions of joy and apprehension: joy at the fact that the new millennium was approaching, and apprehension due to the uncertainty of what it would bring, a state of mind that exactly mirrored my world, since I was going through my own private hell, wanting so much to be with Christina but at the same time seeking any chance to escape because of my inability to provide her with comfort.

The situation was complicated by the fact that I was away most of the time, flying to one city or another, working with companies to strategize their marketing plans. I kept in constant communication with home to monitor how she was doing, but most of the time I spoke with Estelle, since I always seemed to call when Christina had just gotten to sleep.

In late December, I wrapped everything up a little earlier than expected and rushed home to be with Christina after a two week absence, arriving two days before Christmas.

"Good evening, sir," Bascom said, as he helped me off with my overcoat.

"Thank you, Bascom. How is everything here?"

"As well as one might expect," he replied, opening the closet. "Good to have you home, sir."

"Good to be home. Matt may need your help. I did a little Christmas shopping."

"Very well, sir. I'll attend to it straightaway."

I ran upstairs knowing that Christina would be surprised, since I had not let her know exactly when I would return. I was taking off my tie when she emerged from the bathroom.

"Look who decided to finally come home," she said, rubbing her stomach.

As for me, I couldn't believe my eyes. Her hair didn't appear to have been combed for months, her face was covered with unsightly blemishes, and she was wearing an oversized robe. Nothing about her helped foster my thoughts of a romantic evening.

"What happened?" she continued. "No more deals? No—don't tell me! You realized that you have a family?"

I was stunned. I had never expected to hear Christina talk like this. She was having a hard time walking back to the bed so I rushed to help her.

"I don't need your help," she said, pushing me away. "We've been doing fine without you."

"What are you talking about?" I demanded. "What's the matter?"

"He abandons us and then wonders what is the matter with *me*," she said, addressing her stomach. And then, turning to me, "I hate you! I hate you! You left me when I needed you most." She started pounding on my chest. "Get out! The sight of you is making me sick! Get out!"

"If that's how you want it," I said, grabbing her hands. This was certainly not the homecoming I had anticipated. "I don't know what has gotten into you! But if you want to be left alone, I'm leaving!"

"Then go! Do what you do best! Run like the coward you are!"

"Coward!" I squeezed her hand. "Who are you calling a coward?"

"You're not the man I thought you were," she cried. "Did you actually think you were the father of this child?"

I stared at her in astonishment as she continued to lash out at me. Suddenly, I felt as if I was in someone else's house. And, if she had meant what she said, Christina had become worse than a stranger. Was it possible that she had deceived me, and that all the ruses she had employed to force me to marry her had been for the sole purpose of providing some other man's child with a father? It couldn't be true. And yet it would explain so much.

I had to get out of the house. I didn't know where, but I just needed out. Running down the stairs, I startled Lady. Picking her up, I wandered into the backyard. It was hard to believe that only two months earlier we were happy out there. But the frigid wind had sent a chill through me, perhaps as a warning that the demons of my past would not relent in their quest that I should never live in peace.

I went into the den, taking Lady with me, still seething about the way Christina had treated me. Disgusted by the whole ordeal and in dire need of sleep, I flung myself on the leather couch, tormented by my thoughts. I could, of course, tell her everything about my past. Perhaps then she would understand my fears. But I had pledged never to revisit those terrible days, to share them with no one. Even my mother didn't know how affected my life had been by what had happened back then. No, the pain of telling Christina what had happened to irrevocably change my world ten years before would be too much for me to endure.

When I woke up the next morning with Lady still in my arms, I found that someone, probably Bascom, had covered me with a comforter. And then I remembered how I had come rushing home to surprise my wife, only to be the one who'd received the surprise. I had never enjoyed Christmas. I felt the true meaning of it had been lost a long time ago.

Everything was too commercialized now with people buying gifts they couldn't afford and spending half of the next year paying for them. But for Christina's sake, I had intended to make an attempt. Well, all of that was over.

I became furious as I remembered what Christina had told me. Had she actually said that the child she was carrying was not mine? The more I recalled what she had said, the more I was convinced that our marriage was over.

I was contemplating whether or not to call Joan to see if she had any condos for sale, meanwhile booking myself in a first-class hotel, when Christina opened the door and slipped inside. Although she had managed to make a remarkable transformation from the haggard woman that had greeted me last night, I was too incensed to be enchanted by anything about her.

"Dearest, I'm sorry," she said, approaching me with what was for her remarkable timidity. "I don't know what made me say the things I did."

"There's no need to apologize," I said, holding up my hands to keep her at bay. "You said it all last night. Go back upstairs! Better yet, go in the living room! That way you don't have to look at me. I can easily pack."

"I'm sorry, Tony," she said. And I saw tears in her eyes. "I've been feeling so strange lately. One minute I miss you so. And the next I hate you for leaving me the way you do. That's why I told you the baby wasn't yours."

What is she talking about? I thought to myself. Surely Estelle had told her how many times I had called, only to be told that she was sleeping? But that still didn't excuse her for labeling me a coward and saying that I was not the child's father.

"I got the message!" I told her. "It all came through loud and clear. You no longer love me. You needn't explain further—I understand!"

"No, you don't," she protested. "It's you who doesn't care for me. Or for our baby. If you did, you wouldn't stay away from us. Our baby kicks and you're not here to feel it. I'm scared, Tony. I love you! I need you!"

How could I let her know that my apparent lack of emotion wasn't due to unhappiness, but my inability to deal with all the complications of her pregnancy? And worst of all, how each new one sunk me deeper into the abyss, afraid that history would indeed repeat itself? Why couldn't she understand that I loved her and I was terrified of losing her or going through that hell again?

"Princess, I'm sorry," I said, wrapping my arms around her. "I didn't know I made you feel that way. I give you my word; until our baby is born, I'll be by your side."

"I'm sorry for all the rotten things I said," she told me. "I wanted to apologize last night, but when I found you in here peacefully asleep with Lady, I went upstairs and got a comforter. It was the least I could do for treating you so cruelly."

"So it was you," I said. "I thought it was probably Bascom or Estelle. Princess, I don't mind you trying to get my attention if you feel I'm devoting more time to business than to you. But let me make one thing perfectly clear: never, and I mean never, tell me that the child you're carrying is not mine."

Christina told me that perhaps her raging hormones had gotten the best of her and what she had meant was "what happened to the man she married?"

Why had I made such a drastic change from always being with her, to alienating her at a time when she needed me most?

"You've had enough excitement for one day," I told her, unable to provide a plausible answer. "I'm helping you back upstairs."

Later that afternoon, Christina asked me to close my eyes as she led me to the living room. "Dearest," she said, "you can open your eyes now."

Standing before me was the biggest Christmas tree I'd ever seen in anyone's home: seven feet tall and covered from top to base with artificial snow. The trimmings were marvelous, especially the hidden chirping birds. The lights, the garlands, and the different tree ornamentations gave it a special glow. The candy canes and the smell of the tree brought back memories. In our family, only my mother's older sister ever purchased a real tree. I always enjoyed the scent but hated cleaning up the pine needles.

"This is fantastic," I said. And it truly was. The shadow of the night before had been wiped away. "Who's the tree-trimming expert?"

"You have to thank Bascom and Estelle," Christina told me. She was modeling a low cut, crinkled-silk, black chiffon dress that she had bought especially for tonight, and artfully applied makeup which made her skin seem as soft and smooth as it had been the first night I met her. "Matt picked it out and Estelle and Bascom decorated it."

"They did a wonderful job," I said, unable to take my eyes off her. Had my presence in the house produced this effect? "I did a little Christmas shopping, but completely forgot about getting a tree. I used to—this is great."

"I'm glad that it pleases you." She leaned over

and kissed me. "I couldn't bear the thought of your not being here on our first Christmas together. I wanted it to be special."

"It will be," I assured her. "All I need for Christmas, I already have."

We stood at the room's entrance, admiring the tree. So many gifts were underneath it. "Princess, all those gifts, they're not all ours?"

"No, dearest, I thought we could have our families over."

So we were not going to be alone. How could she be so insensitive? Didn't she understand that, particularly given what had just happened between us, I might want to be alone with her? With my luck, we'd probably have to go to her parents' house to ring in the new millennium. No wonder more suicides occur between Thanksgiving and New Year's: the merriment of those silly seasons drove more lonely people to their graves than at any other time.

"Dearest," she asked, "what's the matter?"

"Nothing, princess . . . I was looking at all the gifts. We're a part of so many people's lives. I can't even keep track of all of them."

"No need to worry," she reassured me. "I bought gifts for them all."

I kissed her tenderly. "Thank you for being you," I said, and meant it. Who had that wild man been who thought that his marriage was over?

Later, while Christina tried to nap, I went out on the terrace to admire how Bascom and Estelle had decorated the outside. All through the house, carols played and I couldn't help thinking of Christmases gone by.

Our first Christmas together. We had bought our

first tree on Christmas Eve, I remembered. It was so much fun decorating it. We didn't have much then, but we didn't care. We had each other. That was all we needed.

Our last Christmas, there was no tree. I had lost my best friend. Yes, the silly season. So many times, I came close to joining you. All that was precious in my world was gone. What was the use? If it weren't for the vow I had made, to never give my heart . . . Could it be that history was looking to repeat itself?

"Dearest," she said, clearly startled, "what are you doing?"

"Uh, I was . . . looking at the lights. Bascom and Estelle did a wonderful job."

"Please, come inside," she said, trying to suppress her anxiety. "You shouldn't be so close dressed only in your robe. Aren't you cold?"

"Not really," I said, finally realizing how close I was to the edge. "I went to take a look and saw some of the guests arriving."

Christina asked me who was there, but how could I answer? I hadn't been paying attention, lost as I had been in my musing of the ghosts of Christmases past.

"Dearest, please hurry," she beckoned. "It's a quarter to six."

Christina was trembling when I took her in my arms. I wondered what could have agitated her so. Surely, she couldn't have thought I would have thrown myself over the ledge. But then again, how sure was I that I wouldn't have, if she hadn't come out when she did?

"I love you," she said, burying her head in my chest, "and I always will."

By eight the party was in full swing. Christina seemed to glow around all those people, taking such pride in showing off our home. Cautioning her not to do overdo it was pointless, since on these occasions she seemed to draw strength from somewhere. Maybe it was the euphoria of the moment or having her family and friends around her. I, on the other hand, was content to be in the kitchen, a room that has always been my place of refuge, a sort of sanctuary during these gatherings. I could go in there and nibble and pretend I was giving directions to the extra staff.

"Bascom," I said, "that was a lovely job you and Estelle did decorating the house."

"Thank you, sir," he said, looking into the oven. "I believe this is almost done."

"It seems that you have been bitten by the holiday spirit."

"To be honest, sir," he said, handing a tray full of drinks to a temporary worker, "I mean no disrespect to my former employers, but they were not ones to celebrate anything. Your wife and you, sir, are entirely different. Both of you are why I chose to remain. With your purchase, the house began to live again. We've even begun to call it the 'Richardson Manor.'"

"'Richardson Manor' does have a nice ring to it. I'm glad that you decided to remain. Your presence, my wife and I agreed, adds to the charm of the place. It would not be the same without you. Incidentally, I was thinking that this kitchen could use a face-lift."

"In what way, sir?"

"I always wanted one with an island," I said, looking around. "That way we would have two places to cook. We can keep the wall oven and expand the counter to give us more space."

"That would be helpful," Bascom assured me. "A real gourmet kitchen."

"Only fitting for a gourmet chef. Merry Christmas, Bascom."

"And a Merry Christmas to you as well, sir."

We continued talking, but I should have known that I couldn't hide for long.

"There you are!" Christina exclaimed, taking my arm. "Bascom, may I borrow my husband? Listen, Tony, promise to stay by my side. Everyone has been asking for you."

"I thought everyone was so captivated by you that they wouldn't notice my absence," I told her, forcing a smile.

"I need you near me always," she said, kissing me. "I feel lost without you. No matter how many people are around, I need you to complete me. Besides, I have a surprise for you."

I entered the living room to a chorus of "Merry Christmas" and was led to a seat in the middle of the group.

"Merry Christmas, dearest," Christina said, taking her violin from her mother.

She began to play, and I knew that I couldn't have asked for a better Christmas gift. She had chosen the works of one of my favorite composers, Antonio Vivaldi, beginning with his *Concerto Grosso in A minor*. I was especially moved by the *larghetto e spirituoso*. She played with so much feeling that I was mesmerized, my attention totally fixed on her.

She is so talented. How can she think of giving this up? Why is it so important to have this child? Will she hate me later? What if her talents diminish? Will she ever forgive me? Why now, God? Didn't you hear my prayers? Did I pray in vain? Or have my prayers been answered? Am I simply too blind to see?

Then she was playing the *Concerto Grosso in D minor*, and I forced myself to abandon those thoughts. She was playing her heart out to please me. How could I ever repay her for this wonderful gift, a gift of herself? God, I cast my cares upon you. Who am I to question you? You know the innermost desires of my heart. All I know is that I love her. She completes my world. I would be lost without her.

Then it was *La Tempesta di Mare*, a violin concerto in E flat. She outdid herself with this one, rendering the "presto movement" with incredible virtuosity. I could feel the passion as she poured her heart and soul into the piece, holding nothing back. Never had I seen or heard her play with so much emotion.

The bow flew across the violin strings and her body swayed to and fro. Those soft hands that so often stroked my face then commanded forth music that stirred my very soul. I was in awe, for in that moment, I knew I was in the presence of greatness.

Her talent was truly a gift. She punctuated the end of the piece by hitting the bow across the strings. The room deafened from the boisterous applause. She had indeed saved the best for last.

Gasping for air, she fell into my arms. "Princess!" I cried, "Are you all right?"

"Yes, Tony," she replied, smiling at me. "I'm fine. I love you."

"Let me take you upstairs! Silly me, I shouldn't have let you play for so long!"

"Dearest, really, I'm fine."

The room had become deathly quiet. Her mother and father were at our side. It was Bascom who took charge of the situation. "Everyone back, if you please. She needs room to breathe. Sir, she needs to lie down."

"Yes, you're right. I'll take her to the den."

With Bascom's help, I placed her on the couch in the den. I was worried and upset. In her attempt to please me, had she overexerted herself? Why couldn't she understand?

I told Christina that she looked exhausted and warned her that she had tried to do too much. But she just smiled and took my hand. "Feel our baby kick," she said, holding it to her stomach. "Merry Christmas, Tony, I love you so much."

I knew better than to bring up that conversation again. She wouldn't have listened anyway. "And I you, with all my heart. I'll always love you. Merry Christmas, princess."

We stayed in the den for about a half an hour. Against my better judgment, Christina insisted on returning to the party where everything had come to a standstill, with everyone concerned about her welfare. When Bascom announced that dinner was served, I tried not to venture too far from her, wanting to make sure that the overexertion had had no ill effect. But she was radiant. She glowed the whole night, every bit a princess in her manners and grace.

Still, I blamed myself. We should have waited to have this child. I should have insisted on taking more precautions. I was to blame for the condition she found herself in. All I had had to do was put my foot down. Now the world would be robbed of her talent. A woman that could play the violin like that deserved better than this. It was too late to change the present, but there was hope for the future. I could make sure she had a nanny. Because she must continue to play.

After dinner, it was clear that Harry was itching to take me outside.

"Honestly, dear," Helen said, shaking her head, "you're no better than a child with a new toy."

"Never mind her," he said, pulling me by the arms. "I can't wait till you see it! Tell me what you think of it."

It was a new Rolls Royce. Not just any Rolls, mind you. This one was a Silver Mink. And according to Harry, it would change color depending on the light.

I ran my finger along its body. "What happened to the Bentley?" I asked.

"It's at home," he told me, grinning. "I'm gonna keep them both. It's my Christmas gift to myself. I also bought an Excalibur for Helen."

"I'm surprised you did that," I said, a little green with envy. "I thought Helen didn't care for cars that much."

"She doesn't, but I just couldn't resist. I didn't know which one to get."

"So you got them both."

"You're darn right," he told me, grinning, and handed me the keys. "Want to try her out?"

The new car smell, the rich mahogany wood, and the leather appointments were overwhelming. I knew one day I'd have to get one, too.

"Harry," I said, as I drove down the circular drive, "does Helen interfere with your desire to make money?"

"Does a shark have teeth? She does nothing but! Why are you asking?"

"How do they expect us to be good providers if they keep interfering with our ability to provide?"

"Son, you'll have to learn the same way every man does," Harry told me. "What a woman wants most is security. I had to learn that the hard way. Believe me when I tell you that it doesn't always translate into money."

"What do you mean?" I asked him, although I was afraid of what he might say.

"Each woman is different. For one, security means that her husband is home every night. For another, it may be living within their means. Then there are some that need a man to be the leader in their home, providing for the family spiritually. Then you have the materialistic ones. You don't need me to explain those! So you see, son, every woman is different. You'll have to learn your wife's needs. There is no set rule to follow. It's a matter of trial and error."

"Well, I hope it's her condition that's making her the way she is," I said, parking the car and getting out. "She always wants me near her. I know that one day I am going to be forced to choose between her and my career. I'm driven to succeed, and besides, there's a promise that I must keep, no matter the cost!"

Harry put his arm around my shoulder. "When the time comes, son, I know you'll make the right decision."

I wouldn't be so sure of that, I thought. Christina's constant need to have me near her was only making matters worse. Every pain, every new complication, had me worried that something would go wrong. It was becoming increasingly difficult to hide my apprehension and to suppress the demons of the past. When I was away on business, my mind had been kept busy, but staying home, there was no avenue of escape. Why, Christina, why didn't you listen to me?

At that moment, all I wanted to do was to blurt out to Harry my fears about Christina's pregnancy, but before I could, Bascom appeared in the doorway to tell us that it was time to open the gifts.

I went inside and watched the happiness on the faces of all our family and friends as they exchanged gifts. I was right—Christmas had become too commercialized. I wanted to go to the den, but how could I explain that I needed to be alone?

Christina looked so lovely. Her smile radiated throughout the entire room. I wanted to reach out to her, hold on to her, wrap her in my arms and drift off to a peaceful sleep, only to be awakened after the baby was born.

But as I closed my eyes, that vision eluded me and was replaced by images from the tragedy of my past. And although the laughter in the room should have shielded me, it only seemed to mock me that I was indeed on the same road and would be powerless to prevent my world from being torn apart again.

The day before the eve of the new millennium, Christina and I were having breakfast in bed. Rather, she attempted to eat, while clearly distracted by the fact that I was engrossed in putting my thoughts to paper.

"Tony," she asked finally, "what are you doing?"

"I'm trying to find a way to repay you for the wonderful gift you gave me," I told her. "I'll never forget the way you played that night. One day I hope to find the words that will let you know how much you mean to me."

"I can wait, then," she smiled. "Dearest, what are our plans for tomorrow?"

"I was hoping for a quiet night at home, since you overexerted yourself on Christmas Eve."

"But didn't the doctor say I was fine?"

"Yes, he did," I told her, annoyed at having my

thoughts interrupted. "But he also warned that you should take it easy."

"But haven't I been resting? I feel so much better when you're home. And you have to admit, I've been doing what the doctor requested."

"Okay, princess," I said wearily, "I know this is leading up to something. What's wrong with a quiet night in front of the fire? I was thinking that I could put your gift to good use. I haven't had time to watch it. Just imagine, you and I snuggled up in the living room watching that big screen."

"I suppose that will be fine," she said with a deep sigh. "But everyone will be disappointed."

"Everyone? What do you mean, 'everyone'?"

"It's just that our families and friends expected to be with us to ring in the new year. They didn't want me to travel, so naturally, celebrating the new millennium would have to be here."

"Naturally," I said, although slightly perturbed. "And what part did you play in all of this, may I ask? I will not have a repeat of what happened on Christmas Eve!"

"Tony," she said, all too calmly, "I promise I will not play."

There is as much a chance of that happening, I thought to myself, as there would be the possibility of it snowing in hell. But Christina had given me her word, and I accepted it. What harm could befall her if she promised not to play? Surely this night would pass without any calamity.

I didn't have the heart to refuse her, despite feeling as if I were boxed into a corner. And if I was going to have to contend with all those people again, I reasoned, it would be best if I did it from my own home.

"Okay, princess, we'll do it one more time. I can't help but wonder if I'll ever get to spend any time with you alone."

"You're alone with me now," she said, pulling the ribbon on her chemise. "Are you not? What is it you wish to do with me?"

"I guess I won't be able to finish putting my thoughts—"

"No, dearest, but I promise I'll let you finish this—once you get started."

"Well, princess, I hope you're up to it," I said, easing her onto the pillow. "You know once I get started, it takes me a long time to finish."

"Yes, I know," she teased. "Please show me again."

"As you wish, princess. And may I fulfill all your requests with equal pleasure."

Christina kept her promise not to play. Once again the floodgates opened and poured forth people. The house was overrun with kids.

Harry brought the Excalibur this time, and I was glad, since it gave me a chance to escape the bedlam. I greeted him at the door, and he handed me the key. I had wanted to use the opportunity to finish our conversation from Christmas Eve, but Harry was more interested in eating.

"I'm so hungry I could eat an opossum," he said, rubbing his stomach. "Lead me to the kitchen, Bascom. Besides," he added, turning to me, "you don't need me, son."

But Harry, I do, I thought. Who else am I going to talk to? Where am I going to turn?

"Boss, you mind if I go with you?"

"There you go," Harry chimed in. "Let Matt drive you. Once you've driven one Rolls, you've driven them all."

I told Matt that he didn't have to, but he jumped at the opportunity, saying that he might never get the chance again. While he took a few minutes to acclimate himself to the car, I chuckled at the fact that he did exactly what I had done in the Silver Mink.

"I would love to have one of these," he sighed. "The boys in the old neighborhood would never believe it. Where to, boss?"

I figured a drive to the marina would enable us to get back before the ball dropped. I didn't think either of our wives would forgive us if we didn't make it back in time. Matt started thanking me for all the gifts Christina and I had given them. I accepted his gratitude and quickly changed the subject since I had no clue what those gifts had been.

"How do you do it?" I asked.

"Do what, boss?"

"Three kids," I said, as the Excalibur rolled down the drive. "How do you do it? The fights, the interruptions. You must never get a moment alone with your wife, and I'm not talking about making love to her. Maybe you just want to talk and hold her hand. You know, share a quiet moment together."

"Boss, it's all in the way you look at it," Matt told me. "Sure, if you look at it that way, it would be a drag to anyone."

We turned toward the marina. "What do you mean?" I asked.

"Boss, have you ever smelled a baby's hair?"

"Baby's hair? No. I can't say that I have."

"There is something about the sound of little feet," Matt went on, "coming into the room early in the morning that is different from any other sound in the world. My wife and I would try to get a couple more winks in before the alarm went off again. I can still hear the pitter-patter of those little feet. I'd pretend to still be asleep while she climbed up on the bed beside me. Then I would lay her upon my chest and smell her hair. I would get so choked up inside that I'd start crying."

Why would he become so emotional over smelling a baby's hair? I wondered. Surely the experience couldn't have been all that moving.

Matt then told me about the time when he lost his younger daughter Darlene on a family camping trip. He had argued with his wife about Darlene being an unplanned pregnancy and how it was more difficult to make ends meet. Matt said when they woke up the following morning, Darlene was gone. Luckily they found her nearby, and when he questioned her, Darlene told him she heard them fighting and had run away so they wouldn't fight anymore.

"To tell you the truth," Matt continued, turning into a parking space, "for a long time I didn't want to have any kids. But when God blesses you . . . now I can't think of life without them. So you see, boss, it's all in the way you look at it."

We silently walked the length of the pier. How else could I have looked at it? He had found his child.

"I used to go on camping trips with my father," Matt said, finally. "I remember the last time. It was the year before he died. Life was hell then. I couldn't make ends meet. My wife and I were always at each other's throats. I knew the marriage was falling apart. I figured she'd be better off without me. My dad was sick at the time, this proud man who never asked for anything, who fed and clothed all ten of us. Times were bad, but he kept us together. And now he wanted to go camping. So to make him happy, I took him.

"I still remember what he told me when we got there. He turned to me and said, 'Matthew, even God couldn't make two mountains without a valley in it. So if you're in the valley, there's a side of the mountain to look up to.'"

"Very wise man, your father," I remarked as we stood together, looking out across the water.

"He taught me to keep the faith," Matt told me. "I also learned a couple of things from watching you."

"What could I have possibly taught you that you didn't know already?" I demanded.

"Well, for starters, you never accept defeat. You make things happen. And then there's the way you treat your wife. My wife and I have never been this happy. After all the years we've been married, my wife finally has what she wants. It took me a while to figure it out. All the years she and I fought, money wasn't her main problem after all. What she wanted most was for me to spend time with her and the kids. Go figure. Women."

Harry was right. Smarter men than us have tried and failed. Perhaps that is one mystery God will never allow man to solve.

We got back a few minutes to ten. In the living room, everyone's eyes were fixed on the big screen as they watched the millennium being celebrated all over the world. Estelle told me that Christina was in the kitchen with both of our mothers. I approached quietly, not wanting to intrude if either of them were doling out motherly advice. I thought better of it and started retreating when I heard my mother declare, "Christina, honey, I'm scared for both of you. My son has been acting all his life!"

What on earth was she talking about? Acting all

my life? I couldn't move. I felt like I was stuck in quick-drying cement.

"He plays so many parts," she went on, "and he has played them for so long. I don't know where the acting stops and where his true self begins."

Why, Momma? I thought. Why now of all times? Why are you never on my side? You see the good in everyone. Everyone except me.

"Worst of all," she continued, "I'm afraid that even he doesn't know."

"I too have watched him," Christina's mother concurred. "It's as you say. He's a man of many faces."

I waited patiently. How come Christina was not defending me? Why wasn't she saying anything? After all, she was my wife. I wouldn't allow anyone to speak ill of her.

The fact was that the two women who were most important in my life were discrediting me. One through her words, the other through her silence.

Someone was approaching, so I forced a smile and continued on into the kitchen. I excused myself for the intrusion, greeting both of our mothers before I kissed Christina.

"Dearest, I'm glad you're back," she said, returning my kiss. "I trust your drive was enjoyable?"

Trust, I thought to myself. How ironic that she would have chosen that word. But I acknowledged that it was and told her that I wouldn't intrude upon them any longer.

"That's all right, son," Momma told me, pushing back her chair. "We were finishing up anyway."

Christina's mother echoed the same sentiment and said she must rejoin her husband. I felt like a hypocrite going through the motions, but I had to maintain the deception that I hadn't heard what they were discussing. Bascom interrupted by asking where I wanted to be served and when I indicated the dining room, Christina objected.

"No, dearest," she said, extending her hands. "You may eat here. But remember to join me in the living room before midnight."

I helped Christina to her feet. "Okay, princess, I will as soon as I'm finished." When Bascom started placing the meal before me, I said, "My apologies for coming so late."

"Think nothing of it, sir."

"Well, after this you may retire. I know you'd rather celebrate the millennium, as opposed to serving me. Have you eaten?"

"No, sir. I will right after I'm done."

"Nonsense! Pull up a chair!"

"Sir. That would not be proper."

"Bascom! That's an order!"

"If you insist, sir."

"Yes, Bascom. Have a seat, please."

He quickly fixed a plate and sat down. Imagine a house full of people and I was in the kitchen, my place of refuge. Never before had I felt so alone.

"Bascom, I want to ask you a question," I said. "I know I can count on your frankness. How would you describe me? Would you say that I'm a man of many faces?"

"What man is not, sir? We all have so many masks to wear. How else would one get through life? The only danger, sir, is when one forgets that he has been playing so many parts and loses his identity."

"Is such a thing possible?" I asked, pushing away my plate.

Bascom hesitated for a moment. "Yes, sir," he finally said. "It's very possible. A man can grow accustomed to wearing so many that he becomes lost without them. Waking up one morning, he finds that he no longer recognizes his own face staring back at him."

"How is that possible? How could a man not notice?"

"It starts slowly at first." Bascom became more animated than I had ever seen him. Clearly my question had touched a chord. "A trauma, a painful experience, some deep-rooted emotion, one that he would rather suppress than face. Emotions suppressed in such a way are notorious for making their presence felt in other ways."

Is that what Momma was talking about? Christina's mother said she saw it, too. Is that what they were warning her about? How could that be? If I didn't know myself, then who would? I live with myself everyday. Surely, I would know. I had no problem looking into the mirror. I know the man that looks back at me. But then there are the voices that keep fighting within me. Have they been trying to warn me about something?

"I knew a man," he continued. "He had a lovely wife and two sons. He owned a restaurant. He was working very hard to make it a success. So hard, in fact, that he forgot what he was working for. In trying to provide for his family, he alienated the very ones he cared the most about."

I listened intently, trying to figure out if it was Bascom's story or not. He continued by telling me how the man had come home late one night to find the entire house in darkness. And that should have been the man's first clue that something was amiss, but the man had thought nothing of it as he climbed the stairs. He said the man's wife had not been in their bedroom, and that he had figured she must have been in the boys' room, because she sometimes fell asleep in there.

"Finding his sons' room empty, he began to panic," Bascom said, clearly shaken. "Mad with worry, he started shouting, running like a madman. He searched every room in the house. It wasn't until his second passing that he found the note she had left on the kitchen table.

"'Please forgive me. I can no longer live without a husband. Our boys need a father, and I've tried to explain, but you wouldn't listen. Your business has taken first place in your life. I no longer know you. You're not the man I married.'"

I realized suddenly that Bascom was telling me his own story, but surely I wasn't guilty enough to suffer the same fate. He continued to tell me what his wife had written. Clearly, he had read the message over so many times that he had memorized it.

"'Our sons don't even refer to you as 'daddy' anymore. We shan't return, so please don't bother looking for us. I wish you all the best with your restaurant. I'm afraid I can't be the wife you wanted me to be. To cause you no further embarrassment, you'll not be seeing us again. I've done my best. Love, Elizabeth.'"

I couldn't believe that a woman would have just packed up her family and left her husband over a simple thing like him working hard to provide for her. But clearly that was what Bascom's wife had done. And I wondered, between the love of my wife or the promise I had sworn to keep, what would the outcome be if I had chosen to follow the latter?

Bascom then told me how, in an effort to find his family, the man had spent all the money he had had, ultimately losing his home and business in the process. He choked on his words as he related how the man had been reduced to a vagabond and a drunk. And how, on one ill-fated rainy night, the man, drenched and in a drunken stupor, had decided to take his own life by jumping off a bridge.

"Luckily, there had been a constable nearby," he said despondently, "who had been eyeing the man and jumped in and saved his life."

What does a man say to another after hearing a story like that? I didn't feel like eating anymore and from the looks of it, neither did he.

The irony of the situation had not escaped me. On what was supposed to be a most joyous occasion, Bascom and I sat quietly, both of us brooding, he undoubtedly for the family he had lost, and me, for the family I would hopelessly lose.

The silence in the kitchen was broken by the merriment coming from the living room. I heard someone approaching, and whoever it was moved at a snail's pace. Bascom must have heard it also, because he jumped up and grabbed our plates.

"Dearest, are you not finished?" she asked, clearly flustered.

"Uh, yes, princess. We—I'm done."

"Then please join me," she said. "The new year is almost upon us. Bascom, you, too."

"Madam, I have so much to do. Perhaps another time."

"Bascom, please come here," she insisted. "This will not happen for another thousand years."

We entered the living room, Christina holding

on to both of our arms, just as the final countdown began. When the ball reached the bottom, everyone cried, "Happy New Year!" All but Bascom. Seeing the pensive expression on his face, I knew that Christina and I shouldn't have interfered.

"Happy New Year, old man," I said. "I'm sorry. I should have allowed you to celebrate the way you always have."

"Sooner or later some things must be faced, sir," he replied. "A new year. A new millennium. I can't think of a better time to start. Thank you, sir."

He was right. A new year. A new millennium. So many resolutions made. So much promise for the future. If only I could forget the past.

Chapter 17

THE MONTH OF JANUARY WAS BY FAR THE EASIEST TO DEAL with, since my apprehension of fatherhood slowly dissipated, thanks in good part to my conversation with Matt. Fortunately, although I had plenty of clients, none of them required me to travel at that time. As a result, I chose to do most of my work at home so I could spend as much time with Christina as possible.

Spending time at home had other benefits as well, since it allowed me the opportunity to supervise the remodeling of the kitchen. The architect's plan called for the removal of the swinging door heading into the kitchen, replacing it with one that slid together. I liked the idea of that and was eager to see him get started.

It had become increasingly difficult for Christina to move around, so she spent most of her time in our bedroom where I often joined her to play board games and cards to keep her company. I discovered that she was very good at playing chess. Thanks to my competitive nature, I usually beat her at every game we played, but when it came to chess, she had my number. She seemed to draw energy from beating me. We would be up most of the night playing.

During the month of February, we started reviewing

what each of us would do when the day came. Christina's suitcase was packed and placed downstairs in the closet near the foyer. Her doctor's number was on my nightstand. It was agreed that Estelle would come upstairs to help dress Christina. Bascom would put her suitcase in the limo and call family members to alert them to what was going on.

We repeated this process about four times, with all ending up false alarms. We would make it all the way to the hospital, only to be turned back. I hoped that Christina didn't sense my frustration, but clearly she was troubled.

"Dearest, I'm sorry."

"What's there to be sorry about?"

"All these false alarms," she said impatiently.

"I'd rather be safe than sorry," I said, taking her hand. "I know you feel like the little boy who cried wolf once too often."

"Yes, isn't it awful?"

I quickly changed the subject by asking Matt to take us to Baskin Robbins. That feeling of hopelessness had overcome me, and I was afraid that I would snap at Christina for making me go through this hell again.

The memories that I had fought so hard to suppress all started coming back with resounding fury. Christina's fascination for ice cream had been the key that unlocked all the unpleasantness of my tragic past. She had a penchant for banana splits. I would watch as her eyes glistened while it was being made. I always had to remember to make sure that Christina got extra cherries to top it off.

But this time, as the clerk handed it to me, I couldn't escape the image, albeit a different dessert, of how I had given one to another. There had been no denying it then that the past had indeed come full circle, and to ensure that history didn't repeat itself, I resigned to tell Christina the truth.

Just then she smiled at me. In that moment, as she radiated an overwhelming happiness, I lost the courage to subject her to my anguish.

"Dearest," she said joyfully, "thank you."

"I hope you're feeling better now," I told her, despite being imbued with overpowering sadness. "Should I get you another?"

"Why would I need another one?"

"You know you like your late night snacks."

"My late—Tony, are you all right?"

"How many nights did I have to . . . ?"

I realized just in the nick of time and had caught myself. I told Christina instead that I was sure she wouldn't mind having another as we played chess late into the night.

But how many of these false alarms could I take? With each one, my apprehension grew, and yet I was eager for it to be over because I was certain that the birth of this child would allow me to finally bury the past.

It's funny how there are some things that you will never forget. It was Wednesday, the eighth of March, and I was in my den working late with Lady peacefully asleep on top of my desk. It seemed so much like old times that I was genuinely startled when Christina appeared.

"Princess, what—is anything wrong?"

"No," she replied, rubbing her stomach. "I just miss you, that's all."

I had wanted to continue working, but one look at her face and I could tell that this time it wasn't a false alarm. We timed the contractions and called the doctor. He informed us that she was in labor, but there was no need to bring her in yet. Bascom and Estelle took charge of the situation. Bascom brought a mattress from the guestroom. Estelle made it up and we placed Christina on her side to rest. Sometimes the best laid plans don't go exactly as planned.

There was nothing to do but wait. I held her and felt the movement of the child, somewhat of a rhythmic vibration. I guess, comforted by the fact that I was near, Christina quickly fell asleep.

God, what am I going to do? In a matter of hours, all of this would be over, but which way? You've got to help me this time. I can't afford to lose . . .

"Tony, wake up, please."

"Princess, just another five minutes. After that I'll get up."

"No, the pain grows. Please wake up!"

"Uh, what pain?"

"No false alarm."

I jumped to my feet, screaming as if the house were on fire. Christina no longer rubbed her stomach, she held it. She seemed unusually calm.

"Estelle, Bascom. This is it. Where's everybody? My wife is having a baby!"

"Right here, sir," Bascom replied. "I have called Matt and he's getting ready."

"Don't worry," Estelle answered. "Everything is all right. I have her clothes."

"Sir, while we attend to her," Bascom said, "you may want to put on a fresh shirt and trousers."

"Dearest, they're already on the bed. Please hurry."

While I jumped into my clothes, Bascom timed her contractions. When I returned, Christina was neatly bundled up and waiting in the limo.

"Sir, her contractions are ten minutes apart. I've phoned the doctor and he's en route even as we speak."

"Thank you, Bascom. I should be doing better than this. Heaven knows we've practiced long enough."

"There lies the difference."

"Difference?"

"This time it is irrefutable," Bascom told me as he held the door. "You leave as two, but return as three."

"Hurry," Estelle said. "That child is eager to come out."

The hospital was about fifteen minutes away. It seemed that we no sooner got into the limo than we were getting out. Neither of us said a word, although we kept our hands clasped. I was nervous and didn't want my words to betray me. What a woman thinks at this time, I'll never know. Even if she wanted to share, I don't think I would have heard her. I just wanted to get this over with, to lay all my demons to rest once and for all.

A nurse met us at the entrance and instructed me to register Christina while she took her to a room. As the nurse whisked her away, Christina kept looking back at me. I told her not to worry and that I would be at her side as quickly as possible. It may have been a small comfort to her, since she smiled, but never uttered a word.

"Matt, please accept my apology."

"Apology for what, boss?"

"For getting in your way."

"I don't follow."

"The way my wife looked at me. I understand now. Please accept my apology."

When I entered the room, the nurse told me that I had just missed Christina's doctor. He had examined her and everything seemed fine.

I looked at the machine that was monitoring the contractions. Christina was in so much pain. I forced myself to go over to her. I wiped the sweat from her forehead.

God, I know that we don't talk as much as we should. But this time I need your help more than ever. I don't know why you're making me go through this again. I know I've been cross with you. Please, not for my sake, but for hers. Please help her through this. I love her too much. Life would be unbearable without her.

"I'll always love you," I whispered, as I kissed her gently on the lips.

She wanted to reply but more contractions came, each one more violent than the other. She grabbed the handles of the bed. I knew it was time to go. I couldn't bear to watch. It tore at my insides to see her in so much pain, and to realize that there was nothing I could do to provide her with comfort. How useless were those words to me: provide and protect.

When I had scrubbed, I was allowed to join Christina. The doctor, a silver-haired old fox, instructed me to coach her the way I had been taught in Lamaze class, to tell her when to pant and when to push. Christina was clearly trying to be brave, but she gripped my hand so tightly that I knew the agony she must be in. She began to scream. That scream shot through me like a bullet. For a moment everything went black.

It was then that I realized something was wrong.

The anesthesiologist and the nurses began to scramble. The doctor ordered me out of the room and a nurse ushered me into the hall. The walls started spinning. Oh, God, I thought, it can't be happening again. And then the other doctor who had been in the room was standing beside me. "Mr. Richardson, sir, are you all right? I think you'd better have a seat."

"What—uh, yes."

"Mr. Richardson, you need to listen very carefully. Your wife is experiencing a series of complications," he said grimly. "The baby is in a breech position and the umbilical cord is wrapped around the neck. We have to move quickly or the baby will choke to death. Your wife has been told about the complications and has asked us, if a choice has to be made, we are to save the baby."

My God, this can't be. Didn't I pray for this not to happen? Why have you again forsaken me? How the hell am I supposed to choose? The last time I had no choice, but this time isn't any better. I love her so much. But what kind of life can we have with this tragedy between us?

"Doctor, this is not a threat, but you had better do your best to save them both. So help me God, if I lose either one through your negligence, I'll take this hospital for everything it has. In addition, I'll personally see to it that you never practice medicine anywhere again."

"Mr. Richardson, I can understand how you feel."

"Do you really, doctor? How the hell can you understand how I feel? I love my wife. She can always have another child. The child can't give me back my wife."

"What would you have told her?"

"Told her?"

"Yes, as she clutched on to you, pleading for you to save her baby. Would you have had the guts to refuse her request?"

His words cut through me. I could not answer. But then again, what could I have said? Either way, I would be tormented for the rest of my life. I remarked that Christina and me wouldn't have been in this situation if the birth control pills had worked.

"Sir, unless your wife has been seeing another gynecologist, I have never prescribed any birth control pills for her."

"Excuse me, Doctor, but what are you saying?"

"Mr. Richardson, I must be getting back to your wife. Do you stand by her decision?"

"No. I mean, yes. Doctor, are you sure about the pills?"

"I would stake my medical reputation on it. Besides, why would I prescribe any contraceptive methods for a woman who wasn't sexually active?"

"Are you sure?"

"I mean no disrespect, sir. But you should know better than me if your wife was a virgin on your wedding night. Now I must return to her."

The corridor began closing in. He has got to be wrong. Christina knew how I felt. Must be a reasonable explanation. She couldn't have betrayed me like this.

"Mr. Richardson, are you feeling all right?"

"Let her decision stand."

"Excuse me, sir."

"Let—her—decision—stand."

"The man who will operate is our top obstetrician. He's handled many of these complicated situations.

Sometimes we doctors are put in an awful position, but I felt you had a right to know. No need to worry, though. Our best is handling the case."

How could she betray me like this? She knew of my desire to wait. She deliberately forced us to go through this. Then to make matters worse, she concealed it from me. Did she think me a monster, capable of snuffing out a life, even if it was only in its embryonic stage? Probably on her deathbed, she makes the biggest decision of her life, leaving me a widow, to raise our child alone. This treachery is the deepest cut of all.

The doctor said that Christina would be all right. She was in the hands of an expert. I dropped to my knees. I would ask the expert of all experts to guide his hand. Allow both to return safely to me. Once I knew they were safe, I would leave. She had no right to put me through this. I would take them home. Once that was done, I would leave.

How could a man live with a woman he no longer trusts?

After my little prayer, the gravity of the situation sank in. The hall started spinning. I couldn't focus. I couldn't get off the floor. I covered my ears, but the voices would not stop. I pulled at my shirt. The collar was choking me.

"Mr. Richardson, I'm so sorry."

"No, no!"

"I am so sorry, sir," the doctor told me. "We lost them both."

"Oh—God!"

"We did all we could. But your wife just seemed to give up when she realized that the baby was dead."

"No, it can't . . . "

"I'm very sorry."

I struck the wall, over and over again, tears streaming down my face. My whole world was gone. She had wanted to give me a child. And then I had nothing.

Where was the mercy? How could you, God? I trusted you. Everything that was precious in my world, gone. I could see no lesson in this.

Pushing the doctor aside, I went into the room. Nothing was wrong, I told myself. I'll wake her. Take her home. She wouldn't have given up on us. I don't care what they said. She would never have left me. Never! If one of us had to go, it was supposed to be me. Not you, never one as young as you.

Wake up. Please wake up. Do it for me. Open your eyes. Please open your eyes. Falling on top of her, I cried until no more tears came. I don't know how long I stayed. A nurse finally came in. Putting her arms around me, she led me out of the room.

Chapter 18

"M R. RICHARDSON—SIR, YOUR WIFE AND BABY ARE FINE.
Your wife is resting. She was given a sedative to calm
her down. The baby is being cleaned to remove liquid
that was in the lungs."

I stayed on my knees for awhile, unable to utter
a single word. Finally, I managed to get to my feet.

"Mr. Richardson, sir. Mr. Richardson. Don't you
want to see your . . . ?"

"Boss, is it over?"

"Uh—what?"

"Boss, what's the matter? Anything wrong?"

"Nothing. Everything—fine."

"The missus and the baby?"

"Matt."

"Yea, boss."

"Please take me home."

When he closed the door, I raised and locked
the partition. I needed to lie down. The blackness was
coming again. Someone kept playing tricks. I kept
falling and falling. I had lost everything. And now
where was I going? It all started coming back to me. I
closed my eyes, hoping that would help me not to
remember.

I had been walking home. No limo for me back

then. And all I could think of was how could one so young, so vibrant, and so innocent die? Had the child been that important? And why shouldn't I join her in death? After all, she had been my reason for living.

I had ended up in a bar that time. Had drank myself under the table, spilled my guts to the bartender. I had woken up in my apartment the next morning, lying in my own vomit. Never took another drink after that.

"Boss, what's the matter? You're home. Boss, ya hear me?"

The voices wouldn't stop. Someone, please stop the world. I want to get off this merry-go-round.

"I don't know what's wrong with the boss."

"Matt, help me—get him inside. How are madam and the baby?"

"He keeps mumbling something about everything being fine."

"As soon as he is settled, I will make inquiries at the hospital."

Blackness came again. No vomit this time—no voices. Sleep again.

The sound of the curtains being drawn roused me. It was morning and Bascom told me that four days had passed since I returned from the hospital. The doctor said that I had suffered a traumatic shock.

"Rest is what he ordered," Bascom reassured me. "I'll ring him. He told us to notify him the moment you regained—"

"Bascom. Do you hear them?"

"Sir?"

"Quiet!"

"Sir?"

"The voices. Can't you hear them?"

"Voices, sir?"

"Shh, there they go again."

"Ah, voices."

"Surely, you hear them."

"Yes, sir, I do indeed."

"Good. I know I'm not crazy."

"Sleep, sir."

"Yes. Sleep. No more voices."

"You've had a most frightful experience."

"You're a good man, Bascom. Don't know what I'd do without you . . ."

"Don't worry, sir. We are all here. Sleep, sir. Sleep. The voices won't trouble you any further."

The next time I woke up, a man was standing over me with a needle. "What are you doing?" I demanded.

"This is something to calm you down," he said. "You're suffering from a severe shock."

"Bascom," I shouted, "show this man out."

Darkness came again. Mustn't give into it. Have to fight it . . . The doctor had barely left the room when I fell off the bed reaching for the phone. Thank God for speed dial. I heard Maggie's familiar voice.

"Tony!" she gasped. "You gave us all an awful scare."

"Maggie, please listen."

"Sure, Tony."

"I need to get out of here."

"Why, what's the matter?"

"I can't talk here—this is what I want you to do. Book me into a hotel. I've got to lie low until I can figure out what's going on."

"Sir, I thought you would like—great Caesar's ghost! Here, let me help you up."

"Thank you. Bascom, I need—pack my suitcase." Bascom protested, but when I insisted, he packed my garment bag and helped me into my clothes. My head hurt and I felt dizzy, but I was determined. I wasn't going to stick around and let that doctor shoot me again. But when I asked him to tell Matt to bring the limo around, he said, "I will, sir, as soon as he returns from the hospital with madam and . . . "

I didn't give him a chance to finish. I didn't want to hear anything about the woman who had betrayed me. Uncontrollable rage gave me strength. And then, suddenly, Christina was in the room and Bascom was explaining what was going on.

"But you can't leave," she said. "You're not well."

"No thanks to you."

"I don't understand."

"Stop the pretense, Christina. I know what you tried to put me through."

"But Tony, I was scared."

"Of what? Being found out or getting away?"

"I thought—"

"No, you did not. The condoms were there. What was it you said? 'Let nothing come between us.'"

She tried to console me, but I pushed her away. Nothing she said would have made a difference. "That child wasn't brought into this world through a labor of love, but through treachery and deceit," I told her.

"You don't mean that," she protested.

"You tricked me. All the times we made love, you were never on the pill. All my plans are ruined. I'm leaving. The sight of you is making me sick. I can't trust you. The house is yours. One suitcase is all I need. I don't want anything to remind me of you."

"What about our child?"

"I have no child. The baby is yours. You wanted it. You take care of it. Bascom, where is my suitcase?"

"But won't you at least look at—"

"What part didn't you understand? I don't want to look. You said it before. I'm not the father. Bascom!"

"Why do you say such things?"

"Why! Why the hell not?"

"But you know they are not true."

I wanted to hurt her. Let her feel the pain I felt. She had no right to take away my dreams. "You're selfish," I told her. "You only thought about yourself. You didn't care about my needs. Now you've got what you wanted. I hope you're happy. Bascom, is the suitcase packed?"

"No, sir. It's not."

I turned and glared at her. "So you've turned him against me. The deed is done. The treachery's complete."

When she rushed to me, I brushed her aside.

"There's nothing left for me here," I told her.

"Please, I didn't . . . "

I never heard the rest. Storming out of the room, I hurried down the stairs. "Take care of her," I told Estelle. "Take care of them both. I will not be back."

Matt was outside wiping down the limo, while the gardener was working nearby.

"Morning, Mr. Richardson," said the gardener.

"Matt, never mind with that. I'm leaving."

"Ever seen anything more lovely?" he asked me, holding out a handful of seeds.

"What of them? They're just seeds."

"Yes, they are. Funny thing, though."

"Look, I'm in a hurry. What's your point?"

He held up the seeds. "No one knows what makes them grow."

"That's nice," I said impatiently.

"Isn't it? Man knows so much. Yet he doesn't know what seeds know."

"What?"

"Plant them in good soil. They know what they ought to do."

I remained silent. Anything I said would have kept him talking.

"They must be what God meant them to be."

"I don't understand."

"You will. In God's good time."

"Anything you say." I started walking to the limo.

"You're one of his seeds."

I turned to look at him. Bascom was coming toward me with my bag.

"Wait, you'll see," he yelled, waving his spade at me. "Mark my words. Be not deceived. I will not be mocked. Whatsoever a man soweth, so shall he reap."

"Thank you, Bascom," I said, trying to drown out the old man. "I thought you were against me."

"The thanks should go to Madam. She insisted that I bring it to you."

Matt took the bag from him while I got into the limo. I rolled down the window. "Take care of them, old friend," I said.

"There's just one more thing, sir. Do you remember our talk that evening in the kitchen?"

"Yes, I do."

"I neglected to mention that in order to comprehend the present, one must examine the past."

"What?"

"God speed on your journey, sir. We await your return."

"Thank you, Bascom, but a return here, however, is not likely. One last request."

"Yes, sir."

"Keep the gardener out of the sun. Matt, let's go."

"Where to, boss?"

"I don't know yet. Just drive."

Not surprisingly, I ended up where it all started. I asked Matt to drive me into the city. I didn't want to put him in an awkward spot if asked of my whereabouts, so I made him drop me in the middle of Times Square. Although it was the farthest place from my mind, I found myself back at the Waldorf Astoria. I had no problem getting a suite under an assumed name. I tipped the bellboy and gave him strict instructions that I wasn't to be disturbed.

The minute he left, I threw myself on the bed, unable to hold back sleep any longer. But the reoccurring thoughts that plagued my mind wouldn't relent even in sleep. I found myself running through a series of doors, each one leading nowhere, each seeming to pull me deeper into an abyss. I awoke to a room engulfed in darkness and found myself drenched with perspiration, no doubt because of the overwhelming fear that had consumed me.

What am I to do? I thought to myself. I was having a hard time grasping on to reality. And the moment had come for me to face my fears, and I couldn't. Christina, the baby. They were safe. I had worried for nothing. But the demons of my past wouldn't let it go at that. I would find no solace until I could come to grips with what had happened in the past. But, as quickly as those thoughts appeared, they seemed to vanish, and I once again became victim to an overpowering desire to sleep.

It was three o'clock in the afternoon when I awoke. The phone rang, breaking the quietness of the room. Unable to move, I stared at it. Maybe if I don't answer, it will stop, I thought to myself. But when it continued to ring, I slowly picked it up.

"Howdy, son! You don't know how to pick up a phone?"

"How did you ever find me?"

"Never mind that. I'm on my way up. I'm so hungry I could eat an opossum. I'm taking you to my favorite watering hole. Then we can talk and eat a mess of groceries."

I knew it was useless to complain about wanting to be left alone, given Harry's bullheaded personality. Quickly drying my eyes, I opened the door and waited for him.

"Son, you're a sight for sore eyes," he said, locking me in another bear hug. "How you been keeping yourself?"

"Fine, old man, just fine."

"Hogwash, son. Maggie filled me in."

"I see you're your normal, diplomatic self."

"Now look here, son. You know I've never been one to pull punches."

"I should have known better than to try to fool you, old man."

"Son, let's get a move on. If we stay here talking, I'm going to need two opossums."

Harry's favorite watering hole was a place called the Capital Grille, which we often frequented whenever my business took me to Houston. I was sure that his invitation to dine would have taken place in one of the local restaurants. But it was Harry, and I should have known better. Two hours later we were indeed pulling up to the Capital Grille in Philadelphia, the city of brotherly love.

My fondness for the restaurant was without end. From the giant lion sculptures to the United States eagle and the wine lockers displayed with gold nameplates, everything about the place exuded power. Given the oil paintings that adorned the walls, it could have been a museum. After all the hell that I'd been through, Harry's intrusion was a welcome diversion. After placing our orders, he didn't waste any time picking up where he had left off.

"Son," he said, "what the hell is the matter with you? It's not like you to run away from anything."

How to explain something I had suppressed for so long? Where did the lies end and the truth begin?

"There must be a good reason why you would desert your family."

His words couldn't have cut through me any deeper than if he had been using a surgeon's scalpel. He was upset—no—disappointed, as if I had betrayed the confidence he had in me.

"Son, tell me something. Don't make me believe that I'm a bad judge of character, that after all these years I've befriended a coward."

I knew what he was trying to do. Any other man who had dared to call me a coward would have had to pick himself up off the floor. But for the first time in my life, I didn't want to fight back. "Harry, I don't know," I said. "Maybe you have."

"Poppycock, son. Once a fighter, always a fighter."

He called the waiter over and gave strict instructions not to disturb us. I was to get everything off my chest, even if we had to stay there all night to do it.

"Now go right ahead, son," he said.

I took a deep breath. Where to begin? He was right, of course. It was time that I faced it.

"About ten years ago," I began, "Priscilla came into my life. Back then I dated a lot and gave no serious thought to any kind of commitment. She was unlike any woman I had ever known. Through some odd turn of events, she got me to accompany her to a park nearby. What was to be a half an hour walk turned into four. She had this zest about her. Her joy for life was incredible. She was full of ideas for the future. It was she who taught me to live. To get some focus in my life. Chalk it up to the ignorance of youth, but I didn't realize what a special gem I had. All she wanted was to marry me and have my child."

It was, I thought, too painful to go on. I wanted to stop. But Harry nodded his head and waited patiently for me to continue.

"Her pregnancy was the happiest time in my life," I told him. "She would wake up in the middle of the night. She was remarkable with the many things she craved. I remember when she broke the news to me. I was working late one night. When I got home she was waiting up for me. When I asked her why, she told me she wanted to go to the supermarket.

"I was tired and asked if it could wait until tomorrow. I should have taken her superstitious nature more seriously. She casually answered yes, just as long as I didn't mind having a child with a birthmark."

I told Harry of the plans we had made to be married that summer, how I was really looking forward to settling down, how my life had been so much sweeter because she was a part of it, and how, after a day of shopping, we came home to find a telegram that had been shoved underneath the door that led us on a tumultuous road to the very depths of hell.

I could no longer hold back the tears. In the middle of the Capital Grille, in front of the old man, I wept like a child.

"In a blink of an eye, my world turned upside down. All that I lived for, all that was precious—gone. Life was no longer worth living. Never was I to see what we created out of a labor of love—neither would she.

"I don't know how I got through it. I blamed and cursed the very existence of God. How could he take one as lovely as she? There were so many that were unfit to live. Why take her?

"The number of lives she touched was incredible. So many people attended her funeral. I wanted to join her in death. What was there for me to live for? As she was being lowered into the ground, I had made up my mind to do just that. If it hadn't been for the pastor, I probably would have. After the service, he pulled me over to the side. He said he wished he had known her. She seemed to be loved by everyone. He challenged me to make her death count for something. Then he said the words that have lived with me since that mournful day.

"'It's not what men say about you when you're gone that counts. It's what angels say about you before the throne of God.'"

I told Harry about what happened later that night. How, surrounded by family and friends, what had been supposed to be a vigil of death, had turned into a celebration of life. And how as we had gone around the room, we each had taken a moment to describe how she had touched us.

"Remembering the pastor's words," I told him, "to make her death stand for something, I vowed not to cheapen her memory and to build my business in her honor. Her death gave me the focus to concentrate and accomplish all my dreams in her memory."

I fought hard to regain my composure and told Harry how I had assured everyone that I would be all right if left alone. How I had sat in that lonely house and wondered why there were no tears. I had maintained a pillar of strength around everyone, but when I had been alone, the tears would not come.

"It was then I remembered the pact we had made," I said. "If anything were to happen to either of us, if we couldn't remember the joyous times we spent with each other, then there would be no need to remember anything at all.

"Christina's treachery has been a hindrance to fulfilling my promise to Priscilla. She knew of my desire to wait. Yet she went ahead, knowingly. How can I ever trust her again? Now there's an innocent child between us. How can that child lead a happy life? In my state of mind, I have only bitter contempt for what she has done. Who's to say that it won't carry over to the child? So to make the best of an unhappy situation, I left."

Harry hung on to my every word. Sitting there nodding, his fingers intertwined, he beckoned me to continue.

"I thought that I could bury my bitterness by running away," I told him, "but it seems that no solace will I find even in that. What it has done, though, is cast a shadow of doubt. Why can't I be like most men who cheat on their wives, their taxes, and covet their neighbor's possessions?

"All my life, all I ever wanted was to be one of the boys. I just wanted to be like everyone else. Circumstances, however, seemed intent that it would never be. I'm reminded of something Winston Churchill said: 'I was never the lion, but I was called upon to give the lion's roar.'

"Why, Harry? Why can't I be like everyone else? Why must I always carry the ball? Why can't I relax and let someone else take over for a change? Why must I always lead? In a room full of people, I feel so alone. I can never really get close to anyone. I've always been apprehensive that if I were to get too close to the people who work for me, they would become contemptuous of me. When I worked for someone, I couldn't go to my bosses. To do so would be an admission of weakness. Now that I'm a business owner, it remains the same. No one really knows me. And of the two women that I thought did, one was lost through death and the other through betrayal."

Chapter 19

"SON, ARE YOU TRYING TO PULL THE WOOL OVER MY EYES dancing this little sidestep?" Harry asked me. "I know that this must be very difficult for you, but make me understand why you're blaming yourself for this woman's death."

Why can't he understand? I thought to myself. And then I realized my close-to-the-vest nature had kept me from really telling him what had happened. I took a deep breath as I clenched and unclenched my fists underneath the table.

"Priscilla's desire to give me a child is how I lost her," I told him. "That first day in the park, I became intrigued by her outlook on life. She had this zest for living life to the fullest because she had lost her mother to cancer at an early age. And that may have been where her superstitious nature and self-fulfilling prophecy that she would not live to a ripe old age began. No matter how hard I tried, I couldn't get her to shake that belief. But I didn't understand back then why it had been so important to her and what great lengths she would go to have a child."

I told Harry of the great joy I felt the first time she became pregnant. But I failed at choking back my emotions when I told him about her first miscarriage, how I had grown to hate the doctor who had assured us that it was just one of those things and we would have no problem in the future.

"Against my better judgment, she didn't want to wait," I lamented. "And that's where my blame for her death and our ensuing struggle to bring a child into the world began. It started out so innocently. Six months after her first miscarriage, she became pregnant again. I should have chastised her for not taking her birth control pills. But she was happy again after months of depression and wanted nothing more than to marry me and give me a child. And for a time, so was I as we planned our future, but I couldn't suppress the nagging fear that again she would not carry the child to term."

I took comfort in that Harry's facial expression had never wavered throughout my story so far, but all of that changed when he put his hands to his lips as if in prayer, perhaps sensing that the worst of my tale was about to be told.

"She began to complain about a variety of pains. And I tried to comfort her that it all must be due to the pregnancy. But perhaps each of us knew and was afraid to tell the other that another miscarriage was imminent. It happened three months later, and I became adamant that no more attempts to have a child should be made. I tried reasoning with her. I told her that her body needed time to heal, that it was physically and mentally taking a toll on her, and that my guts were being wrenched out at the thought of her losing another baby.

"And yet, through it all, she refused to listen to reason. She wanted to know why she couldn't have her baby, why both times they were lost a third of the way. She submitted to a battery of tests. She became so depressed awaiting the results that I was left with no choice but to take an untimely vacation. But the change of venue didn't help. She deluged me with article after article of procedures to keep a baby from falling out."

I told Harry that it was the worst time in our lives. The vacation to uplift her spirits and return the woman who had had such a positive outlook on life turned into the retreat from hell. She began to complain of pains in all parts of her body. She became listless and spent most of her time lounging on the couch, her only comfort those medical magazines detailing steps to avoid having a miscarriage.

"My nerves were becoming overwrought watching her slip away from me, and so I decided it was time to return home. The hospital had tried in earnest to contact us while we were away, and their last ditch effort was the telegram that we found shoved underneath the door. I called at once, but all they would tell me was that I needed to bring her in. I'll never forget that day as long as I live. She was placed on a gurney in an overcrowded emergency room and we waited for hours. I was consumed with fear. She seemed dispirited but content that her self-fulfilling prophecy had borne fruit."

Slamming my fist upon the table, I told Harry how I had been unable to take seeing her carted among the sea of human suffering. I had become adamant for the results of all those tests she had undergone. They were to either supply us with an answer or I would take her somewhere else.

"We were finally told about the abnormality in

her blood test results. The doctor advised me that she should be admitted and that more tests would be needed. I created quite a scene when the nurses tried to make me leave, citing hospital regulations. They finally acquiesced to my demands and I stayed with her. She cried the entire night. She didn't want to be in the hospital. She kept telling me that she wanted a last look at our home. She wanted to have my baby. She kept pleading to God to let her have her baby. She asked me to bring a picture of us to put in the room. She told me that she would be joining her mother. Nothing I did or said provided her with any comfort. And so I asked the nurse to see if the doctor would prescribe something that would allow her to sleep."

Harry sat upright with a sad expression etched on his face. Once again, I wept like a child. "In the morning, my worst fears were realized," I told him, "when the doctors delivered the news that the woman I loved with all my heart had been diagnosed with a rare form of leukemia . . . "

After a moment of silence, Harry motioned to the waiter to bring our food. "It's a pity we're not in Houston," he said. "I would have loved to show you around the farm."

Dumbfounded, I thought Harry had taken leave of his senses. I just poured out my inner thoughts and he wanted to show me a farm he had just purchased.

"I love walking on the farm and watching the animals," Harry continued, "especially the chickens and turkeys, because they always flock together. You never see either by themselves. It's amazing how they all stick together. When I go hunting, it's the same thing. I see a flock of geese flying in formation. The strangest thing is that no matter how I shoot at them, no matter how many fall, they still try to maintain their formation."

Was Harry really serious or was he dancing a little sidestep of his own? What purpose would it serve for him to tell me this?

"Now the eagle is another story," he went on. He said that it never flocks and always flies by itself. He told me how he likes to sit and watch it spread its wing and soar with the wind. He asked me if I had ever seen it go after its prey.

"The majestic eagle has long been admired for its beauty and strength," he said enthusiastically. "As soon as it can fly, it must fend for itself. That's why it must be strong. That is why it's revered by so many. It stands alone and is content to be that way.

"Some men are born to be chickens and turkeys. Like the geese, they don't have enough common sense to go it alone. Because they always follow the crowd, constantly needing the approval of others, in the end they're shot down since they cannot think on their own. So they go through life being told what to do, when to do it, and how to do it.

"Then there's a rare breed of man. Like the eagle, he must go his own way. He must pave his own road, control his own destiny. He's never understood, and neither does he care about the approval of others. Men despise him, they fear him, but if he truly has eagle qualities, those same men come to envy him and eventually respect him. It seems to me that a man can do a lot worse than to be considered an eagle."

The waiter brought our food and Harry excused himself. He said that he had an urgent call to make. I guessed that it was just an excuse to give me a chance to compose myself. When he returned, he pushed his plate aside, called the waiter over, and asked for the check.

"Son, you know that God never gives a man more than he can carry," he told me, as we waited for the valet. "Instead of blaming yourself for Priscilla's death, why can't you think of how he put you and her together?"

"For what purpose?" I shouted. "So that I could become an emotional wreck, almost destroying my life in the process?"

"You could look at it that way," he said soothingly. "But I choose to look at it from another angle. He needed a man of courage, who could go through the ordeal and help that young woman have a small degree of happiness, despite her time being cut short. Most men who have done anything great in life were tested by a tremendous tragedy.

"I think back to Saul of Tarsus," he said, pulling onto the highway. "Of all the men God could have picked to lead his people, why would he have picked one who was persecuting them?"

Why would he have indeed? I asked myself. Surely he couldn't have thought that a philanderer would have had the conviction to abandon those ways and devote himself to one woman's happiness.

But that was exactly what I had done and saw nothing come from it other than five years of agonizing and blaming myself for doing nothing to prevent her death.

And yet what could I have done differently, I've asked myself countless times, as she battled that deadly disease? Although the doctor pointed out the fallacy of my thinking, nothing he said could make me abandon the notion that Priscilla's desire to give me a child, which led to her subsequent miscarriages, was not what had triggered it at all.

"He chose a man of courage . . . that's one way to look at it," I told Harry. "But why not the latter? A man tormented by the loss of his first love, cowering in fear, similar to an ostrich burying its head in the sand, tried everything possible to make sure that love would never cross and darken his path again."

"But an eagle would never have buried his head in the sand, and neither could you."

I didn't have the energy to spar with Harry any longer and drifted off to sleep. I was awakened by the slam of the car door and realized that we were back at the Waldorf.

"You've got to stop blaming yourself," Harry said, as he patted me on the back. "What would you have done differently the second time around? From the way you described the young lady, Priscilla was hell bent on having a child with the man she fell in love with. Be grateful that you and she were able to share a moment of happiness, no matter how brief it was.

"Son, God doesn't make mistakes. He chose you to be with her for a reason. You said it yourself, how she wanted you to remember her. It would be foolish of me to tell you to forget the past, but now you must look to the future. You have a wife that loves you and a child that needs you. So Helen and I will be expecting you and yours to join us in Houston for Christmas, ya hear."

That night it seemed as if the devil himself had taken ahold of me. I was besieged by images of roads leading nowhere. I kept running away from something that I couldn't see. Finally, I came to a fork in the road, but the sign indicating the path of each direction was obscured by darkness. And then I heard it: the sound of a child crying. But where it was coming from eluded me. No matter which direction I moved, the sound seemed to move with me. It intensified to where I thought that a thousand babies were weeping. At last, a light illuminated a single door. I ran to it. But try as I did, it would not open. The hair stood up on my neck as I realized that something was charging at me. I pounded on the door in hopes that it would give way. Whatever it was lunged at me. I sprang from my bed, only to realize foolishly that it was room service knocking on the door.

Feeling like Dickens's Ebenezer on Christmas morning, I threw open the door, startling the chambermaid as I did. No doubt she thought I had taken leave of whatever good sense I had left.

"Never mind with the room," I cried, as I hugged her. "Dear woman, if it took a thousand lifetimes, I would never be able to repay you for waking me from the nightmare I was in."

I emptied my wallet on her, grabbed my garment bag, and stormed happily out of the room. A limo took me to the marina, where I claimed I wanted to admire the boats, when secretly I knew I was trying to delay the inevitable. All around me was a bustle of activity: couples walking hand in hand, fathers teaching their sons or daughters how to fish, runners, kite flyers, people busy barbecuing. I wanted to sit and be a part of this wonderful salute to nature. As he waited for me, I took a seat on a familiar bench. It was here that I had sat and watched a father teach his son to ride his bike. It was to this marina that I had brought Christina when we thought our chance of getting our home was lost. What a difference a year makes. This place, filled with so many wonderful memories, had come to that. All around me were individuals enjoying life. Enjoying the beauty that nature had to offer. Was I lost to all of this? Surrounded by so much beauty, I sat alone, frustrated and angry, contemplating what to do about a perceived damage to my honor.

"Pardon me, sir."

I looked up to see an old man, very neat in appearance, standing in front of me.

"Do you mind if I sit with you?" he asked.

"Sure, why not? The park is for everyone."

"Thank you very much. I hope I'm not disturbing you?"

"No. In fact, I was getting ready to leave."

"The only reason why I mentioned it was that you look troubled."

"It's nothing really. I'm trying to cast out some demons."

"Demons must always be excised," he said, as he rested on his cane.

"Sounds like you know about them firsthand?"

"I should say so," he said. "I've just been casting out my own."

"Well, from the looks of it, you must have been successful."

"Yes, I have. It's remarkable what can happen in a year. You see, one act of kindness helped me appreciate life."

"One act?"

"Yes. A man with courage told me that I had to face life."

"I don't understand."

He went on to tell me how he had lost his wife and business due to alcoholism. How he had lost every measure of self-respect and would beg for enough money to get a bottle for the night and that this park had become his new home.

I looked closely at the old man. Surely, he couldn't be the drunk I had given money to that night? I thought to myself.

"A young man, perhaps troubled himself, took the time to tell me that life was worth living. I took his advice and took a good look at myself. Ashamed at what I had become, I vowed to get my life in order and reclaim the love of my family."

"I'm very happy for you," I told him, meaning it. "That is a very touching story."

"Yes, though living through it was no picnic. But in spite of it all, there's still a debt I must settle."

"How is that?"

"Since my recovery, I've come to this park often, each time hoping that I would see that special young man. I know I can never repay the debt I owe him. I just need to thank him, and perhaps one day do something that would be of help to him.

"Well, I must be off. I appreciate your taking the time to listen to the burdens of an old man."

I watched him leave the marina, proud, erect, a man who had fought a good fight and had won. I got up to take one last walk on the pier, when something caught my eye. Neatly folded on the bench was a brand new fifty-dollar bill. Wrapped around it was a note.

"To whom much is given, much is required. Thank you."

I got back into the limousine and asked myself if I could really go home again. If I did, would I be as fortunate as the old man had been? Would I be welcomed with open arms? Or would I, like Bascom, return only to find that my wife had fled, taking our baby?

At my request, the driver left me outside at the end of the circular drive. As I approached the front door, I heard music playing. I was home. But what would I find? My heart was pounding as I opened the front door and walked inside.

Chapter 20

WHEN I FIRST ENTERED, THE SONG THAT WAS PLAYING started over again. I saw Christina and my heart nearly stopped. I was hoping to see either Estelle or Bascom first, in order to judge the temperament of the house. But there she was, standing in the kitchen. From where I stood she couldn't see me, and judging from how loud the music played, I doubt she could even hear me either. Suddenly she began to sing . . .

All my feelings of love resurfaced when I recognized the words to the song.

I stood against the wall, unable to move. Tears were running down my face, but I didn't care. I loved her so much. How could I have ever doubted her love? She was singing along with so much emotion. "I love you, Christina," I murmured, "and no matter what happens, I always will."

Looking around the house she had decorated, filled with simple treasures, I was fully aware, for the first time, of the warmth and happiness that exuded from it. And Christina was actually baking. I wanted to reach out to her, take her in my arms and kiss her passionately. But first there was someone else whose forgiveness I desperately needed.

Going up the stairs, I went into the nursery

Christina and I had so carefully furnished and breathed a sigh of relief when I saw my bundle of joy peacefully asleep.

Getting a chair from the other side of the room, I gently placed it by the crib and lowered the side.

"I know that you're asleep and won't understand a word I'm going to say," I told her. "If you were awake it really wouldn't make a difference. It's just that I would feel that at least somehow you understood me. I steal into your room like a thief in the night, begging your forgiveness. Filled with fear that something would happen, I tried to delay your arrival. I wanted to force your mother to wait many years before attempting to have you, when secretly I knew I couldn't face the ordeal and would have postponed it indefinitely.

"But your mother was determined. I said some awful things to her. Believe me, I regret that those words ever came from my mouth. Imagine creating one as precious as you. I had the nerve to tell her that you were not made from a labor of love, but brought into this world through treachery and deceit. I still have a hard time with that. What I tried to do was hide my own inadequacies—blaming the child I never had for the death of my first love—vowing never to attempt another, since I felt it would be the same with you. Can you forgive me for having such silly thoughts?

"I want to be the best father the world has ever known. I want to be your pal, your friend, and the one you can always come and talk to. I'm not perfect. I'm probably going to make a lot of mistakes, but together we'll solve them. I'll read books, confer with other parents, and use a degree of common sense in order to make you proud that I'm your father. Even with all that, I'll make mistakes. I'll probably be too protective and overbearing, but through it all, I guess we'll learn together. So I steal into your room today to let you know officially that I'm proud that you're my child. Yes, you were created out of a labor of love. I can't envision the world without you, even though we just met.

"I'm sorry. I didn't mean to wake you. Whew, you have a strong grip. You're smiling like you understand. Does that mean that you forgive me? I hope it will be this easy with your mother. I keep putting it off, deluding myself that I'm waiting for the right moment. I love her so much and need to let her know that life is miserable without her. God knew what he was doing when he sent her to me. Only your mother, with her lovely obstinate ways, could have helped me see that I needed you.

"Why am I telling you all this, when she's the one who should be hearing? Oh, God, I love her so much. Finally, I realize what she means to me.

'If I lined up everything that's supposed to be important in life,
It would pale in comparison to the love I have for my wife.
A greater love, no man has ever known,
Her expressiveness of it and the way that it is shown.

Many nights, in front of the house,
Sitting in the car before entering in,
I would wonder how could this ever be,
That she loves me, now, and for all eternity.

Going into the kitchen, to find a snack waiting and a little note,
The beauty of her thoughts is what it all denotes.
'In this house alone, wondering what to do,

You can't imagine how I love and miss being with you.'

Entering our bedroom late at night, to find you fast asleep,
Sitting at the edge of the bed, gazing at you,
Can't imagine the wonderful memories I keep.
Those bewitching eyes, the softness of your voice,
As I watch an angel sleeping, so contented with my choice.

Sensing I am in the room, you awake and extend your
Tender arms to me and gently stroke my face,
Sheltering me from the coldness of this world,
With your loving warm embrace.

On the threshold of greatness, there I stood alone,
But your faith in my dreams turned this empty house into a loving home.
Imagine my world now, free from stress and strife,
All because you consented to become my wife.

You questioned me often, am I sure that you're the one?
Well, I can answer now; yes, my quest is done,
I no longer need to wonder if this love is true,
May the humbleness of these words reveal how much I love you.'"

I walked over to the wall and turned on the music. Anita Baker's "I Apologize" was still playing. I took the baby in my arms and started dancing as I sang along.

When the song finished and was starting over, I decided to take the baby downstairs. There was something I needed to do. I went back into the kitchen. "Now where did your mother go?"

The kitchen was warm and the counter bare except for an empty pitcher. Remembering what Matt had told me, I went out to the backyard. I lay down in the hammock, breathing in my newborn's hair as she lay across my chest. The movement of the hammock was soothing, and I felt myself drifting off to sleep when I heard the sweetest sound. It was Schubert's *Ave Maria*. And Christina! She was there, holding a pitcher of lemonade in one hand and the baby monitor in the other.

"That was so beautiful," she said, overcome with emotion. "You. The baby. I never expected . . . "

"Shh." I put my hand up to her lips. I didn't need to hear the rest. How could I forget her tears of happiness? Thank you, God, you knew what I needed even when I was too stubborn and blind to see. True happiness isn't in amassing a fortune, but in being surrounded by the ones you love.

The old man was right: what a difference a year could make! Contentment overwhelmed me, the likes of which I had never known, as Christina, setting the pitcher on the grass, lay down beside me. The birds serenaded us and the trees sheltered us as the hammock swung back and forth in the gentle breeze. The wisdom of Maggie's words dawned on me.

We do not always look for love,
Yet love finds us,
We believe it is our right to choose,
Never realizing we were chosen.

Everything is as it should be: my queen safely at my side, my princess peacefully asleep on my chest. As I drifted off to sleep, *Ave Maria* played on.

ACKNOWLEDGMENTS

Where does one begin in expressing their gratitude to the many individuals, who in one form or another have contributed invaluable assistance in bringing this story to fruition? As I pondered these thoughts, it dawned on me that the answer I had been searching for, was staring me in the face, on a faded piece of paper on the refrigerator.

"Visionaries are charged with an image that no one else sees. Often as they go in search of their dreams, they are met with resistance from small-minded people, but if they have the temerity to hold on, and not fall victim to the lugubrious outlook of others, they'll see that those people will fall by the wayside, and be replaced with people that not only offer help, but the resources they need to fulfill their vision."

It would be impossible to recount the innumerable ways this particular statement has aided and consoled me on those bleak days when, *I Apologize* was in its infancy. Even more, how it guarded me against the naysayers and the prognosticators, who were eager to informed me of the arduous road that laid ahead and the countless failures of others that had traveled on it before me.

First I must give honor and glory to God, for through him all things are indeed possible.

I'd like to thank Robert Aulicino, who took the hazy image that I had held for so long and crystallized it into a magnificent dust jacket.

Special thanks to my editors: Charity Heller Hogge, Nancy D'Inzillo and Karli Clift.

Charity, the Senior Editor of the group, your edits gave clarity to what I wanted to say, while maintaining the characters' unique voices.

Nancy, your perspicaciousness and attention to detail is without equal.

Karli, the way you hewed what was superfluous in the beginning has helped me tremendously in writing the next novel.

I would like to also thank the people at Affluent Publishing and Malloy. Their dedication to excellence and the professionalism of their respective teams made the completion of this project that much easier.

A warm thanks to Elizabeth and ReBékah. The two of you have taught me that laughter is the spoonful of sugar that sweetens a sour disposition.

And of course, words don't do justice when it comes to you, Irena. Your tireless and unwavering devotion, to illuminate the path from which at times, I seemed to have lost my way, is a testament to the faith you have in me. May I, always be worthy of your love . . .